The Square Mile Murder

James Ward

COOL MILLENNIUM BOOKS

3

Published in the United Kingdom. All rights reserved. No part of this publication may be reproduced, distributed or transmitted in any form or means, without written permission.

Copyright © James Ward 2017

James Ward has asserted his right to be identified as the author of this Work in accordance with the Copyright, Designs and Patents Act 1988.

First published 2017.
This edition published 2021.

A CIP catalogue record for this book is available from the British Library.

ISBN: 978-1-913851-33-0

Cover picture shows the view to Mansion House from the steps of the Royal Exchange.

This novel was produced in the UK and uses British-English language conventions ('authorise' instead of 'authorize', 'The government are' instead of 'the government is', etc.)

To my wife

Chapter 1: Because I Spoke Out

A million ways to say goodbye, so they said.

Songs, some of them.

Like, *It's a Long Way to Tipperary.* Probably. Though why that - ?

God, he was hyperventilating!

At his age, manic breathlessness might even signal a coronary. Mind you, how long since he'd felt, or even looked, forty-two?

Some part of him definitely wanted to giggle. Stop thumping, heart! Stop!

Goodbye, Piccadilly, Farewell, Leicester Square.

Oh, they always came for the bloody blogger first, yes, yes, in every film that had ever been made.

No, not *first:* that was wrong. *First* they came for the Socialists, then the trade unionists, then ... And no, that didn't work. *They came for me because I spoke out?* Not Niemöller's thought, no way. Sacrilege! Stop giggling!

The hard drive, unscrewed. Fingernails both sides; shaking as he succeeded in prising it out. Momentary self-glimpse: a terrified middle-aged male in the sheen of the unplugged old-style glass monitor: clean shaven, short hair, blue eyes, chin made long by the curve of the screen, like in one of those bendy mirrors in old fashioned fun fairs, places where they commit murder for fun, like how the hero thinks he's shot the bad guy and it turns out to be just another reflection, a menacing infinity of regress, and then the prolonged ghoulish cackling.

Scratch that magnetic platter, man! Letter-opener. Shiny surface. Make it unusable. But take it along, just in case.

That urge to giggle again. Like none of this was real.

Stay calm. Gulp four deep breaths.

Retch – no, no, not part of the cure.

Retch again. No, can't help it. Don't cry, don't cry.

Nine hours earlier, that barrage of texts and emails. Someone in the same building, because they'd proved they were watching him. *We know who you are. We know what you do in your spare time. We're coming to get you tonight. Say good-bye.* One hundred and sixty three variations on that over the space of two hours, ten minutes and twenty seconds. Then radio silence. Close of trading on the London Stock Exchange. Time to clock out from your dismal little job. Time to relax. Time to go to your little room and pray.

Because you couldn't go home to Irma.

Back to the present. Get a grip. Think. Any - anything to do with his identity?

But he'd taken care of that long ago. DNA, he couldn't control, but they wouldn't know what to do about that. Even if they did, he wasn't on any database.

Turn the screwdriver inward, gash your arm. Way in, that's it. Whoa, whoa, whoa! Coming out nicely, and not half as painful as he expected. Drip it round the room, then bandage. A long way from feeling faint! Then overturn the computer, kick the little knick-knacks shelf over. Hoped they couldn't hear him downstairs, but in his list of concerns now, not high up. Break the chair leg for good measure. It had to look like there'd been a struggle in here.

Hard drive, what's left of it, in a bespoke pouch inside jacket, coat on, say fare thee well to thine room. *It's a long way to little Mary, to the sweetest girl I know!*

Hannah would know what to do.

Risky, but she'd get it. Definitely. She would.

In any case, what choice did he have?

One final, pointless look around before locking the door. Hardly space to move about in. A prone, gutted computer, a bare desk, a restricted view of Mansion House EC4 from behind a net curtain.

Just a cupboard really. Even so, the landlord could probably charge top dollar for it now, City of London epicentre.

So, down the dark, rickety old staircase with the smelly carpet and the greasy walls – amazing, the dilapidation just a stone's throw from the Bank of England – and exit through the pub lounge. The Frederick and Elizabeth, marmoreal walls, tiled floor, ornate bar, gilt-framed mirrors, everything stylishly lit.

Eleven, the clock said. Chucking-out time. Not too many punters tonight. Eyes on him, how many? Try not to return the gazes. Put the key discreetly across the bar for Brent. Don't walk too fast, no sudden movements. Where *was* Brent? Did it matter? Breathe normally. You're just leaving after a run-of-the-mill Thursday night. You've had a quick few pints, that's all, now you're off to your nice little semi- in Belgravia. Stroll casually to the door, calmly as you can, steady on. Then walk briskly.

They wouldn't pounce yet. Of course they wouldn't. They'd wait till he was alone.

Push open the door. Step out into the cool.

Another deep breath. Nicer, much nicer. But still, the lingering taste of bile.

Not too many people out on the street.

Good or bad? Easy to see when his attackers approached, harder to lose them.

Should have rung for a taxi or an Uber, ideally. But there'd been no phone signal, they'd seen to that.

Left or right?

Left, towards Mansion House. The intersection. Where the traffic lights were. Easiest place to flag down a ride. *Still no bloody signal!* Getting quieter now. Thursday: not really a going-out night. Spooky at the best of times, round here. Right now, as deserted as any village centre in rural Nowhereshire.

Perhaps it'd have been better to turn right.

It was starting to rain. Still no bars.

His stomach wriggled simultaneously with the recognition of a sinister *someone* on the other side of the road. Same direction, same speed, same gender, recognisably the same aura of grim determination, five or six paces behind. At this time of night, the correspondence too rare to be coincidental.

He sped up. *This is it then!* Almost a relief in a grotesque sort of way. Whoever they were, they'd shown themselves. They weren't supernatural monsters any more. Just natural ones.

Two more ahead. Same side of the road.

My God, they were wearing masks.

Those – *were* masks, weren't they?

Too much, too much. But nearly at the Royal Exchange now. Ought to be busier there. Create an almighty scene, draw attention to them. Or double-back… depending on how many of them there were.

What if there were ten? Twenty?

Screaming would be his best option then. Hollering blue murder in as public a place as he could find.

Had it not been for those *horrible* masks, he'd have just about held together. But his nerves were shot. Had been for a while now, truth be told, which he'd have known had he only stood back and taken a good look at himself.

Too late. All his short-term plans disintegrated, but like he was watching them from so far away it didn't feel like anything to do with him. Biology kicked in – flight because there were too many to fight, and because those masks made them too utterly *repulsive* - and he began to sprint.

Behind him, and around him, he could hear them yelling to each other. Perhaps they hadn't expected this.

And the magical thing was, he was so super-saturated with adrenalin, he was outstripping them. He felt almost like he was flying.

That weird urge to giggle again.

… Yet he was crying, had been all along. The only question: how long could he keep this up? The weeping Usain Bolt of Cheapside.

Then he remembered his intention to scream. Part of his pre-considered 'effective strategy'.

So he ran for his life and he screamed.

Chapter 2: Another Kind of Farewell

It was a memorial service rather than a funeral. No coffins, because the dead bodies were already deep beneath the earth three thousand miles away, buried without a shroud, still covered in their own blood probably, because that's what they did with martyrs over there.

John Mordred, thirty-two, blond hair, clean shaven and a little over six foot, occupied a chair halfway up the pew-less nave, sandwiched between two strongly scented middle-aged couples. Every seat in the church was taken, and about a hundred people stood at the sides and near the exits. London's Kurdish community was well represented, some in the front row, alongside the parents. Mordred's MI7 colleagues were also here somewhere, probably as alone as he was: Alec Cunningham, Annabel and Tariq al-Banna, Phyllis Robinson, plus – so he'd heard - a clutch of Thelma's former colleagues from White Department (none of whom he could be expected to identify, even by sight). They all had cover stories, because it was unthinkable any-one should ever discover the deceased couple had, until three years ago, been on British intelligence's payroll. The entire world would draw the wrong conclusions.

Ian's and Thelma's deaths had been announced a month ago by the Kurdish militia alongside whom they'd been fighting ISIS. In an online video tribute, Angela Barnes, the last surviving member of the trio who'd left Britain in 2014, spoke of her terrible sadness, the courage both her friends had repeatedly shown, the deep affection in which they'd been held by their fellow combatants, how much they'd be missed by everyone on the front line.

Details of their last moments were sketchy, but accord-ing to their Kurdish commanders, they'd died in a rocket attack somewhere on the outskirts of Raqqa. In their last Facebook message, recorded together a few days before-hand, the pair had apologised yet again for leaving the UK without telling anyone, and expressed a desire, should things end as they had, to be buried in Syria, alongside their fallen comrades. On receiving the news, both families im-mediately assented.

Mordred was surprised the couple had a Facebook page. He'd never been there, not even for a look. Which made him feel doubly bad. What kind of a former friend was he?

The vicar spoke of Ian and Thelma's deep similarity, switching from one to the other at a point in their lives be-fore they'd met, and their shared passion for fighting in-justice. He illustrated his abstract claims with biographical anecdotes, presumably obtained from friends and relatives, and spoke without notes. He was about their age: mid-thirties.

No one had approached Mordred in regard of stories about Ian, and no one would. After the service was over, he was supposed to make his excuses and leave. All his former colleagues were. No post-ceremony reception for them.

Which made sense. If anyone got to hear that Ian, Thelma and Angela had once worked for MI7, they'd make the usual stupid assumption: *once a spy, always a spy*. Which would sully everything. Their courage, the respect in which their memories were held, their integrity. And it would put Angela in a hell of a lot of danger.

Because they *hadn't* been working for MI7, any of them. Mordred remembered the icy underground meeting at which Ruby Parker had first informed her team of Ian's de-parture, three years ago. *Sometime yesterday evening, Ian Woodward boarded a flight from Heathrow to Ankara. An hour ago, he saw fit to inform us that he's in northern Syria, in com-pany with the YPG, preparing for an assault on Rojava. The YPG are the Kurdish People's Protection Units. Rojava is held by ISIS.*

I'm assuming – I dearly hope - no one here knew anything about his intentions beforehand.

At the time, she'd seemed furious. She wasn't here today. Afterwards, they'd all had to sign formal declarations to the effect that they knew nothing of the trio's plans. They'd been in shock for the rest of the week. And conflicted. Half-full of guilty admiration.

Probably why he'd never looked for that Facebook page. As a spy, he was spied on. All the time. Or that's how it felt sometimes. Couldn't afford the risk. Better just to put Ian out of your mind and get on with life. Work was like that. This morning, for example, when they'd all been given that form to fill in, accompanied by an *under no circumstances discuss it*. Which they all would. Especially after Ian and Thelma. Right now, they weren't in the best mood for mindlessly obeying orders.

It wasn't like an old person's funeral, where just the immediate family shed tears. The more the vicar honed his depictions of Ian and Thelma, the more intense the grief became. Mainly over the minutiae, because it was always there that people become fully human. The fact that, at university, Thelma had owned an ant farm; that, in his spare time, Ian played the oboe in a jazz band; that he complained of never being able to get a pair of shoes to fit; that he'd dressed as a giant banana to run the London marathon in 2012, which is where he'd met Thelma (who'd gone as a giant pear), and they'd both been raising cash for cancer research; that together, they'd taken six hours, ten minutes, which, they proudly acknowledged, was pretty close to the slowest time ever; that Thelma was a devoted auntie and loved to take her two nephews to Chessington. As detail piled on detail, more people's lips trembled. Men and women you thought were relatively indifferent suddenly broke down. Tissues were produced from bags, dissolving eyeliner was wiped away, noses got blown.

Mordred wasn't one for crying, but neither was he immune to strong emotion. When they played Ian and Thelma's last video message on a widescreen to one side of the pulpit, he found himself struggling to remain outwardly phlegmatic. Confronted with Ian dressed all in khaki, halfway across the world, how tanned he was, how apparently at ease with that rifle, and how unaffectedly he and Thelma spoke to the camera, he began to hear a little voice: *What have YOU ever done, John? What is YOUR life worth?*

However, as usual, the sucker punch was dealt from afar; from thousands of years before anyone present was born. "For what shall it profit a man," the vicar asked sonorously, "if he shall gain the whole world, and lose his own soul?"

Then silence.

Then the organist.

It took Mordred, as it took a lot of people, a few seconds to realise it was all over. The vicar walked solemnly through the nave and took up position by the door. A general uncertainty, then people slowly stood and began to leave, some in a semi-daze.

He scanned the church and spotted Alec, looking pale. Phyllis was still seated, crying. An old man had his arm solicitously round her. Annabel and Tariq looked wretched.

They were meant to be meeting in a pub, in half an hour's time. Twenty miles from here. In just the right mood for a wake.

The Electress Palatine was just off Cornhill, near Bank tube station. Tariq chose it because it was his turn and because, he said, it looked like the kind of place you could mourn in. Velvet curtains, ornamental coving that apparently hadn't been painted for a decade, a bar as plain as a post office counter, lights in suburban-bedroom-style beige lampshades suspended from the ceiling, a dark carpet that probably hid a multitude of stains. Amazing such places still existed in central London, but then it was probably the same everywhere: the brewery was at fault, but it didn't care; it just wanted to skim off the profits. ('I didn't know you were a Communist,' Mordred said, when Tariq told him this). They ordered soft drinks to begin with, because they knew they'd be staying a while, and couldn't afford to get blotto, however much it might appeal. Today was Thursday; tomorrow was back to work.

Apart from the fact that they were all dressed in black, they looked like any gathering of young professionals at the end of a working day. The women had long hair, suits, and the best shoes; the men had short hair, suits, polished brogues. All were reasonably attractive. To add to the impression of office workers set loose, they kept looking at their phones. In this part of London, that might conceivably mean you were checking the latest share prices.

They got their drinks and Alec kicked off. His memory centred on Royal Ascot in 2011. Ian lost his top hat when Hurry Up Lazenby came in at 20-1 and the crowd surged forward in excitement. He'd retrieved it crushed to a pulp twenty minutes later, plus five hundred pounds in winnings. Later, on the way home, they'd stopped at a pub, and Alec had ritually consumed a few threads from the hat-lining along with his poached lobster, in recognition of his hackneyed promise to 'eat his hat' if they won. Later, they got smashed, swam in the River Cut and ate the entire thing with Heinz tomato ketchup. Neither of them ended up in hospital.

Phyllis's memory centred on how incredibly kind and patient Ian had been when she first arrived. Annabel spoke of his nervousness during a burglary he and she had committed in the cause of defending the realm. "I realised later that it wasn't being caught *in itself* that bothered him. It was the perceived lack of respectability involved in house-breaking, the immoral *appearance*. He didn't want to look bad in front of a group of police officers."

"I happen to know he was a big fan of *Inspector Morse*," Alec said, as if that explained it. "Then *Lewis*, after John Thaw died."

"I knew he was heavily into Miss Marple," Annabel replied. "What's your favourite Ian-memory, John?"

"When we were all in Ussuriysk, in Siberia," Mordred said. "I met him after Gina disappeared, then we lost you, Annabel, or seemed to. Ian remained calm. And when we all got together on that rooftop for a crisis-meeting, he was the one trying to forge compromises."

"I don't remember that much about him," Tariq said, when the eyes turned to him. "Except he was good at CSS."

"Which is?" Alec asked.

"A kind of computer code," Tariq said.

They raised their glasses, whispered Ian's name and drank. Phyllis's phone beeped. She took it out, pressed it and listened to a voicemail. She blinked slowly as if someone had thrust a pin in her foot and she wasn't supposed to react. "Bloody hell," she whispered.

Time for a quip, but no one was fast enough. Phyllis pressed the screen twice, and spoke. "Hi, Mum. It's lovely that you're in London. I know you wanted to surprise me, but I'm with a group of friends, and we've just been to a funeral. Someone at the office. You didn't know him. We've already ordered food and we're planning to stay here until late. I'll come to the hotel when I've finished. About eleven, maybe half past. And don't argue. I'd love to see you both. Love you. I've got to go. Ciao."

She rolled her eyes as she hung up. "Why does she always try to surprise me at the most inconvenient times?" she asked everyone. A second opportunity for a one-liner. "Don't answer," she said, while everyone's brain was still working.

15

They talked about Ian's and Thelma's Facebook page, then about Angela, whom none of them had ever met, although they'd heard things about her. Their meals arrived and they ate in silence. They played *American Pie* for Ian – the only vaguely appropriate track the jukebox had, and that only because of its closing line, 'This'll be the day that I die'. Phyllis became teary again, and embarrassed by the fact. "It wouldn't be so bad if he hadn't been so sodding decent," she said. "Why did he have to be such a nice guy?"

Alec bought another round of drinks. By now, they'd been talking and thinking about Ian and Thelma for so long that it was as if the grim reaper himself had pulled up a chair beside them. Each knew that, once they broke up, they'd have little option but to go home. After all, tomorrow was back to routine. And what would they do there? Too early to turn in for the night, so they'd carry on thinking about Ian. Only, alone; or relatively so: Phyllis and John were together, so were Annabel and Tariq. Everything considered, though, when you'd been touched by death's chilly fingertip, you were best off with as many friends as you could muster. So they each had a vague, but accurate, sense of clinging to the others. They were here for the long-haul - until last orders at 10.30, or possibly even 11 - the aim being to go home, get undressed, get into bed and fall asleep, all on autopilot with no pause for thought.

It helped that, at eight, the pub began to fill up; then they could converse more freely. In the din, there was less chance of them being heard. "What did anyone make of that form this morning?" Alec asked quietly.

Everyone looked at him with *you shouldn't be discussing that in public* expressions, but without facial components usually considered integral, such as anxiety and indignation.

"I don't know," Phyllis said. She took a sip of her drink and shrugged. "It's got to be normal, hasn't it?"

"Given that everyone in the building was taken aside in-dividually - " Mordred began.

Tariq drew his face back an inch. "The whole *building?*"

"You didn't know?" Annabel asked him.

"No, I ... "

Mordred finished his own earlier sentence. "We don't even know whether we've all signed the same thing."

It seemed a fair point. After a second, they put their heads together in the centre of the table, and Phyllis whispered: "That we all agree to carry on working as usual in the event of a national emergency." She paused and ad-ded: "Essentially locking us into our jobs in that event."

"And they don't have to pay us," Alec said.

"Although in practice, they will have to support us," Tariq replied. "Food and shelter, at least. They can't let us starve."

"Quite the contrary," Annabel said. "We'll become key workers. I'm not sure what the fuss is, really. It's consistent with what I expected when I went to work there. Obviously we'd be vital in a national emergency."

"That's exactly the point," Alec replied. "Don't you think it's odd that they're asking us to sign up formally to that *now? Why now?* What are they expecting to happen?"

"I take it you're talking about Donald Trump and Kim Jong-un," Phyllis said in a bored tone. "It doesn't necessar-ily mean anyone's *expecting* a nuclear war. It may just have focussed people's minds a bit more."

"Alec's got a point," Mordred said. "If that's all it is – just the sudden realisation of an administrative lacuna – then why would they make such a festival of it? Everyone in one day? That looks like urgent action to me."

"Or to use another term," Alec said, "panic."

"Well, I don't know what they're panicking about," Phyl-lis said. "And I've signed now, anyway. I guess we'll just have to wait and see what Santa brings."

"I can't believe you're so blasé," Alec said. "Presumably, we're allowed a 'cooling off' period."

Phyllis laughed. "I don't think consumer protection laws apply."

"We're not supposed to be talking about it, anyway," Annabel said. "And we're here to pay our respects to Ian and Thelma, remember? I'm depressed enough already, without you throwing Armageddon into the mix."

"Just trying to prepare us all for what could be a nasty shock," Alec said. "Remember, you heard it from me first. I'll shut up now. Pointless speculating anyway."

"I can't really think of anything more to say about Ian," Phyllis said. "Much as I loved him, I think if he was here, he'd want us to cheer up a bit. Besides anything else, and I know it sounds selfish, I can't meet my mother tonight while I'm in this mood. It's not as if she's young. And any of us could die. Statistically, we're not in the safest of jobs."

Mordred got up and returned with a Monopoly set. No one objected: the unspoken consensus was that they'd eaten, and drunk, and now it was time to make merry in precisely the minute quantity a nineteen-hundreds board game allowed, and that, if Ian was here, he'd probably give it his blessing. When the barman announced last orders two hours later, they were still playing.

"I don't suppose you want to join me at the Beaumont?" Phyllis asked Mordred at 10.50, after they agreed to declare Tariq the winner, and left the pub in a group. It was cold outside.

"I don't think I'm invited," he replied. "Your mum wants to see her daughter. She doesn't want to see her daughter plus her daughter's boyfriend. There'll be time for that later."

"Don't bet on it. Are you going back to your place, or mine?"

"I'm going to walk a bit," Mordred said. "Then I'll toss a coin."

A black cab pulled up. She waved discreetly to the driver, who acknowledged her with a half-smile. "This is mine," she said. She kissed him lightly on the lips. "See you later maybe. Or tomorrow. Love you."

"I love you too," Mordred said.

"Can I share a taxi?" Alec asked her.

"You'll have to squeeze in with Annabel and Tariq," she replied. "I'm going halves with them. But I can't see why they'd object. We're all in roughly the same direction."

Alec gently slapped Mordred's upper arm. "Don't mope too much. Remember what you're always telling everyone: there is an afterlife. You've got more reason for optimism than me and Richard Dawkins. What exactly's up, anyway, if you don't mind me asking? I mean, apart from the obvious."

"It hasn't got a name."

"Describe it then."

"When someone you loved dies and you feel the need to re-evaluate your own life. Don't worry, I'm not going off the rails."

Alec shrugged and smiled. "Hey, it used to be considered normal. So I've heard. See you tomorrow then."

"Thanks for the concern."

"What friends are for. Call me if you get suicidal."

"He's more likely to call *me*," Phyllis interjected. "I'm the love of his life, not you. You're okay, aren't you, John?"

Mordred laughed. "I'm fine. Just ... not that tired."

When the others left in the taxi, he set off westwards. If you wanted to walk at this time of night in London, that's what you had to do: choose a direction and stick to it. The sky was starry, the smells of the air changed as you walked along – diesel, nothing, curry, diesel again, something putrid, then nothing again, then diesel – and, as usual in this part of the city, there was hardly anyone around. He put his head down and his hands into his trouser pockets. He hadn't brought a coat.

Ian's death had shocked him perhaps more than he realised when he first heard. That form filling-in this morning, just before they were allowed out to the funeral, had made things worse. As if MI7 was taking advantage of their vulnerability to get them to sign something they wouldn't otherwise have touched. Alec was right. They didn't know what the hell they were volunteering for. None of them had read the small print... probably. Maybe Annabel? He'd have to ask her. They were all focussed on grieving. In any sane, normal job, it could easily have waited till tomorrow. Not at Thames House.

Funny thing about Ian, though. How Mordred had hardly thought about him since he'd left. Three years ago, when he first heard he was in Syria, his immediate concern was about how he'd be treated when he got back; who would employ him; how far the intelligence services would interest themselves in his case; how he'd fit back into a civilian routine; what tales he'd have to tell. Even about whether he'd hack it over there, or whether he'd realise he'd done something stupid and quietly hop on the next plane, boat or coach home. Slink back into Britain under cover of darkness, brimful of self-contempt; get a job at Tesco, night-shift, stacking shelves.

At no point had it really occurred to him – not really: once or twice, perhaps, as an academic possibility – that Ian might not be coming back.

And now he wasn't, ever.

He hadn't even visited Ian and Thelma's Facebook page; hadn't even looked at it.

He was a complete bastard, really. That was how Ian had probably thought of him, on the few occasions he reviewed his time as an intelligence officer. He'd probably expected his MI7 colleagues to make some sort of comment on his decision. Even just a *Good luck*.

But no.

In fairness, they'd been ordered not to. *We were only following orders*, how did that sound? And Ian must have known that would happen.

And it could have exposed him to ungrounded suspicions.

That was the crucial thing, really. The one thing Mordred and his colleagues had to say in their defence. *We'd have happily dropped you a line, Ian, but your new friends over there might have twigged we're all spies.*

How true was it? Or was it just an excuse? After all, they'd all been to his funeral, even if they hadn't stayed to express their condolences.

The truth, if there was one, was that it wasn't possible to know. Life can only be lived going forwards, but you only understand it looking back – who had said that?

Whoever it was, they were wrong. You *never* understood it. All you did was tell yourself a story about it, loosely based on the facts – although your memory of *those* was never perfect, and sometimes probably not even adequate – and you filed it away somewhere in your mental hard drive, and every so often you'd bring it out and polish it up. If you were good at telling stories, you made it consistent with all the other half-arsed yarns you spun about yourself. If you weren't, you didn't. Either way, you got what cod psychologists called 'closure'. Not understanding. 'Closure'. A stupid word that no one bothered to use thirty years ago before the world got self-obsessed and soppy.

Ian was gone forever – at least from this world. This was now an *Ian-less* planet. Stegosaurus, Triceratops, *Homo Erectus*, William the Conqueror, Henry VIII, Anne Boleyn, Ian and Thelma. All equally extinct now. *Equally.*

21

It seemed both incredible and horrible in equivalent measures.

He stopped and looked up at the stars. Normally, you couldn't see them that well, because of the light pollution, but somehow, he'd reached a lull in the glow.

This is where you start having clichéd thoughts, he realised. *The smallness of everything.*

But we *were* small! We *were* nothing! And he couldn't express it to himself in any way that hadn't been done a million times before, in exactly the same way. Ian was gone; he and Phyllis were next.

But the weird thing was, we'd been nothing before. Billions of years had passed during which we hadn't been here. And that was coming back, far faster than everyone knew. Part of you thought: why isn't everyone screaming? But you knew why. Because what would be the point? It was work tomorrow, and someone had to take the bin out. Recycling this week; waste next.

He put both hands on his head. *Don't mope too much. Remember what you're always telling everyone: there is an afterlife.*

There was. He didn't know how he knew it, but there was something more than this. It wasn't even that there had to be. There didn't have to be. But there was. Ian and Thelma weren't dead, not in the absolute sense. He'd see them again. And he'd explain why he'd never visited their Facebook page.

He wiped the water from his eyes.

They'd be okay with it. His phone rang. *Phyllis.*

"Just checking you're okay again," she said. "I didn't like to do it while the others were there. Are you on your way home yet?"

"Just about to flag down a taxi. I love you, Phyllis."

He heard her chuckle. "Two specks of life holding on to each other in a cold, indifferent universe. That's what something like today does to you. Forces you to think. And it's not unhealthy. Makes you realise what you've got. I love you too."

"Good luck with your mum."

"Thanks. Now go home and get some sleep." She hung up.

Probably best place to find a taxi this time of night would be the crossroads at the Royal Exchange, where the traffic lights were. Two seconds away. If that didn't work, he'd call one. It was starting to rain.

He was about to put his phone back in his pocket when he heard it. It took him a moment to realise what it was, then his brain went into recognition mode. A middle-aged man, running and screaming for help, being pursued by others – two, three, four, maybe more – in some kind of... dragon masks?

Because he was attuned to the complex nuances of speech and behaviour – part of his job as Red Department's expert linguist – he immediately grasped what the few other passers-by apparently couldn't: that this wasn't some kind of prank. Here was a man in desperate fear of his life. Probably about to be assaulted or worse.

Where the hell were the police when you needed them?

But he was already running, pursuing the pursuers and accelerating fast.

Five of them, all in masks, shouting encouragement to each other. They more or less herded him into Princes Street, with its huge blank wall on one side and the offices on the other: at this time of night, about as deserted a spot as you could hope for anywhere in London. The timbre of their voices confirmed what Mordred already knew: this was a deadly hunt, nothing frivolous about it. Whoever these men were, they were intent on murder.

His one advantage lay in the element of surprise. He came up behind the last chaser, grabbed his collar and braked hard, yanking him off his feet. No time for explanations. He pulled the mask off in one motion – it was rubber, enclosed the whole head, and clearly designed to resemble a griffin – and punched the man hard in the face. Then, painfully conscious that he was already losing the others, he rived the mask over his own head and resumed chasing.

Whatever was happening, it had reached the last act. The victim had collapsed in exhaustion against the wall. He hugged himself and whimpered as the rain thundered down on and around him.

The others looked in no hurry. They gathered round him and took out knives. Mordred ran up and inserted himself amongst them. No idea what he'd do yet, but two versus four could just work. And the police might conceivably be on their way. Or not. Perhaps he could give them a call. The emergency button on his phone. He'd never yet used it, but -

It was gone. It must have missed his pocket in the mayhem.

Then something happened that changed everything. The man Mordred thought he'd punched unconscious staggered up behind him, looking like a blood-soaked monster yes, but also gasping and pointing.

Too late Mordred realised he'd walked into a locked room. If he hadn't been dressed for a funeral, perhaps he wouldn't have stood out so starkly. But the mask was no disguise now its original owner was back on the scene. His black suit and tie marked him out as blatantly as if someone had painted a target on his chest.

Which is where the knife went in.

He gasped and looked down at himself, like an idiot.

His shirt was… red. Boy, it had gone in quite a long way! So why didn't it feel like anything?

He was cold. His head seemed to float away. He thought of Ian.

Chapter 3: Good Knife and Sweet Dreams

Meadows laughed when he saw what had happened. The way the blond guy went down, like a sack of coal. The funniest thing wasn't that, though, but the look in his eyes when he realised he was dead. Spaced out, man. Not your usual, by any stretch. And of course, the way Paul was freaking out, that was also hilarious: laughing and crying, a bit of both, yet weirdly, neither. He wasn't used to stabbing people to death. Not in the least. He carried the knife as an ornament, essentially.

No undoing it now, though. And Paul looked awful, poor guy. Like his entire face was gushing blood.

On the other hand, he'd done well. One thrust, straight in. A natural, you'd think, if he hadn't immediately lost control of his reactions. Still, over time, he might get used to a little recreational killing. They'd see.

The blood thing was good. His mask had been removed, so the CCTV would probably have picked him up. But looking like that, identification would be impossible. And it was raining. If he'd left a trail – as he almost certainly had – it'd be washed away.

No time to dwell, though. They still had the blogger to deal with.

Theoretically, they could take their time over him. They had him surrounded. He'd dropped to his arse next to the wall and he was trying to make himself small, hands over head, curling up, like he thought a good kicking might be all that was on the cards. But, not so deep down, he must know it'd be more than that. Crucial thing was, he'd stopped believing he could escape.

But it wasn't a pretty sight, Paul *and* the blogger blubbing like babies, and it was sapping the others' morale. Meadows got his own knife out, grabbed the blogger's hair, raised him from the ground like a wounded animal, and thrust the blade into his chest. He died with a little whimper, like a gasp. No point in prolonging it.

The expected Ford Fiesta with blanked-out number plates pulled up. Its driver, a young male hipster with a plaited beard and wraparound sunglasses, got out and opened the boot. Tony and Hilldy took the canister of acid out and administered it slowly and methodically, like the corpse was a potted plant that required sensitive watering. Calm, professional; beautiful in a way.

Paul lit a cigarette. He shook.

"You did well," Meadows told him, putting a supportive hand on his back. "No need to look so *cut up* about it." He laughed.

"Good *knife* and sweet dreams," Hilldy said.

Tony threw the plastic canister away like he might as well give the police a little something. And they were all wearing gloves, so no worries. "I bet he's sorry you *holed* him up," he said, giving Paul's shoulder a supportive squeeze.

Meadows roared with laughter. They were probably out of the CCTV range here, which was almost a shame. The murders had both been clean as a whistle, not a trace of sadism, hardly even enough to frighten the kiddies, and this was top-level banter. They should be on TV, really. Five clean-cut early-thirtysomething guys, handsome as hell, rich, athletic, lethal in a corner, and great company. Like *Fight Club*, but better.

Meadows took his own knife, put it in the blond guy's hand and squeezed the limp fingers to the handle just long enough to leave prints. It wouldn't fool the police for long, but it would buy a little time.

He had the sudden feeling the blond guy wasn't dead.

If so, pulling Paul's knife from his chest would finish the job.

But why bother? If he lived, he wouldn't be available for interview for some time. Unconsciously, the police would pin their hopes on him, which meant they'd be just a tiny bit less punctilious in other crucial areas. Which could be very useful. After all, Mystery Guy hadn't seen anything the CCTV hadn't, and what he had seen, he probably wouldn't remember. When they finally got round to questioning him, he'd likely be the biggest dud since Jell-o Salad.

And the police too might actually be completely useless. It did happen. They might even swallow the fit-up.

"Leave it," he said, stopping Paul as he leaned down to retrieve his knife. "It's better where it is, believe me. I'll explain later. Get in the car."

They had to split, pronto. This might be a deserted part of the city, especially at this time of night, but someone would have seen. The police would be on their way.

A siren in the distance, right on cue.

They piled into the car. It pulled away at a respectable, non-suspicious speed.

Chapter 4: Scene of the Murder

Nicholas Fleming was at home in bed when he received the call. He got up without disturbing his wife, and dressed quickly in the bathroom where he could check his appearance in the mirror before leaving, ensure there was no hint of sleepiness such as might undermine anyone's confidence in him: tall, dark eyes, dark eyebrows, firm jawline, all alert. He descended the stairs, closed the front door quietly and drove to Princes Street in the heart of London's Square Mile. Four police cars had already arrived. The area had been cordoned off and floodlit with moveable arc lamps so Forensics could collect samples. It rained heavily. Detective Sergeant Ava Bach – almost as tall as he was, thin, with a habitually serious expression and blonde hair almost entirely tucked beneath her hat – stood ready to brief him. He put on his police coat and showed his Met ID as he got out of the car. He raised his umbrella.

"What have we got?" he asked solemnly.

"Double stabbing, sir," Bach said. "Two white males. Both in their early thirties by the looks of it. One fatality. The other's been taken to hospital, condition critical."

"Any witnesses?"

"No one's come forward. We're retrieving the CCTV."

"Any indication as to exactly what happened?"

"We're still working on it."

"From what you've told me so far, it sounds like a simple knife fight, right?"

"Except it can't have been. True, both men were holding knives when we arrived, so they could have stabbed each other, but we don't think that's likely. First, the dead man's face and fingertips have been... significantly eaten away with sulphuric acid. Post-mortem. But the other guy was several metres away, and we think he was stabbed first. There's no discernible trail of blood running from him to the deceased, although the rain would have washed most of it away, in any case."

"But he did have the acid container next to him, I assume. Empty."

"That's right. But there was no acid on him. According to the initial assessment, anyway. Which may change. You'd expect a little in the way of splashback, at least."

"So we think… there's a third party, someone who tried to frame the second victim?"

"It seems likely. It may or may not be significant, but the murder victim was carrying a damaged hard drive in a pouch sewn to the inside of his jacket. The acid almost certainly destroyed it beyond retrieval."

"What was he doing down here? In this part of town? Do we know that?"

"We don't even know who he was. Or what he looked like."

"What about the second guy? Description?"

"Tall, well-built, blond curly hair, about six-two. Wearing a black suit and tie. We're checking out nearby funerals today now."

"Maybe he saw himself as a *Reservoir Dogs* character. There's a lot of fantasy in the gangland world. Lack of a funeral would count, in my view, albeit infinitesimally, against his innocence. You say he wasn't carrying any identification. Not even a phone? Did either of them have phones?"

"If they did, they don't now."

"It's starting to look like a professional job. In any case, we need to get hold of the CCTV asap."

"That should be available any minute."

"Keep looking into those funerals. Might turn something up, though how he got from a funeral to here's a mystery in itself. We'll put out an appeal for witnesses tomorrow, and hope our casualty makes it through the night. He should supply us with at least some answers, though it may be a while before he's up to being interviewed."

"If ever."

"Get a good picture of him, if you can. I know it sounds insensitive, but before the family gets involved. Put together a team to ask around in the vicinity, see if anyone saw anything. Someone must have. And let me have any forensics results as soon as you hear anything concrete from the team."

"Yes, sir."

Jeffries, the head of the forensic scene investigation team – small, balding and middle-aged, with a stereotypical line in graveyard humour – came to stand by them. "We're ready to move the body now," he said. "Can't say anything for certain yet, but it looks like the two victims were attacked separately by a third party or parties. In case you're wondering, that hard drive's obliterated. The acid would probably have ruined it, but it looks like whoever it belonged to made determined attempts to destroy it beforehand. It was already useless, in other words, when the attack commenced. You got the CCTV up yet?"

Fleming shook his head. Jeffries made a face as if that's what he'd been expecting and it was typical of life generally. "Given that you're probably considering house-to-house enquiries at some point, why not start there" – he pointed to Mansion House, the Palladian style manor at the crossroads in front of them – "with the Lord Mayor?" He grinned. "I've heard the latest incumbent's a real live wire."

Bach and Fleming exchanged looks. They both picked up London's free newspapers every day, *Metro* in the morning, *Standard* in the evening. They'd both heard the same thing. Probably everyone in the capital had.

"If we're lucky," Fleming replied airily, "it may not come to that. CCTV, a possible witness lying in hospital. We haven't all the pieces by any means but it could be enough to yield a few suspects."

Jefferies shook his head. He hadn't taken his eyes off Mansion House. "Maybe," he said. "Maybe."

Chapter 5: Meeting with Mum

One day, someone would write a novel about AXW51.

The only problem would be getting people to believe it was based on fact. Because 'based on fact' was important with novels. Readers loved it. It helped propel sales.

But how to persuade anyone that there was a sealed-off department in the basement of Thames House, London SW1, manned exclusively by retired civil servants whose job was to take delivery of information from the police – information the police weren't officially supposed to give - and match it to unnamed passport photos of active British spies?

Bet Leveson was determined to capture the market as soon as it materialised, so she had her own novel fully worked out. *Misidentification*. It helped with marketing if the title was a single word.

Chapter one was set down here where they all worked. B43, a poky little room with four filing cabinets, a pair of PC's, two telephones, a fax machine, a nice little table lamp that someone had bought in a car boot sale (and which, to everyone down here's surprise, MI7 Security had certified as fit for use), and two elderly personnel always on duty.

The action began when one of AXW51's contacts in the Met sent it a bodycam picture of a murder victim. *Time of death: 01.53* – twenty minutes ago! Using the latest face-recognition software, and the anonymised material in the filing cabinets, the two duty staff quickly identified the dead man as 'one of ours' – no more than that; the relevant information was passed to whoever was on the other end of the phone that night, and AXW51 did nothing more about it, because that was where its job ended. All 95% real stuff.

But then, the next day, the duty member of staff – Elsie, she was called: a 75-year-old widow with a flat in Camden - actually *saw* the murder victim *in Hyde Park!* And the way she and he exchanged glances gave her recognition away. She realised with a start that 'one of ours' didn't necessarily mean a *British* spy. It could mean *any* spy. Just 'known to British intelligence', that was all.

Next thing, she was chased through five different continents by shadowy figures determined to kill her. Her only hope of rectifying the *misidentification* – hence the title – lay with her son (an unemployed former car salesman with two failed marriages behind him), her seven-year-old granddaughter (a computer wizard, Mensa 162), and eleventh hour contact with the other OAP's who worked in AXW51. But it wasn't easy, oh no. Lots of people got shot dead along the way. In Chapter 25, an eighty-five-year-old colleague was hurled from the top of the Eiffel Tower.

Exactly the sort of thing any decent literary agent would jump at, and just begging to be made into a film, never mind a novel.

So the likelihood that no one would believe its real-world counterpart even existed was a serious annoyance.

Thankfully, it wasn't the only novel she planned. She might be old but she'd long since learned never to put all her eggs in one basket. It wasn't a lesson she'd forget, either, no, no, not after she and Arno broke up.

The thing was, you got lots of time to think about possible plots down here, because there was nothing else to do. Officially, you had to stay alert. Upstairs had banned all card and board games, prolonged conversations, recreational reading, leisure pursuit puzzle-solving, and accessing your phone for other than emergency family calls.

Bet puffed up her dyed-black hair and sipped her tea. She only worked the night-shift four times a week. There was an average of one murder every three days in London, so most of her sessions were quiet. A hundred or so murders a year, and of those, how many were spies? None, as far as she knew. Spies' deaths were as rare as hen's teeth. It was a wonder the government kept paying for AXW51, but then, given how fawningly the intelligence services were treated, it probably didn't even realise it was.

Behind her, Albert sat in a wicker chair dipping a digestive into a coffee. It was like being married, only with a lot of electrical equipment, no available vacuum cleaner, and the odd inclusion of a murder victim.

Suddenly, there was a beep. Bet was closest to the monitor, so she moved the mouse. The UFO screensaver vanished leaving a police message in its place. *Two victims: one dead, second critical, Princes Street, EC2R.*

"We've got two vics," she told Albert solemnly.

But he'd already come to sit at the second monitor.

A series of six photos came through, three for each victim, all from slightly different angles. Both young men. Lots of blood.

Terrible, terrible.

The pixilation increased, revealing the detail.

Oh, my God. Oh, the poor -

"I'll take the… disfigured chap," Albert said in his cut-glass accent. "Not the sort of thing I'd expect a lady to deal with."

Bet had never found out what Albert had been before retiring – they weren't permitted to ask each other personal questions – but she always pictured him in the Foreign Office. He was in Chapter 19 of her novel.

The instructions for how to apply the recognition software and what to do next were written on laminated cards next to each mouse mat. Just as well, because she'd never remember them without. Especially after seeing that.

Five minutes passed. Albert gave a sigh. "Mine's completely unidentifiable. Another bloody acid attack, I suppose, God help this country; it's going to Hell in a handcart. What about yours, Bet?"

When she didn't reply, he leaned over, clocked her monitor and spoke without emotion. "Well, well, well. Bingo."

Annabel and Tariq got out of the taxi five minutes after Alec, and it set off for the Beaumont Hotel, half an hour's drive away. Phyllis sat on the back seat in her funeral clothes and looked out of the window. Not many people about, even in the brighter parts of the city. But then this was Thursday – Friday now? – *was* it Friday yet? She looked at her phone. *12.01*. Just.

Hopefully, her mum wouldn't keep her up too long, although it would be nice to see her again. *She'd* be tired too, wouldn't she? No, because the moment she'd heard her daughter wasn't coming till late, she'd have got down for one of her celebrated 'naps', an officially designated 'brief few moments of light sleep' that usually segued into three or four hours' deep slumber, sometimes in bed snoring. She'd be fully refreshed by now, ready to talk the hind legs off a donkey till at least sunrise.

And her dad? He'd definitely be asleep somewhere, although he'd likely put his head round for a dazed hello on one of his five or six nightly trips to the toilet.

What would they talk about? Always the same problem, there. What did you talk about to your mum when you were a singleton, no children, and a spy?

You made things up and tried to keep the details vague. When they seemed to be getting too complex, or you added something unnecessary (usually under pressure), you wrote down the details so you could revise them before your next meeting. You tried to steer the conversation to impersonal topics, or got your interlocutor to talk about him/herself. The last was generally easy, but not with your parents. Mostly, they wanted to talk about *you*, and *you alone*, and in minute detail. An utter bloody minefield. Not so bad if you were like John, one of five children. Phyllis only had one sibling: a brother, Francis, four years younger than her, married with two daughters, and the owner of an estate agent's in Stoke-on-Trent.

Maybe they could talk about him.

Or maybe she should be brutal. Say she was too tired for an interrogation.

Conversation. Not 'interrogation'. Definitely not. Never use that word with your mum.

She needed a coffee before she even walked in there. Ideally, an espresso.

Suddenly, it hit her. Of course, she knew what they'd talk about. They'd talk about her new boyfriend, John Mordred.

Good or bad? Her mum tried to give the impression she didn't mind him, though she definitely found his vegetarianism irksome. She'd tried to keep off the subject of politics during his one visit to their house, on the grounds that he'd been advertised as a woolly liberal and everything in the Robinson household was bright Tory-blue. She disliked his being a glorified travelling salesman who hawked machine parts to big companies abroad, and she'd even hinted that she didn't think such a job existed (although what she meant by that, neither of them knew).

She'd definitely want to know if he and her daughter were still together. The truth might be disappointing enough for her to consider releasing Phyllis from captivity and turning in for another epic nap.

But that seemed unlikely.

Thinking of John... She picked up her phone and called him.

"Just checking you're okay again," she said. "I didn't like to do it while the others were there. Are you on your way home yet?"

"Just about to flag down a taxi. I love you, Phyllis."

She chuckled. "Two specks of life holding on to each other in a cold, indifferent universe. That's what something like today does to you. Forces you to think. And it's not unhealthy. Makes you realise what you've got. I love you too."

"Good luck with your mum."

"Thanks. Now go home and get some sleep."

She hung up.

The fact was, it had been a long day. That form they had to fill in this morning: shouldn't have been remotely stressful, but it was. The sudden way it had appeared out of nowhere, the secrecy, the way they'd been allocated individual time-slots. All very reminiscent of *some of you will emerge with your jobs secure, some of you are going to be 'let go'*. Then straight off to the funeral and a completely different set of emotions. Then friends, a few drinks, a board game. Nice that her boyfriend had been the one to grab Monopoly. Most guys wouldn't have seen it as cool - for good reasons. But they'd thoroughly enjoyed themselves. Ruthlessly buying and selling chunks of London was a breath of fresh air. But it had taken it out of her, even just that.

Where was she going to get a coffee now? There were enough places open this time of night, definitely. The trouble was, would the taxi pass one? Even if it did –

She could order one at reception when she got there. Places such as the Beaumont, they'd probably do whatever you wanted whenever, providing you looked like you could pay the bill.

The taxi pulled up. She paid and went inside. Polished walnut, prominent browns and greys, Art-Deco style. She gave her name at the desk and ordered an espresso. The receptionist – a thin, middle-aged woman with an orange bouffant - rang her mother's room, then informed her politely that Mrs Robinson was on her way, and added that, if she'd like to take a seat, they could bring her coffee to her here.

The lift doors swished open and her mother stepped out, arms extended, beaming. She wore a blue trouser suit, heels and lots of jewellery. "Phyllie!" she exclaimed. She clasped her daughter's forearms and leaned forward and kissed her. "You finally made it!"

"Why didn't you tell me you were coming to London? I could have taken the day off."

"We didn't want to inconvenience you. And we wanted to surprise you. We'll catch up for ten minutes, then I'm packing you off to bed. I've booked you a room here, just for tonight, so you don't have to go home. I've brought some of your clothes from home, so you can change too, if you want to, before going to work. And I've booked a taxi for 8am, although I wasn't quite sure where to tell it to go. Still, it's fully paid for, for an hour."

Phyllis laughed. "Oh, my God. Where do you get the money?"

"Your father won the lottery a few years ago. We never told you, because… I'm *joking!* Don't worry, we can more than afford it. We may not have won anything, but we're crafty investors, and we've got very – oh, who cares? We're not here to talk about accountants and offshore banking and all that guff – most of which, frankly, I don't understand anyway. We're here to talk about *you*. And we've only got ten minutes. How are you, anyway? Are you and 'John' still together?"

"He actually asked me to marry him a while ago."

"Oh my word. You…?"

"I said no."

"Oh, thank God. I mean, not that I don't like him. He's sweet enough, and he's got an attractive face. But I'm not sure he's in your *cultural* league, Phyllie. There, I've said it. Anyway, you've got to make your own life-choices. Whatever you decide to do in life, you'll always have our support, that goes without saying. But we're here to give advice too, obviously. Anyway, enough about 'John'. What about you?"

"I kind of wish I'd said yes. If he asks me again, I probably will."

Her mother laughed. "You're teasing."

They walked into the lift. Her mother pressed 4, then continued, "Anyway, even if you're not, what's it matter? There's no such thing as a ready-made husband. Even the most promising prospects are, at best, half-formed. It's for *us* to make them into the finished article. I fully admit 'John' will probably require a fair bit of polishing, but I'm sure he's not completely beyond a woman's redemption. He can cook and iron, I take it?"

The lift doors opened. A man in a uniform stood in the corridor with Phyllis's espresso on a tray.

"What's that?" her mother said.

The uniformed man uttered the words, "Your espresso, ma'am" at the same time as Phyllis said, "I ordered a coffee", and at exactly the same volume. The result was a noise, and Phyllis's mother had to ask again.

"Coffee," Phyllis said.

"For you?"

"Yes."

"Where did it come from?"

"I ordered it at reception."

Her mother clicked her tongue. "I do wish you'd consulted me. I don't want you drinking coffee. Not so that you can jabber away into the wee hours, anyway. No, I want you to get a good night's sleep. Take it away, please," she told the man, as if it was entirely his fault.

They went into the room. "You must see Antony Gormley's *ROOM* while you're here. It's amazing. He's the man who did *The Angel of the North*, you know. Not entirely to my taste, but then, who am I to judge? I'm not an art expert. Mind you, a lot of modern art's complete rubbish."

A big double bed, in which her father was pretending to be asleep, a chaise longue, a matching sofa and chair, lots of framed pictures on the wall, lamps with expensive shades, gladioli in fluted flower bowls.

"Keep your voice down," her mother whispered, removing her shoes, sitting on the sofa and patting the space next to her in one continuous gesture. "Your father's asleep."

As if in response to this, her father half sat up, gave a little wave and said, "Hullo, Phyllie."

"Hi, Dad."

He swung his feet over the side of the bed, trudged past them, dressed only in a pair of Union Jack Y-fronts, and went into what was presumably the toilet. A few seconds later, they heard it flush, then he plodded back the way he'd come, got back under the covers, and said, "Well, see you both in the morning".

"Good night," they said in unison.

Her mother rolled her eyes. "Right, well now you're here - "

There was a knock at the door. They looked at each other. Her mother sighed irritably and got up. It was the uniformed man who'd met them from the lift with Phyllis's espresso.

"There's a man downstairs asking to see your guest, Mrs Robinson," he said to Phyllis's mother. "He says it's an emergency. Name of, er" – he looked at a card – "Alec Cunningham."

It took Phyllis a second to digest this. *Alec?* What did Alec want?

She couldn't just walk out. Not now. "I'll call down to reception," she said. "See if it really is an emergency. Friend from work," she added in a feeble stab at an explanation.

Even as she picked up the receiver, she knew she was wasting precious time, entirely to placate her mother. *Of course* it was an emergency. Alec wouldn't come out at this time for nothing.

"Alec?" she said, when reception put him on. "Why didn't you call my mobile?"

"Some news you need to get personally," he said. "Ruby Parker's out of the country, so I've been deputised. Long story short, John's been stabbed and he's lying in hospital fighting for his life."

Phyllis gasped like she'd been thumped in the sternum. "Are you sure? I've only just spoken to him!" Then it sank a millimetre further in, enough to seem real. "Oh, my God! Who? When?"

"We don't know the culprit, but when: shortly after we left him. Come downstairs. There's a taxi waiting to take us to the hospital. You can tell your mum what's happened, by the way. Apparently, it's not classified information."

"John's been stabbed," she told her mother. "I've got to go."

She didn't stop long enough to register her mother's re-action, although she expected she'd be equally horrified, whatever she thought of 'John'.

She descended to reception via the stairs. She passed Alec without breaking stride and they went straight to his taxi. She recognised the symptoms in herself. She was in shock. And shocked that she was in shock. She'd been in the army, for God's sake, and nowadays she was supposed to be a bloody spy. How could someone with her training have any truck with shock?

But this was different. She'd been sitting with her mum; it was about the man she'd just admitted she was seriously considering marrying, the one she'd been on the phone with only … which was part of the unreality. *I've only just spoken to him!*

She got a grip sufficiently to listen to what Alec was telling her. A combination of information and instructions.

"There was a dead guy at the scene. John was holding the murder weapon, but we expect the CCTV to exonerate him, quite apart from the obvious – to us - fact he couldn't have done it. A member of the public found his phone lying in the road nearby, and turned it in to the police a short while ago. No one knows exactly what happened, but Ruby Parker's going with the available evidence: random attack by a gang of thugs. Probably a robbery that went wrong. For that reason, we're not putting out an 'official' version. Nothing we need to hide. You also need to ring his family. The police will anyway, but it's what's expected in a situation like this. You can tell them the truth. John was attacked and stabbed by a bunch of gutter rats in London City centre. We don't know the details."

"How bad is he?"

"I've already told you: he's fighting for his life. Critical. But he's made it to hospital, that's a start."

"I don't know his parents' number. But I've got one of his sisters on my phone. I'll call her."

"You don't have to do it right now."

"Which hospital?"

"Saint Thomas's."

She held her phone limply in her right hand and robotically rehearsed what she was meant to say. "John's been stabbed. He's in intensive care in Saint Thomas's hospital. Police think it was a random attack by a gang of thugs. Probably a robbery that went wrong. John's been stabbed. He's in intensive care in Saint Thomas's hospital. Police think it was a random attack by a gang of thugs. Probably a robbery that went wrong."

She took four deep breaths, opened her contacts list, scrolled down to *Hannah Lexingwood* and pressed Call.

Chapter 6: The Return of Murgatroyd

An hour after returning from Princes Street, Fleming sat in darkness in his first floor office at New Scotland Yard, reviewing the CCTV footage. DS Bach stood close behind him and next to her, Sergeant Alan Green, young, close-cropped brown hair, well-trimmed beard. On the desk, Fleming's papers sat in careful order, otherwise, the room was cramped and impersonal with a vague smell of carpet cleaner.

"It's pretty good stuff," Green said. "I make it five of them. The other guy's definitely not with them. Given that he actually pulls one of their masks off."

"Pity he then stands in front of the guy and punches his face," Bach said. "The angle and the whole aftermath make the whole thing pretty useless."

"Some kind of have-a-go-hero, presumably," Bach suggested. "Unless he's a friend of the murder victim."

"He could be a friend of the *murderers*," Green said. "At least in theory. Someone who knew them, but didn't share their antipathy to the dead man."

Bach shrugged. "You mean the fact that – maybe - he tried to stop them doesn't necessarily entail his not knowing them."

"Exactly," Green replied. "It could even have been a fight over the masks. Six men, five masks. Sounds weird, but I've known weirder."

Fleming frowned his disagreement, but didn't express it yet. There was a more important consideration. "How is he, our second victim?"

"Still critical," Bach said. "Still hanging in."

"Presumably the perpetrators are wearing masks because they're aware of the CCTV," he said, returning to

Green's point. "And those masks all match. So it must have been premeditated. Making it unlikely the second victim knew the attackers. They wouldn't have exposed themselves to such a potential hazard."

Green let out a flute of air, frowned and nodded. "Agreed."

"Matching masks?" Bach said. "And rather – I don't know – 'reptilian'? Could it have been some kind of… ritual killing? Maybe? Like a Satanic thing?"

"Jefferies mentioned the Lord Mayor," Green said. "Those look to me like griffin masks. They're the spitting image of the dragons you see around the City. I know Jefferies wasn't entirely serious, but maybe there is some sort of connection. I've heard some odd stuff about the present Lord Mayor, and he's a very different proposition to anyone who's held the post before. There've been lots of… parties at Mansion House since he was installed. Not normally a party venue. Not his sort of party."

"There wasn't one last night," Bach said. "I've checked."

"Where would you *obtain* masks like that?" Fleming said. "If we can find out - "

There was a knock at the door. Sengupta, from the ground floor night-duty squad, put her head round. "There's someone to see you, DCI Fleming, sir," she said casually. "A 'Mr John Murgatroyd'. Asked for you by name, and requested a meeting alone. 'Without his colleagues', was how he put it. Says he has information about the murder in Princes Street."

Fleming straightened. "He's got my name? Where from?"

Sengupta shrugged. "I'm afraid I don't know. Not from us. I've put him in A11, sir. Nice and comfortable, so as to put him at his ease. Thought you might want to talk to him informally first. Find out if he's *bona fide*."

Fleming walked decisively into A11, an empty room with three or four padded chairs, and a low-level table strewn with well-thumbed car and cookery magazines. He extended his hand to the seated occupant, a white male, middle-aged, stout, balding, in a dishevelled grey suit and scuffed brown shoes. A carton of nectarines perched in his lap, one of which he was eating. Juice dripped down his chin.

Obviously a crank.

"Detective Inspector Fleming," he said cordially. He could warn him about wasting police time later, if necessary. "Pleased to meet you... Mr Murgatroyd? I understand you have some information about tonight's murder."

The man surprised Fleming by neither standing up nor accepting the proffered handshake. That, plus his glower, plus the hard eye-contact he made, his inexplicably relaxed body-language, the tub of fruit, and the mystery of how he'd even obtained Fleming's name to begin with, turned the temperature in the room down several degrees.

"Sit down, Detective Inspector," he said stonily.

As if he wasn't just anyone. That mixture of contempt and authority. Like he knew things about Fleming and his little world.

Like he was a spook.

Of course. A ritual, possibly occult, murder from one angle. From another: very like the kind of twisted thing British intelligence might have a hand in. The hard drive, the clumsy attempt to make the whole episode look like a knife fight, the acid: all bits of a puzzle. One that, given the involvement of the espionage fraternity – assuming that's what this was - would now probably never be explained, like that poor guy found in the bag padlocked from the outside, several years back. Weird, true - and yet still, all this time later, essentially mysterious.

"I guess you're going to tell me to back off," Fleming replied bitterly. "The case, I mean."

The man smiled for the first time, like they were on roughly the same wavelength. He paused to take the pip from his nectarine and transferred it to a tissue "What makes you say that?"

"Because I know who you are. MI7 – or 'MI5', as you still like to call yourself for PR purposes."

"Very perceptive. I trust you're not wearing a wire." He held his hands up. "Joke, just a joke. Of course, you worked for MI7 yourself for a brief period, Nicholas. Until you realised it was incompatible with a happy family life. Although I happen to know your wife's still very much part of the setup in White Department. Really *going places*, I understand."

"Stop showing off, whatever your true name is, and get to the point. What do you want? Because if I really, really have to drop this case, fine. In that case, we might as well get this conversation out of the way so I can return home and get back in bed."

"On the contrary, like I told PC Sengupta only a few moments ago, I want to help you."

Fleming scoffed. "Oh, really? In what way?"

"Although I can tell you roughly what happened, I can't tell you much more than you've already got from the CCTV footage. You'll find the perpetrators' burned-out car soon, if I'm not very much mistaken. It won't help you. My novel contribution is that the second victim – the one who's now in hospital - is an MI7 agent called John Mordred. You met him once, I believe, very briefly, just over a year ago."

"My God, that was *John Mordred?*"

"The same."

"This must go deeper than I thought."

Murgatroyd shrugged. "I'm pretty certain Mr Mordred stumbled on the whole thing by accident. He saw a man in trouble and tried to help."

"You want me to cooperate in covering his name up, is that it?"

"We're not going to cover it up. Like I said, he was there by chance."

"But of course, I'm not allowed to share my knowledge that he's a member of British intelligence with my colleagues."

"Don't blame me for that," Murgatroyd replied. "Ask yourself: how to explain that you know who John Mordred is without letting on that you were once intimately involved with MI7? Which, if you do, puts you in breach of the legally binding non-disclosure agreement you presumably signed when you joined up. No, I'd keep it to myself, if I were you, Nicholas. We're not going to cover up his name, or the facts about what happened to him tonight. We're simply going to conceal the fact that he's a British intelligence officer. In my world, that doesn't really count as a cover up."

"So what is it you want that merits a personal visit? So far, you've simply told me the name of the second victim. Which I'd have discovered soon enough anyway."

"Not if we didn't want you to."

"Oh, come on. He's in intensive care. Even *you* can't make a man disappear when he needs urgent medical attention. You can only conceal so much. We might not have found out he was working for MI7, but we'd have discovered his *name,* for God's sake. Give us *some* credit!"

Murgatroyd wiped his lips with a tissue. He didn't look fazed. "Let me come to the point then. *I* – and for all practical purposes, you may take that pronoun to mean the deepest levels of British intelligence – believe there's something significantly amiss in the City of London at the moment. I can't be any more precise than that, not here. Somehow, what happened tonight is part of it. I don't know how. And, with respect, I'm pretty sure you don't have the means at your disposal to find out. Left to your own devices, you'll go round in circles. Two facts. First, there's been a murder committed; that makes it your business. Second, I'm interested. That makes it my business."

Fleming laughed. "And that's your idea of 'coming to the point', is it? Thank goodness you decided not to beat about the bush."

"Quiz me."

"I've still no idea what you've got in mind."

"A partnership, Nicholas."

Fleming hooted. "You and me?"

"You and John Mordred."

"Whoa." He took a sharp breath and frowned. "Sorry, slow down, that seems disrespectful. Firstly, from what I've heard, John Mordred – assuming it is him - might not even make it through the night. But even if he does, since you said he was there by chance, that must mean you haven't yet asked him, and I might not need or want him."

"He'll pull through. And by that time, you'll have worked out for yourself that you're not going to get anywhere without some kind of *deus ex machina*. And he'll reach the same conclusion about his own involvement even faster."

"Don't be so sure. We've got a lot of leads."

"I've seen them. They're junk."

"Forgive me if I don't take your word for that."

"I wouldn't expect you to. What I *do* expect is for you to spend the next few weeks chasing your own tail and becoming increasingly frustrated. I could be wrong, of course." He gave an acerbic smile, picked another nectarine from the carton and bit a chunk off. "Except I'm not."

"Omniscience must be a wonderful thing."

"He'll find *you*, incidentally. On this." He took a cheap mobile from his pocket and laid it on the *Good Food* magazine, on the edge of the table. "You don't have to do anything. You don't even have to wait. If it helps, you can forget we ever spoke."

"Was he at a funeral this afternoon?"

"That won't help you in the slightest. Probably no one there remembers him. And those that do won't come forward."

One last desperate bid for a lead. "The Lord Mayor. Is he involved?"

Murgatroyd stood up. "Time for me to depart now. Would you like a nectarine? They're not poisoned."

"No, thanks."

"In answer to your question: he could be. He could very well be."

He put the carton under his arm like it was a despatch box and strode casually towards the exit. He paused in the doorway and turned a wistful look on his interlocutor. "Good luck, Nicholas. I don't just mean in solving the case. I mean, in literally surviving it. Coming out alive. You and John both." He smiled. "Hey, cheer up. I'm rooting for you."

Chapter 7: Good Old Gajapathi

The journey from the Beaumont to St Thomas's hospital took just over five minutes. Alec escorted Phyllis inside and sat with her for ten minutes, then his mobile rang. He got to his feet, shook his head apologetically and said, "Things to arrange. Really sorry", before walking out.

The waiting area was predictably glum and anonymous. Almost all the seats were occupied, mostly by tired, miserable looking people, and in pairs, since the conventional wisdom was that being somewhere like this alone was just too pitiable. Some sat in hoodies with the hoods up and their legs outstretched, apparently asleep. Others conversed in low voices, or gazed into space or at the floor. Occasionally, someone would struggle to their feet and visit the coffee machine or the water cooler, more like it was an integral part of their ordeal than an attempt to relieve it. Something made it feel as if the darkness outside was permanent; that the sun wouldn't rise again until you got exactly what you came for, which might be never. Nurses and doctors appeared at random intervals from beyond double doors, sashayed about at a distance, stopped for whispered conferences with colleagues, then disappeared back behind the scenes.

Phyllis got a vivid sense of the Mordred clan determinedly on the move in distant places. After her initial contact with Hannah, she got a call from Charlotte, who lived in Devon, to say she was on her way. Then Charlotte got back in touch to say another sister - Julia, a novelist who lived in Norway - was coming. Hannah texted to say John's parents had set off from Hexham; thirty minutes later, Hannah herself was at JFK, about to board for Heathrow. Mabel, the youngest sibling, was in Italy, and *en route* by bus to

Rome Fiumicino Airport. None of them asked what exactly they could do for John, practically speaking. That didn't matter, or rather it was a subordinate consideration. All that counted was a member of their family was in serious trouble. Their reaction was immediate, decisive and automatic, as if they meant to deploy a ritual, learned long ago, to merge wills by his bedside and make everything right.

Yet the practical details weren't entirely neglected. One of the first things Hannah did was call the hospital and authorise Phyllis to receive information as a family representative. Then Phyllis's phone started going with messages of concern about *her*. From John's mother, for example. *Sorry you're alone at the moment. We're on our way. If you need anything, call me. Thank you so much for being there.* Then a call from her own mother to ask if she was okay ('I'd come along, but I suppose John's parents'll be coming, and they won't want a newcomer getting in the way. I do hope he'll be okay. If you need *anything*...') Then another text from Hannah to say that 'Tim' would be arriving any minute.

She knew she was tired, but who was 'Tim'?

A middle-aged man in a white doctor's coat stepped through the door behind the reception desk. Someone she vaguely recognised. Bearded, balding, circular wire-framed glasses, and about average height and build. He surveyed the waiting room with a grim expression and his eyes met and locked on Phyllis's. His mien stayed the same.

Her heart sank horribly and she rose to her feet. He came from behind the desk to meet her.

"Phyllis?" he said.

"Er, yes?"

"Tim," he said, offering a handshake. "We met once at John's parents' house."

Oh God, she remembered now. The notorious 'Brexit meal', where they'd all ended up arguing - mainly with her.

Hannah's husband, this was: John's brother-in-law. The paediatrician. Tim, yes.

Paediatrician. Okay, *that* was why he was in the white coat. He worked here. And he was *Tim,* so he might not have bad news –

"Hannah told me to come and fetch you," he said. "Put you somewhere a bit more comfortable. John's still in surgery, I understand. Since he's made it this far, there's a good chance he'll make it more generally. But let's not tempt fate. Anyway, I'm on duty, but I'll keep you updated if I hear anything first. All being well, he should be out of the operating room in just under an hour. The surgeon will brief us then. It may still be just you and me at that point. Devon and Hexham are several hours' drive away."

"Thank you," she said as they began to walk, him subtly leading.

"I'll get you a strong cup of tea. How did you hear?"

"Police. I called his mobile to check he was okay, and they answered. We'd been to a funeral together earlier today, and we went to a pub this evening. I had to meet my mother. He said he'd make his own way home. I never imagined… "

"Good, God, you mustn't start thinking like that. John's a grown man and we're supposed to live in a civilised country, therefore it ought to be reasonable for him to think he can proceed from Point A to Point B on a map without being accompanied by a friend. Here, sit down. I think you're in shock. Don't take that the wrong way. I think we're all in shock. I'll get you a strong cup of tea with a lot of sugar, and I'd like you to drink it. I'm speaking with my medical hat on now. Look upon it as a prescription."

They entered in a room with a few padded armchairs lined up against a wall, and a long coffee table with magazines in neat piles and a flower bowl. Still anonymous, still harshly lit, but somehow just a touch more human.

There was no one else in here. Tim left and came back a few minutes' later with her tea.

"Anything you want," he said, "there's a nurse just round the corner. Simply ask her."

He left. Phyllis put her elbows on her knees and ran her hands through her hair. She'd passed the point of tiredness. Just a case of waiting now, and she could do that forever if need be. She looked at her phone. *3.10.* Tim had said under an hour – so four am?

Ten years ago, the army had trained her to 'power nap' in situations like this. Times you knew for certain you'd be waiting and you needed to conserve energy. But then she thought of her mum's naps, and she couldn't get started. Besides, if the family turned up and she was dozing, it would look inexcusable.

She loved John. If he died, what would she do? Women nowadays didn't 'need' men in the way they'd so often imagined they did in times past. If the worst came to the worst, she didn't 'need' to look round for another relationship. She'd like a family, true: two girls and a boy; or even better, what John had now: some sort of close-knit, super-talented community of x young people with the same two parents. And John to be the other parent.

It had to be him. No one else she'd ever met was remotely qualified. They wouldn't even know what she meant if she tried to explain it.

Her phone rang. *Alec.*

"How's John?" he asked when she picked up.

"No word yet. In surgery."

"You've got tomorrow off. Stick close to the family and even closer to John. He'll be on drugs. Don't let him let slip he's a spy. I mean, I know you can't stop him, but be prepared to gloss it over if necessary."

"Understood." Brutal, but this was MI7.

"There's something else."

She took a deep breath. "Go on."

"We've been back in touch with the police. It looks like there were some distinctly... *weird* aspects to what happened out there when John was knifed. For example, the attackers poured acid on the dead guy – enough to make sure no one still has any idea who he was."

"My God."

"It gets odder. These men – probably all men, they think – who chased the dead victim: they were all wearing identical rubber dragon masks."

"Dragon masks?"

"Yes, you heard right."

She rubbed her forehead and sighed. "I'm not in the best state to consider ramifications right now. Tell me: does it change anything? I mean, gangland contract or teenage robbery gone wrong, John was still collateral, right? Either way, it doesn't directly concern us?"

"What I'm trying to say is, that's not a question there's a definitive answer to yet. Watch this space."

"I'll watch it later. Right now, I'm only thinking about John."

"Just keeping you informed. Annabel sends her love. She says to tell you she's thinking about you. Tariq ditto."

"Any idea when Ruby Parker will be back?"

"She's cut her official business short and she's returning on a government-chartered jet. Should be sometime in the next few hours. Hey, I'm pretty sure he'll be okay. He's stronger than you and me put together. Look after yourself. Sorry I had to leave so abruptly."

"Thank you." She meant it. He didn't have to offer supportive sentiments. A lesser man wouldn't have. And there were plenty of lesser men in Thames House.

Plus, he cared about John, however much he might play the macho tough-guy a lot of the time. And so did Annabel and Tariq. You weren't supposed to have close friends in this job, or at least that was the myth. If circumstances required it, you were expected to betray anyone and everyone besides the Queen and your line manager, in that order.

But they'd never been like that. It was mainly John that stopped them. Because he'd never bought it, not one iota.

The way he'd brought that Monopoly set over. From being something he'd just *done*, it suddenly became a signifier of *him*. Who he was. He was the man who brought the board game over when everyone else was too cool.

She was becoming delirious. And sentimental. She wiped her eyes. If he asked her again, she'd say yes. They wouldn't have to give up spying. Not yet. It wasn't even like spying had been the thing that had got him stabbed. Gangsters of one stripe or another, that's all. To think of all the times in the past they could have been killed, and it had come to *this*.

Delirium, sentimentality - now anger.

She lowered her head, put her hands together and tried to pray. "Please, God, I know I don't believe in you, but if John lives, I'll really, really make an effort. You can't expect me to defy reason, that's not what you made me for, but I'll go back over all the arguments. I'll listen to believers with respect, even when they sound a bit ludicrous. I'll even go on a pilgrimage, if you want me to. If I can do it without committing myself to anything irrational in advance. A long pilgrimage, like the Camino de Santiago. I won't scoff - "

A sound as of someone politely clearing his throat. She looked up. Tim stood in the doorway next to another much older, smaller man in a white coat. Asian, balding, big eyes and a bulbous nose.

"This is Mr Gajapathi," Tim said. "John's surgeon."

Something in the way he announced it seemed to suggest it wasn't all bad news. Phyllis got desperately to her feet and they shook hands.

"Well, so far, so good," Mr Gajapathi said after a portentous pause. He spoke slowly. "Luckily, whoever arrived first at the crime scene had the presence of mind to leave the knife where it was. Most cases where something like this proves fatal, it's the bleeding out and the difficulty of restoring blood pressure that creates the problems."

"Apparently, it wasn't a particularly long knife," Tim said, as if this was crucial.

"Mr Mordred suffered a puncture of the right ventricle," the surgeon continued, at the same measured pace as before. "We performed an Ashrafian thoracotomy, an incision into the chest, enabling us to go straight to the heart. His sinus rhythm's good, and that's often a predictor of survival."

He paused to allow this last clause to sink in. Phyllis nodded to confirm she'd got it.

"Right now," he continued, "he's out of the woods surgically, but there's still a long way to go. Post-operative complications - possible: intramural thrombus, cardiac enlargement, anomalous wall motion, things too complicated to go in to, presently; bridges we'll cross if and when we come to them. He'll be unconscious for a while, I'm afraid, so you won't be able to see him for at least another three hours."

Another pause. Phyllis nodded again.

"When you do go in," he went on, "be prepared: he'll be attached to a monitor, and he'll have tubes coming out of his chest to remove air and fluid from the pleural cavity, help prevent complications. And, of course, he'll be asleep. When he finally wakes up, he'll probably be in pain, although we can manage that with analgesics. I don't want to stick my neck out, but most cardiac injury patients who survive surgery go on to live full, healthy lives."

For the first time since being a teenager, Phyllis broke so spontaneously and violently into tears that, almost immediately, the main feeling behind them was embarrassment. It felt like vomiting, only with her eyes spouting all the fluid.

As the two men either side of her offered words and gestures of comfort, her mortification was slowly doused from one side – but assiduously fanned from the other - by a little voice at the back of her mind that repeatedly whispered: *don't worry! Let those tears flow! This is perfect for your cover!*

Chapter 8: Mordred's Theory

The police made persistent, but fruitless, attempts to jog Mordred's memory, beginning three days after he was stabbed. A week later, he was discharged to the care of his parents and girlfriend in his flat in Islington, and his sisters went their separate ways. Within another fortnight, he was walking around, and six weeks after being attacked, he stood on the verge of fitness for work. By this time, his parents had been back in Hexham for a fortnight. Yet Ruby Parker, his boss, a small black woman roughly twice his age, insisted on 'giving' him another three weeks' sick leave. Hannah, his oldest sister, invited him to Connecticut, where she was touring with the band she managed, slumming it in trailers and motels. She promised to upgrade his visit.

Still no one was any closer to finding out who the attackers were or what their motive had been. Even the victim's identity remained a mystery; only that he was a white middle-aged male of average height. His DNA was on no database, which, if this was a gangland killing, was unusual, and from the point of view of the investigation, frustrating.

Progress seemed to hinge solely on Mordred eventually recalling something. Visually, since the men had been wearing masks, he probably couldn't add to what the CCTV showed. But he might have picked up some auditory detail – what did the men say? What sort of accents did they have? Did they let slip names? Something with the potential to break the case wide open.

But memories resolutely refused to surface, even under hypnosis. By this time, the broad sequence of events leading up to his attack was a matter of public record, and available for scrutiny on the internet. So he devised his own theory. It took all the known facts into account. It also explained, in passing, why the investigation was doomed; why both perpetrators and victim would remain permanently undetected.

He and Phyllis sat on the sofa. They'd just finished eating a plate of tacos, and watching the last episode of *The State*. His flat was what estate agents called 'compact'. It contained a living room, a bedroom just big enough for a bed, a tiny bathroom, and a kitchen so small every object was always easily reachable. It was owned by the British government, and sat within a secure block accessible only by typing a six-digit code-number into a keypad - presumably so that assassinating him would be slightly more challenging for hostile foreign governments.

Phyllis had switched to BBC News. The newsreader, a middle-aged woman with a thin mouth, turned grimly from the National Health Service to World News and the latest regarding the consultant, Martin Curzon, who'd been abducted and murdered in Venezuela.

"Following the kidnappers' announcement early this morning," she said, "Mr Curzon's supporters held a press conference in Florida. His wife accused the British government of doing 'virtually nothing' to help her husband. According to our South America correspondent, Arfon Thomas, the government in Caracas withheld its cooperation with attempts to reach a settlement after the Foreign Secretary Boris Johnson's criticism of the Venezuelan Constituent Assembly and its alleged abandonment of fundamental democratic principles. The Foreign and Commonwealth Office issued a statement this morning - "

Phyllis switched the TV off. "I'm bloody glad you're not going there."

"Sad," Mordred said. "I really thought he'd make it out alive."

Phyllis shook her head. "His kidnappers were gangsters. You can't pay them because the authorities won't let you; you can't frustrate them because they hold all the cards. In other words, you're completely out of options from day one. In the end, you simply run out of time. Tragic, you're right." She pulled her feet onto the sofa, and her expression changed. "Talking of gangsters, are you going to tell me this 'theory' of yours at any stage? About why you were attacked?"

He gave an I-thought-we'd-get-round-to-that-sooner-or-later sigh and turned to face her. "I'll tell you now if you like. Spoiler alert: it's speculative. It just fits the facts better than anything else."

"So?"

"Informed guesswork suggests gangland activity. We both agree on that. The masks suggest premeditation, as does the acid. And the fact that I wasn't assaulted with acid suggests a group of men in charge of their emotions. The natural reaction to my intervention would have been anger or panic. But they'd brought enough to erase the identity of their victim, and they weren't going to jeopardise that part of their itinerary by revenge-dousing me. They kept their cool. All very methodical."

She shrugged. "So they were professional gangsters, and this was a 'hit'. So far, so predictable. Go on."

"The next question is, if it *was* so professional, then why am I still here? Put it this way: I was stabbed with a relatively short knife. And it was left in my chest, instead of being pulled out. Removing it would probably have killed me, and it's the obvious thing to do when you've stabbed someone. You try to retain your weapon in case there's another round."

"What are you saying then? That perhaps it wasn't as professional as it looked?"

"If you're doing things professionally, you make sure you've eliminated any witnesses. You check they're dead."

"There were no fingerprints anywhere, including on the knife. Which looks pretty pro to me."

"Then tell me why they didn't remove the knife."

"It's a busy part of London. They wanted to get down to their main purpose as quickly as possible. Anyway, if you're suggesting leaving the knife in your chest suggests amateurism, I disagree."

"But it might do," he said. "If the attacker wasn't used to killing. Remember, there were five of them. They don't all have to have been hardened killers. It only needs one of them to do the ultimate deed."

"Sorry, I've no idea where you're going with this. So what if one of them was a bit squeamish? What actually *is* this theory of yours?"

"They stabbed me in the heat of the moment. Ideally, they'd have punched me unconscious, but they had to think quickly, and there were too many variables. They were professionals, I agree, but they weren't gangsters. They were British secret service agents from another department in MI7, one with which we've very little interaction – Blue, or Grey, probably. The victim was a foreign agent in possession of something we'll never ascertain. Presumably, something on that hard drive. I'm pretty sure someone, in some embassy somewhere in the capital knows exactly what was on it. The murder was a message, in other words: *we know what you're up to. Back off.* The victim 'had' to be killed – in the twisted way some MI7 departments use the word 'had' - but they recognised me, possibly at a late stage. Ideally, they didn't want me to die because I'm a fellow spook."

"So they left you with the knife sticking out of your chest. How kind."

"Well, Blue and Grey aren't exactly famed for their charity work."

"When you said your theory was speculative, I thought you meant in the Sherlock Holmes sense. Not the Baron Munchausen sense. I hate to sound brutal, but it isn't underpinned by much evidence. Your stabbing apparently doesn't fit the gangland-professional stereotype. Yes, agreed. And that's it."

"It explains why poor DCI Fleming isn't getting anywhere, and isn't likely to."

"And you can't tell him any of your theory because he's not an MI7 agent. Okay, so that's two little points in its favour. Maybe. But it's still way, *way* too suppositional."

"I haven't yet mentioned the clincher."

She let out a stream of air through her nose. "You're such a showman," she said irritably.

"When Fleming first came to see me in hospital, you might remember he asked to see me alone. No family, no Phyllis, no fellow police officers. Just me and him."

"I did think that was a little strange, I admit. But he was a member of MI7 very briefly. You knew that, right?"

"Yep."

"And? I'm assuming he pulled out some kind of, 'Look, John, could British intelligence be involved?' Wink, wink, nudge, nudge. 'Speaking as someone with a bit of inside experience. Come on, John, you can tell me' stunt."

"It wasn't quite that upfront. But roughly, yes. Then he asked me whether I'd come across a certain 'John Murgatroyd' in my professional capacity. Small, white, middle-aged, balding. Well, I couldn't say yes. I was a bit out of it anyway. So I said no."

"Bit vague. 'In your professional capacity'? Did he actually put it like that?"

"As I say, I was still slightly woozy. But I believe so. I think he deliberately left it imprecise. Like the whole thing was a game of cards, and he didn't want to show too much of his hand."

Phyllis smiled knowingly. "Just enough to get you interested."

"Precisely."

"I'm still in the dark here. Who *is* 'John Murgatroyd'? I'm pretty sure I've never heard of him."

"Remember a couple of years ago, when I was flagged up as supposedly at risk of being 'radicalised'? Because of my support for Tax Justice Network and a supposed qualification concerning my loyalty to the Queen?"

"That was funny… I mean, in retrospect," she added when she saw his look. "Anyway, it was bogus."

"John Murgatroyd was the man who interviewed me. Top floor of Thames House. Quite hostile, as I recall. I'd never seen him before that day, and I've never clapped eyes on him since."

"And you think Fleming's had contact with him?"

"He met a spook going by that name who fits Murgatroyd's description. On Day One of his investigation, apparently. That's good enough for me."

"Right. And so?"

"The thing is, I'm pretty sure 'John Murgatroyd' wasn't his real name. And I'm reasonably certain Fleming suspects the same thing. Now consider: what would be the purpose of someone like 'Murgatroyd' turning up to see Fleming, in precisely the way he did?"

She drew a breath and nodded. "I get it, yes."

"Grey, or Blue, or whoever it is, is sending me a message. *We're responsible for this.*"

"Two years ago, you said you thought Murgatroyd worked for Black."

He scoffed. "That was just me being melodramatic, although I may have believed it at the time, I can't remember. I doubt any of us will ever have any contact with Black. I'm not entirely sure it even exists. No, I think he's been sent as the recognisable face of another department. A *warning* face, if you like, because we didn't exactly hit it off first time round."

"*It ends here, John.*"

"Something like that. *Don't go sticking your nose in where it doesn't belong.*"

"*Stay in bed, have lots to drink and keep taking the tablets.*"

"And I don't get to see him face-to-face, so I can't ask any awkward questions or punch him in the mouth. It's all done from a safe distance, through the medium of DCI Nicholas Fleming. And the genius is, because he advertised himself as British intelligence, Fleming wasn't able to ask questions either."

"And now 'John Murgatroyd' fades back into the woodwork, job done. Okay, it's a very good theory."

"But?"

She paused, looked away and blinked. Then she shrugged and turned back. "But… okay, nothing, really. No one's come forward to claim the victim, so it's obviously about something more than money. You know, I think you may be right. It's Murgatroyd that clinches it, though."

"Good old Murg. Case solved."

"Like a Le Carré solution, though, where it's all a bit shoddy, but that's the best you're going to get. Are you going to tell anyone else?"

"I'll have to tell Ruby Parker at some point. I don't expect her to do anything."

"Probably not."

"Apart from that, I can't see any point in advertising it. So I was stabbed. I lived, and now I'm going for a holiday in Connecticut."

"Without me."

"I'm mainly going to humour Hannah. It'll be all travelling down freeways in lorries, getting sandwiched by 200lb roadies with bushy beards, ponytails and aviators, listening to the same songs night in, night out, lugging instruments around, drinking Jim Beam till 3am, having to laugh at Soraya's jokes - "

"Poor you. I thought Hannah was putting you in a top hotel with all mod cons?"

"That's what she thinks."

"No 'lugging about'. I mean it. Lifting and carrying isn't good for you right now. I know that sounds boring, but hey."

"I'll be sensible. I'll probably enjoy it when I get there. The Coal Tar crowd are good fun as a rule. I still wish you could come, though."

"You're only going to stay with Hannah because I can't get any holiday. Otherwise, we'd be going to Cannes or Stintino. Alone."

"If only."

"As it is, I've got two weeks with Microsoft Excel, and only a smattering of Powerpoint slideshows to break the monotony. Assuming I retain the will to live, I might go to one or two of the after-work lectures. There's one on female alt-right radicalisation coming up. It's the next big thing, apparently. Or rather, it's the present day big thing; we're still catching up with it. I suppose I might as well develop my career while I'm thrashing about in the Slough of Despond."

"Always look on the bright side of life."

"Send me a postcard. Every day."

"Or, given that 1973's now over, I could just text you and attach a photo."

"Doesn't show enough commitment. And I can't pin a run of SMS messages up at work and go, 'They're all from John. Yeah, he loves me so much he actually put pen to paper *every day*, then went out of his way to buy a stamp, then looked all over Connecticut for somewhere to post it because he's so devoted.'"

"Time to change the subject. I'm not leaving till next Saturday. If your lecture's before then, I'll come with you."

"No, thanks. Too work-related, given that I'm only seeing you after six every day till then. I was thinking more of a series of romantic dinners at my place, then Netflix and chill."

He considered. "Sounds good on paper, but I think we should go: chill, dinner, Netflix."

She hooted. "Chill on an empty stomach?"

"We could have a starter."

She sighed. "Okay, we'll give it a try. Once. But only because I feel sorry for you getting plonked among all those Rock Till You Drop types for a fortnight."

Chapter 9: The Party Invitation

The next day, Phyllis arrived at Thames House to find a meeting scheduled with Ruby Parker for 10am. The email didn't say what it was about, but that was normal. Annabel had also been invited. Since Annabel never put a foot wrong, it probably wasn't an admonishment.

She sat at her desk, set her phone alarm for 9.55 then forgot about it. Alec came over at 9.30, asked how John was, and went away again. Suki came over with a batch of files sent over by White Department, relating to an Islamist preacher in Leicester, then left. Ten minutes later, a soft, persistent ding – Phyllis wasn't a fan of personalised ringtones – said to get moving. She took the lift to the basement and Ruby Parker's office, expecting to meet Annabel *en route*. She didn't. When she knocked and heard 'Enter', she found Annabel already seated, her long blonde hair pinned as usual in a hundred places to stop it wandering. She wore an expensive grey trouser suit and brogues, and her sharp features were mitigated by a barely perceptible expression of relief that her colleague had finally arrived. God knows how long she'd been sitting there.

Ruby Parker, a sixty-ish black woman in a grey skirt suit, sat on the other side of the desk. Her office was whitewashed and painfully small, with a variety of house plants on different levels. Up till recently, she'd kept a tankful of tropical fish in here, but she'd given them away – so it was said – after her mother's death, a year ago. No one knew the precise connection.

"I'll come straight to the point," she said, when Phyllis was seated. "I want both of you to attend a party on Friday night. I hope that won't be a problem."

Phyllis and Annabel said nothing. Friday: John's last night, but Ruby Parker would know that. And Annabel hated parties. Which she'd also know.

"I know John's leaving for America on Saturday," Ruby Parker went on. "And it also means you'll have to come in on Saturday morning for the obligatory de-brief. Believe me, if I thought anyone else would suffice, I'd have plumped for them. On the other hand, you're the best people for the job, and it's your name on the invitation."

"Whose party is it?" Phyllis asked. *Her* name? She was baffled.

"Viscount Henry Greysonwell," Ruby Parker replied. "Which should ring a bell, especially if you pick up the free dailies on your way to and from work."

"The Lord Mayor of London," Phyllis said. The penny dropped. But not all the way. "Is this something to do with ...?"

"When you were 'held against your will', yes, in the City, several years ago. You'll recall the Lord Mayor's office tried to make it up to you once, when you went to meet William Chester, Lord Willoughby de Vries, at Mansion House shortly afterwards."

"And it succeeded," Phyllis said. "I don't need the institution to repeatedly apologise. It wasn't even as if even Chester was anywhere near at the time. It was his predecessor, if anyone. And the office passes to a new incumbent every twelve months. Even Chester's gone now. I don't want to sound ungrateful, but nor do I want to come across as the kind of person who needs mollifying on an annual basis. It implies that I hold a grudge, which I don't. It's all forgiven and forgotten, as far as I'm concerned."

Ruby Parker gave a deprecating smile and shook her head. "That's not the reason we decided to inaugurate this. The idea was that the City of London looked to have come unstuck for a while. As a show of goodwill, and as a means

of maintaining the kind of ties we'd need to help us investigate any wrongdoing directly, discreetly and effectively,
the Lord Mayor's office opened a permanent slot in its annual diary for an informal meeting with a senior MI7
officer. Because you were personally affected, you'd already
got an introduction of sorts – albeit a rough one – and the
agreement was that you'd be our representative until further notice. You, plus one other. Last time, it was John. But
John's not available at present. Which is why I've chosen
you, Annabel."

If it had been possible for Annabel to sit up a notch at this
point, Phyllis got the impression she would have. But all
her notches were fully used up. "I'm not very good at
parties," she said. "I mention that, not to dissuade you from
sending me, but because I think it's my duty to remind you
that there are probably many other, more qualified candid-
ates."

"That's very considerate of you," Ruby Parker said, in a
tone that suggested she knew, like Phyllis, that this was
likely as close to lying as Annabel would ever get within the
confines of Thames House. "But I'm sending you precisely
because it's a weakness in your otherwise impressive reper-
toire of skills. I'm giving you the opportunity to improve, in
other words. And Greysonwell's is a friendly invitation,
from which no harm can possibly come. If either of you
needs suitable attire, by the way, I can arrange that through
Amber."

Annabel and Phyllis exchanged glances involuntarily.
They'd both had the same thought.

"I take it you'd like to say something," Ruby Parker said.

Phyllis saw that Annabel wasn't going to volunteer: it
would only increase her own discomfort. It fell to her to
speak. "A moment ago, you mentioned us picking up the
free daily newspapers on our way into and out of work,"
she said.

Ruby Parker nodded. "You're concerned that this may be a somewhat more … *raucous* party than you're accustomed to."

"What I know about Viscount Greysonwell is that he's the office's youngest incumbent for some time - "

"He's thirty-two," Ruby Parker said. "Roughly the same age as you."

"And from what I've read, he's a kind of unreformed Geraint Anderson figure."

"Who's Geraint Anderson?" Annabel said. "If you don't mind me asking."

Ruby Parker smiled. "He's the pseudonymous author of a 2008 memoir entitled, *Cityboy: Beer and Loathing in the Square Mile*. The title probably speaks for itself."

"There have been lots of reports of his 'legendary' parties in the press," Phyllis went on. "I've no objection to attending one, but from what I've heard, he has a reputation for going off-piste when he's had a drink too many. How do we know he won't expose Annabel and I?"

She realised as soon as the words were out how stupid a question it was. Obviously, they'd just deny it, laugh in his face and walk out.

Ruby Parker chuckled. "You're actually saying you think this may be a *dangerous* assignment?"

"That wasn't quite what I intended to ask," Phyllis replied, feeling herself flush. "What I meant was, going by what you've told us, this whole thing was originally intended to function as the opportunity for an informal discussion of matters of mutual concern between legitimate representatives of our two organisations. Is this really the right occasion? Can we be certain he's not… making fun of us? William Chester invited John and I to a face-to-face afternoon tea. Under those circumstances, we could talk. This strikes me as a very different proposition."

Ruby Parker frowned. "Are you suggesting we should decline his invitation? Because that might be seen as a snub. Not just by him, but by the officials who set everything up in the first place. Or perhaps you're suggesting we set terms and conditions for our yearly encounters? I take your underlying point, Phyllis, but don't forget: next year's incumbent is likely to be a very different kettle of fish to Henry Greysonwell, and when he or she appears, I'd like us to be remembered favourably."

Phyllis nodded. "You're right, of course. I'm not looking at the longer term implications."

"Just go along, try to have a good time, and come away as soon as you feel is consistent with good manners, if need be. And make sure you show the appropriate respect to his mother. She's supposed to be the power behind the throne."

"I know you'll probably say no, for good reasons," Annabel said, "but could we take two men? Whenever I go out somewhere with another woman, just us two, men try to … they, er, I don't know what the phrase is…"

Phyllis laughed. "'Hit on you'."

"And Phyllis used to be a model. She still looks very attractive."

"Thank you, Annabel," Phyllis said. "As do you."

"The two of us together might find the evening a bit more wearing than is consistent with a truly 'good time'," Annabel went on. "Especially as there's likely to be a lot of alcohol present in the equation. And, from what I've heard, some of these City types don't know how to take no for an answer. Sorry if that sounds prejudiced. I'm just trying to imagine the worst-case scenario."

Phyllis laughed again. "Given that you're not allowed to punch them."

"Er, yes," Annabel said.

Ruby Parker sighed. "This discussion is turning out to be vastly more complex than I anticipated. Very well, I'll try to get invites for partners. If I'm successful in generously sticking my neck out for you, you can take Alec and Tariq."

"Thank you," they both said in unison, feeling horribly as if they'd turned the clock back on feminism by about forty years.

Ruby Parker passed two gilt-framed envelopes across the desk. "The details and the official invitations are in there," she said. "Have a good time," she added, in a tone of bitter disillusionment.

Chapter 10: The Sister Wendy Chapter

When Phyllis got ready for work that morning, Mordred stayed in bed. There wasn't room for two to rush about in a flat this size, and she needed to concentrate. Shower, hair - 7.05 - make-up, clothes, bag - 7.45 - keys in bag, phone in bag, bus pass in bag, final mirror check, final adjustments to hair, final farewell, 8.00. Bang on time.

After he heard the front door close, he got up. His chest was sore, and he still felt the occasional twinge, but otherwise, he was okay. He'd probably take the bus somewhere today. Hampstead Heath, maybe. Or somewhere even more rustic. Colne Valley, maybe. He went into the living room and pulled back the curtains. Sunshine. Then he checked the forecast on his phone. Sunny all day.

Bus – or train?

The trouble was, everywhere was the same when you weren't with anyone. Phyllis, specifically. He'd used to think he'd like the hermit's life. Not any more. He didn't have the powers of concentration necessary to reach any sort of truth about his place in the world.

Probably why so many people spent time on their phones. Looking for company. In the end, it became a habit. You saw people looking for company even when they were in company.

He wouldn't be like that. Not today. He'd leave his phone at home so no one could contact him. And the internet couldn't tempt him. Nor the possibility of a game. Nor music. Nor reading the news. Nor taking photos.

Strange how that made him feel. Abandoning his poor little phone. What if there was an emergency?

No, all right, he'd take it with him, but switched off.

And he wasn't going to think negatively. He just needed a plan for the day and a book, that was all. Something spiritual perhaps, counter the anti-imaginative soot of modern life.

He didn't have that many books in his flat, there wasn't room. Most of what he owned was textbooks on languages, but they were all in storage at Thames House now. Immediately to hand were mainly books given to him as presents by his sisters, on birthdays and Christmases.

He opened the drawer beneath the TV. *The Illustrated Pilgrim's Progress* might do, but mainly for the pictures. He'd already read it twice. Oswald Hanfling's *Philosophy and Ordinary Language* ("A superb introduction," according to Julia) was too heavy for a day in the country. Piero Scanziani's *The Entronauts* would probably work. *The Desert Fathers: Sayings of the Early Christian Monks* looked too disjointed: he needed something he could get into. Not *Sister Wendy's Story of Painting*.

A novel perhaps?

Except he didn't have one. Not a physical one. Lots on his e-reader. But that would be like taking his phone. He'd spend time flicking about.

Flicking about. The malaise of the present age in two words.

He ate two Weetabix in front of the TV, flicking about between *BBC Breakfast*, *Good Morning Britain* and *Nadiya's British Food Adventure*. Afterwards, he boiled the kettle, made a pot of tea, showered and dressed, then combed his hair to give it some exercise.

Ready to go.

Books, a book, which one?

Suddenly he had an entire-day-altering epiphany. He could join the local library! They'd obviously have novels there!

My God. Why had he never considered it before?

Because weekdays he was always working, that's why. Saturdays he went shopping; Sundays it was probably closed.

My God. *The library.* Whole new vistas opened. He wouldn't even need to go in the countryside now. He could probably sit in among the bookshelves. All day. Reading. They'd definitely let him. Usually, they actively encouraged it.

Likely all he needed to join was two utilities bills, confirm his identity.

He hurried to the kitchen drawer, rummaged about for a few moments and emerged with a gas bill, a salary slip and his passport. Three different types of proof. Best to be on the safe side.

It was a dream come true. And they'd actually *expect* him to turn his phone off.

Then, as suddenly as he'd had his epiphany, he stopped to take stock of himself.

Bloody hell, it had to be the medication. He wasn't thinking straight. He tried to look at it from Phyllis's point of view. *This is a* library *you're talking about, John, what's got into you? Get a grip!*

Yet it wouldn't go away. The thought of sitting there, just reading a book. Heaven. He put his hands on his temples. Perhaps whatever was now exploding in his head had been triggered by the possibility of a day out on his own. Maybe it had released endorphins or something, and they'd reacted with the drugs, he wasn't a neurophysiologist, how could he -

His phone rang. *Hannah.*

Thank God. Because the next stage was probably some sort of panic attack.

"Hi," he said, as casually as he could.

"Is something wrong?"

"I've only said one word."

"You sound odd. Maybe it's the connection. Hannah here," she added unnecessarily, then still more unnecessarily: "Your sister."

"I know. I saw your name on the screen."

"Sarky. Is Phyllis there?"

"She went out about an hour ago. Why? Did you want to speak to her?"

"I've got her in my Contacts list if I do. No, I was hoping to speak to you while she's out of the way. Not *about* her. We're friends now, obviously."

"Is it about me coming to see you? Because if you have to cancel - "

"Why would I?"

He sighed. "I'm not saying you would. Just *if*."

"Reset."

"Okay."

"This is the reason for my phone call, John. Before you come and see me on Saturday – and I'm really looking forward to it, by the way, so is Soraya – I need you to do me a big favour. I mean, a big, *big* favour."

"One that you don't want Phyllis to know about."

"Or anyone. We've been through this. The only people you can really trust in this life are family members. And people like Soraya, people you've known for ever."

"Is Soraya actually *there*, by any chance?"

"Cooee, John," Soraya said in a bored tone.

"What is this favour?"

"I want you to go round to a specific location, in London, to see if someone I know is there."

He shrugged. "Easily done."

"At night-time. When Phyllis isn't around."

"I retract my last sentence. I'm actually staying at Phyllis's all this week. She thinks she's looking after me. And she's my girlfriend. And we're going to be apart for two weeks beginning Saturday."

76

"So… it has to be before Saturday."

"Er, did you hear the beginning bit?"

"No. You'll just have to find a way."

"Who is this – person you want me to check on? Can't you just ring him or her? Or send a text, or an email?"

"I'm not stupid, John. I wouldn't be ringing you if it wasn't a complete last resort. And before you take offence: I didn't mean it like that."

"Why does it have to be at night?"

"Just take my word for it: it does. He – or she – isn't in during the day."

He sighed. *He – or she*: cagey with a capital 'C'. He could see where this was going. Since she'd organised a global demonstration against corporate tax avoidance a few years' back, she'd become convinced MI5 and the CIA were monitoring her phone calls. She might be right. If they were, he didn't know anything about it, but then he wouldn't.

"So are you going to give me this man – or woman's – address?"

"Dictionary. Get a pen."

"Right." He had a distinct sense of humouring her as he retrieved a pencil and a notepad from the kitchen drawer. But he had no choice. She'd almost certainly make him read it back afterwards. "Fire away."

"One-five-nine, column three, W-one, *name*," she said. "*And*… two-five-eight, next to three-zero-one, W-one, *name*. Sixteen, L-four, two-four-two L-6, N-4."

"How long has this person been missing?"

"Read it back to me."

He obeyed, then repeated his question.

"We're not in that frequent contact," she said. "But I haven't heard from him – or her – for… I don't know, over a month. I usually get regular updates."

"About 'financial matters', I assume." Their soubriquet for her brand of low-level anti-capitalism.

"Yes."

So he – or she – was a radical of some kind. A police check of missing persons might turn something up, although Hannah probably wouldn't be entitled to go down that route, even if she wanted to.

"When you get there, ask for *Brent*," she said. "He'll give you a key. I'll let him know you're coming."

"If Brent has a key, and he's on your side – I'm assuming he is - why don't you just ask *him* to go in?"

"Because one: I'd have to ask him outright to do that, and I'm working on the assumption that my calls are being monitored. Two: the key doesn't unlock the door, only the access box to a six-digit entry keypad."

"I assume you're now going to give me the code," he said, trying not to sound weary.

"Yes indeed. Pen ready?"

"Go ahead."

"P-5, L-8, P-6, L7, P-5, L-3. Read that back."

He recited her letter-number string in a monotone and added, "I'll do my best."

"I'm counting on you."

"Thanks."

"Don't let me know how it went till we meet face-to-face on Saturday. And *don't* look it up on Google maps. Go to the library, get a telephone directory. Love you, John. Bye."

She hung up.

He went back to the drawer beneath the TV. 'Dictionary': their code for whatever book she'd given him, mock-innocently, at their last face-to-face meeting, and of which she would always own an identical copy. Right now, one of his Christmas presents: *Sister Wendy's Story of Painting*.

Page 159, third column, first word, name... It had to be... Frederick. Frederick *the Wise*, in this case, but his wisdom was irrelevant.

And...

Page 258, next to 301... Aha, yes: the plates were numbered. Plate 301 was a portrait of Elisabeth Vigée-Lebrun, Countess Golovine. But just the first word again.

Frederick and Elisabeth. Probably Elizabeth with a 'z' – Sister Mary might not cover all the permutations - but he'd see. A pub somewhere?

Page 16, letter 4... *E.*

Page 242, letter 6... *C.*

And number 4.

Frederick and Elizabeth, EC4.

EC4?

But that was where he'd been attacked. Could this missing person be...?

No, of course not. Hannah would have twigged.

On the other hand, maybe she had. Maybe she was using him to play detective. A kind of *Hannah Lexingwood, PI,* with him as her trusty assistant.

Unlikely, though. She had her limitations, but lack of compassion wasn't one. If she suspected her Mr X was the man who'd been killed that night, she definitely wouldn't be sending poor, dopey John to investigate him. Or anyone. She'd take full charge.

He replayed her words. *"He – or she."* Then *"him – or her."*

In both, a slight rise in pitch on the feminine pronoun. Probably inaudible to someone who hadn't known the speaker since birth, and wasn't trained to recognise such things. Whoever this radical person was, Hannah obviously thought of 'him or her' as a woman. And so strongly that it didn't occur to her to question it.

Anyway, most people compartmentalised their lives. In her mind, 'my brother and his doings' might not even occupy the same continent as 'my radical friend'. And when a member of your family was at death's door, you didn't stop to ask about the bigger picture. So she might even not know about the dead guy. But even if she did, it might just be as a free-floating fact with a purely coincidental relation to John Mordred and none at all to Hannah Lexingwood. She might have mentally registered, filed and forgotten it.

And 'EC4': she wasn't a Londoner by birth, upbringing or residence. She might have no real idea where that was.

And she was busy. Fully Magic Coal Tar Lounge were storming the Billboard Hot 100 right now with *Eve of Destruction*. No time to make speculative connections between a pair of things three and a half thousand miles away.

Over a month, she'd said. Whoever her mystery contact was, she obviously wasn't in contact with 'him or her' that frequently. One month plus could easily encompass six or more weeks.

If this Whoever was an Internet friend, the fact that 'she' presented as a woman could simply be irrelevant. If 'she' sold herself as your radical friend, however, you'd probably believe 'her'. There was supposed to be honesty in that sort of thing, even in small matters.

He was interested now.

Time to go to the library.

As long since agreed, he wrapped *Sister Wendy's Story of Painting* in a few sheets of newspaper and dropped it in the British Heart Foundation book bank on Seven Sisters Road, removing and retaining its cover on release. He spent the rest of the morning in Islington Central Library, a building so old and imposing he'd previously mistaken it for a museum. One of the librarians, a middle-aged man in a T-shirt that said, *I Like to Party and by Party I Mean Read Books*, examined Mordred's ID, got him to fill out a form, and gave him a card. He chose a science-fiction novel about gendered robots conquering Bode's Galaxy in the year 2345, then took a look at the telephone directory in the reference section. It confirmed his conjecture. *The Frederick and Elizabeth* was a pub – presumably, it had some sort of annex or private flat adjoining it – thirty seconds' walk from where he'd been attacked and the man he'd been trying to save had been murdered.

The question now was, who to tell? The police? Phyllis?

No one yet. It might turn out to be nothing. He might knock on the door, an old lady might answer, he'd tell her to call Hannah, she'd say, 'Gosh, thanks for reminding me', and that'd be that.

But he didn't think so. Here, somehow, was the heart of the mystery.

Funny how it had come back to claim him. Like he was getting a second chance at something.

Assuming it was anything to do with that.

The medication? Could the medication still be speaking? Maybe that's why he was reading so much into it.

Had it even been speaking in the first place?

He didn't care.

He spent the afternoon at a pine table in the Reference section half-heartedly reading *Robot, All Too Robot* – ending up, after three hours, no further than page 55 – and, more seriously, trying to concoct a plan to evade Phyllis on at least one night before Saturday. Maybe he could go out for the day, somewhere like Colne Valley. Then 'meet a friend' just as he was supposedly about to hop on the bus home.

No, a stupid idea. He'd be on his way back by five at the latest. He couldn't stretch that to 10.30pm, which was prob-ably the earliest he could complete a sinister-looking night mission like this.

Nothing else occurred to him, but it would. He just had to keep thinking. At three o'clock, he looked at his watch. He was due at Phyllis's flat at 5.30 in time to cook her din-ner. He got up, checked *Robot, All Too Robot* out at the desk, and caught the bus to Camden. He spent an hour in the market, shopping for the ingredients for butternut chilli. He let himself into her flat and started cooking. He'd finished when she arrived home at 6.30.

But as she took her shoes off, she looked dejected.

"What's the matter?" he asked, putting his book down.

She sighed. "You're never going to believe this. I've got to go out to a party on your last night. Ruby Parker's orders."

"A party?"

"Annabel's going too. I'm going to be chaperoned by Alec. She's taking Tariq. At the Lord Mayor's. Remember when we met Will Chester? A kind of lurid continuation of that. As Ruby Parker pointed out, we've all read the sort of thing the current Mayor gets up to in the freebies."

"It might be good fun."

"Not impossible, I admit. But I wish you were coming. Or I was staying here."

He served their meal and continued to commiserate with her, but underneath he had a grim sense that the universe had contrived the whole thing solely so he could revisit EC4. Somehow, what had happened first time round was an awful mistake, a sacrilegious tearing of space-time. As a result, the universe had gone awry, and who knew what strange creatures had crawled through the rent?

This was his chance to right whatever had gone wrong. He'd better take it. Or else.

Chapter 11: Underground Texting

Friday, 8pm. Mordred sat on the carpet, in his flat living room, dressed in old oxford shirt and chinos. Alec and Tariq crouched either side of him because the only other option was standing, and, although they were both wearing tuxedos, that seemed too formal. They wanted to express solidarity. Annabel and Phyllis sat on the sofa in evening dresses, looking glum and holding glasses of white wine. Tariq had an orange juice. Alec and John weren't thirsty. A sense of guilt hung in the air, as of four partygoers obliged to leave a friend behind, and whose expensive clothes make that friend look vaguely like a tramp. No one spoke about the party. They talked of America and Hannah.

"She's convinced MI5's watching her," Mordred said.

Alec shrugged. "Could be. If so, I haven't heard about it."

"I'd be surprised if White Department don't have their eyes on her," Annabel said. "They'll be trying to work out when she's planning to launch her new 'world war' on tax avoidance. Or is that on the back burner now?"

"She doesn't tell me everything," Mordred said. He wasn't enjoying this conversation. He was waiting for everyone to go, so he could get changed and head out to EC4. In the meantime, he had to look as if he'd been condemned to spend Friday night alone, trying to cram clothes and toiletries into a suitcase.

"I'd love to manage a rock band," Tariq said. "I mean, in another universe. Mind you, I don't know how they make any money nowadays, not with so much download-sharing."

"Mostly live performances," Mordred answered. "And maintaining a reputation."

"I remember when Fully Magic Coal Tar Lounge was an innocuous little indy band," Phyllis said. "I don't know how they've morphed into this kind of Sex Pistols-Joan Baez hybrid. Hannah, I presume."

"Every band needs a Svengali," Tariq said.

"You'll probably get your fill of the rock and roll lifestyle at tonight's party," Mordred told them.

Alec scoffed. "Is 'rock and roll' even a term any more?"

No one replied, and Alec gave no indication of expecting them to. The world's most boring conversation on an already depressing evening, and it had reached its terminus. Annabel switched the TV on. BBC4. A rock documentary.

"It's the Lady Julia I'm worried about," she said. "His mother. The tabloids seem to think she's more out of control than he is."

"Don't believe everything you read," Tariq said. "The woman always gets the blame."

"Blame for what?" Phyllis asked rhetorically.

"Nero and Agrippina, they call them," Annabel went on, ignoring her.

Tariq shrugged and sipped his orange. "I rest my case. When people can't find specific charges, they always fall back on name-calling."

"No smoke without fire," Alec told him.

"God help us," Mordred said. They all turned to look at him in surprise. "Listen to yourselves. You're all pretty young, even you, Alec. This is a party. You've been invited to one of the most sought-after social gatherings in London. There are people who've literally paid thousands of pounds to get in tonight where you're going for free, but anyone would think you're going to a wake."

Alec laughed. "Truth be told, John, we're doing it for you. We're trying not to make you feel bad. Thanks for including me in the youth constituency, by the way. Mildly patronising, but much appreciated."

"I really am nervous," Annabel said. "I'm not putting it on. But I'm also excited. Like Ruby Parker said, it's a challenge I have to accept."

Phyllis clapped her hands excitedly, stood up and beamed. "Alec, you're one hundred per cent right. Okay, John, you've rumbled us. Especially me. I'm actually really, *really* looking forward to tonight. The one thing that's spoiling it for me – apart, obviously, from having to go into work tomorrow morning for the de-brief – is that you've got to stay here. But do you know what? I'm not even that bothered about that! Because I know you'll be safe, and if you get jealous, or anything silly – which I'm pretty sure you won't: you're a wonderful boyfriend and the love of my life – I've got Alec to vouch for me." She sat down again. "You can ask Alec if I behaved myself, and he'll say yes, and thanks to your supernatural ability to read micro-expressions, you'll know he's telling the truth. So everyone wins. Let's stop looking glum for John's sake. He can read us like a book anyway."

"Let the revelries begin," Tariq said.

"As Agrippina said to Nero," Annabel remarked. But she didn't say it in her previous maudlin tone. She said it like a witticism. Suddenly, the whole atmosphere changed. Mordred, to his relief, had been left to pack his M&S suitcase. Everyone else had entered Partyland.

Surreal. How much wine had Phyllis and Annabel *really* had?

It didn't matter. They'd all gone from being eighty-five to whatever their actual ages were in the space of a few seconds, and he'd uttered the magic words that caused it. Their wrinkles smoothed out, they threw away their walking frames, and Phyllis's mobile gave a loud ding.

"The taxi's here!" she exclaimed.

"Yay!" Alec, Annabel and Tariq exclaimed in unison.

Phyllis and Annabel hurriedly refilled their glasses from the bottle next to the sofa, drank half of what they'd poured, and grabbed their coats. Mordred saw them to the door, like he'd suddenly become the elderly guy, and he hoped they'd all come to see him again sometime soon, maybe stay a bit longer next time. Phyllis was last out. She grabbed him and gave him an alcoholic kiss on the lips.

"Behave yourself while I'm out," she said. "I love you. I mean it."

"Have a good time," he told her. "And ditto about the love."

Alec was waiting a few steps further on to chaperone her. Just as well. He watched her disappear down the stairwell, arm-in-arm with his best friend, obviously looking forward to a fabulous time – he loved that aggressive *embrace of life* speech she'd just given - and breathed a sigh of relief. Now the evening could really begin.

Beanie and aviator sunglasses – both new, so Phyllis couldn't recognise them if, by a dark twist of fate, they crossed paths tonight, hidden in the little gap at the back of the kitchen cupboard. EC4 was right on top of the Lord Mayor's party, so a good disguise was imperative. Those, plus an old coat he rarely wore. Plus black brogues.

The geographical proximity seemed almost *too* coincidental. Could MI7 be testing him? Had his colleagues actually been told to look out for him?

Seemed unlikely. How could they have got Hannah on board?

If that had even *been* Hannah. Maybe MI7 had hired an imitator.

Something like this, you always became paranoid. Or worse, actually mad. Forced into uncharted territory, in this job, perfectly ordinary men and women turned into King

Lear. Best to just make a firm decision then mentally shut down your critical faculties.

Anyway, why would they be testing him? Why would anyone?

Annabel had left the TV on. 8.30. He'd wait another half hour, watch *Gogglebox*, then head out. In the meantime, he'd pack for the USA, make it look like he'd been working his socks off when Phyllis got in.

An hour and a half later, he left his flat and walked to Angel tube station. The length of the descent – this escalator was supposedly the fourth longest in Western Europe – usually left him unfazed, but tonight, he had the eerie sensation of getting an inch closer to all things dark and decayed. Thoughts of Ian and Thelma returned. The accompanying feeling he had of being watched was perfectly normal, and, although he knew not to ignore it, nor was he about to dwell on it.

But just as he stepped off the escalator, he saw what had been staring him in the face all along.

Of course he was being followed! White department!

It wasn't as if he hadn't entertained the possibility himself, but Alec and Annabel had confirmed its reasonableness just two hours ago. If White was monitoring Hannah's phone calls, it would know he was running an errand for her. And, since she'd been so secretive, it would want to discover where he was going. White had probably been watching his flat ever since she'd called, waiting. For all he knew, it might even have 'prompted' the Lord Mayor to invite Phyllis to his bash. If he was honest, the whole thing had seemed just a little too pat all along. Too many coincidences.

He looked around. Friday night was going out time all over the world. The place was packed, and sadly, spies hadn't looked like middle-aged bank clerks since at least the 1970s. Nowadays, they could be anyone at all.

He stepped onto the southbound platform. Smell of engine oil and disinfectant. His 'disguise' was useless now: in fact it probably made him more conspicuous. Why hadn't he considered all this earlier?

Because he'd been so intent on evading Phyllis, that's why. And he was an idiot.

The key now was to give the impression he thought nothing was wrong. Emerging from the flat in a beanie and aviators had been a start. You didn't go out like that if you thought you were already being watched. More like the behaviour of someone clueless. Which was how he had to keep acting.

On the other hand, it might be entirely his imagination.

Only it wasn't. Or better: he couldn't afford to think like that.

They'd have anticipated him going straight to the tube station. If Hannah was sending him anywhere local, that would have been easy to evade Phyllis for. He'd have been already. No, it had to be a fair distance away. And the tube was probably his most secure way of reaching it at this time of night.

But that would mean they'd have a team on him, in case he suspected them. Easy to avoid a single tail in a tube station: the old step-on-the-train-and-step-off-at-the-last-second in every undercover cop film ever made. That would get you away from one shadow. But not usually five or six.

His destination – Bank tube station – was just three stops away. He could deliberately overshoot to London Bridge, get the eastbound Jubilee to Canada Water, London Overground to Whitechapel then south to Monument and walk the rest. A series of subsidiary detours and feints along the way might just do it. By the time they realised he was on to them, it'd be too late.

Completely bonkers, when he thought about it: the way he was actually jeopardising his job because his sister needed a favour.

Still, whose fault was that? It wasn't his. It wasn't hers. She didn't know he was a spy. He was entitled to take phone calls from family members. If MI7's White Department wanted information about that, they could just ask him. They could do it through Ruby Parker if need be. He might be reluctant to cooperate, depending on how they framed the request, but he wouldn't necessarily say no.

Instead, they'd chosen to do it the furtive way.

More fool them.

The tunnel roared and the tannoy gave information about destinations. The crowd on the platform shuffled nonchalantly closer to the yellow line along the platform's edge and the train came racing through with a subterranean howl like a low whistle. Already, through the glass, you could see it wasn't overly packed. King's Cross St Pancras was the station before this, and maybe most Fridaynighters had already arrived in the capital. Either way, a non-crowded train would definitely work against him.

Still, mustn't give anything away.

He got on and sat down on one of the middle seats, so he could get a good view. On his left, an empty seat; on his right, a student wearing headphones and playing *Candy Crush Saga* on his phone. That had been going to be part of Mordred's disguise: play a game on his phone, look inconspicuous. He was in two minds now. Still, he'd better keep up the pretence of insouciance.

Outside, a short, middle-aged white guy with a large bald patch and round sunglasses had knocked into a tall and athletic black guy with a beard. For a second, it looked like no more than a verbal face-off, but then the middle-aged man pushed the younger one over, and, as the tannoy said, 'Mind the gap', he stepped into the carriage. The doors closed behind him. The bearded man slapped furiously on the glass, but the train was already moving. The middle-aged guy grinned. He waggled his fingers in a goodbye wave.

The simple pleasures of a Friday night out in Islington.

Then he came and sat next to Mordred, took out his phone and jabbed the screen.

Slight chest ache now, nothing to worry about, but irritating. It had taken something like this to remind him he still wasn't 100%. Normally, he'd relish trying to give a team of professionals the slip, especially when there wasn't much at stake – no one was planning to kill or maim him, they just wanted to see where he was going. The fact that he wasn't enjoying it – found it mildly dispiriting, actually – was concerning. It probably meant he'd underperform. Might even fail.

Not that he'd even know about it, not if they did their jobs properly. And as for the consequences, he hadn't –

"Excuse me," the middle-aged man next to him said, offering him a cheap phone. "Would you mind just holding this for a moment?"

Not normal to address another person on the tube, much less hand your phone over for safekeeping. But this guy could obviously take care of himself, as he just proved. Probably drunk, though.

Mordred shrugged. "No problem." As soon as he accepted it, the screen changed. *Good evening, John. I took care of your little hanger-on from White – one of them. I trust you're grateful.*

Whoa. He turned. But the owner was fully focussed on texting.

Don't speak to me. We haven't much time. Text your reply.

90

How is this even working? Mordred typed. There wasn't an internet connection on the Underground, everyone knew that.

No idea. You'd have to ask GCHQ.

His heart sank. *Who are you?*

John Murgatroyd. We met once.

Mordred nodded. It all made sense now – almost.

Or not.

In any case, he'd been wondering if Murgatroyd would make an appearance, ever since DCI Fleming mentioned him.

What do you want? he typed.

Where are you going?

Out. 😕 How about you?

Cut the emojis, John. I need your help.

I've already asked what you want. Why weren't you more specific first time round? 😕 What sort of help? Just out of interest.

The train pulled in at Old Street. As far as Mordred could see, none of the people who got on looked remotely anxious. Probably nothing to worry about – although that young woman…

Another gap-minding admonition. The doors slid to and they zoomed off again.

See that woman with the braids? Murgatroyd typed, *standing near the door, to your left? Another White agent. You must be going somewhere really exciting.*

I sure am. 😕

Remember that contract we all had to sign, the day you were stabbed?

Nope. Amnesia. But I've been reminded of it by my colleagues.

We want to know why everyone had to sign it.

Who's 'we'? Mordred typed.

Let's just say, a deeper level than Blue or Grey.

Black? You mean even YOU don't know?

That's why we need your help, John. We all love you down there. Really. ☺

How on earth am I meant to find out why we were all meant to sign a contract, when even YOU don't know?

Because you're a good detective.

Thanks, buddy. ☺ *But no one's THAT good. Sorry, pass.*

Not an option, John.

I'm going to the USA tomorrow, so maybe we should call it quits. I got stabbed, remember? You went to DCI Fleming to cover your friends' backs.

That's rubbish. I've no idea who attacked you. And it's not why I went to Fleming. As you'll soon discover for yourself.

Why? Mordred typed. *Is Fleming in America?*

No, and neither are you.

Not yet.

Not this year.

Pointless texting a reply. It was getting silly.

But Murgatroyd's next message came through un-prompted: *Scotland Yard has information about the death of five financiers in a pile-up on the M23. It was covered up – but why? A blogger's saying it was murder. Goes by the name of 'Guanyin'. But no one can trace her. It may not even be a 'her'. Why hasn't MI7 been informed? The contract and the financiers are connec-ted. How? By being the only two things we don't know about and no one seems to want us to know about. That can't be a coincid-ence.*

Mordred sighed. Incredible, but he was bored. *Informa-tion overload. Sorry, I'm concentrating on the braids woman.*

I'll take care of her. And you can keep the phone. Read it offline later. I can remotely disconnect it from the net once we part.

Brilliant. ☺ *Sorry, I meant: NOT brilliant.*

I'm intelligent enough to know you're not going to tell me where you're going, and I'm not going to press you to change your mind. I'll take care of the White agents. What I can tell you is: whether you realise it or not, you're already on the case.

Hooray. 😊

We want you to work with the case detective, one DCI Fleming, a friend of yours from the past. He's expecting a call.

Assuming I ever begin to care, why shouldn't I go straight to Ruby Parker?

Because she'll claim it's a purely police matter. As regards the five missing financiers, she'll struggle to understand why it's any of Red's business, even if she believes you. She certainly won't want to look into why we had to sign those forms.

Sorry to seem a spoilsport, but isn't it obvious? About the forms? If there is a national emergency, intelligence will become more necessary than ever. Emergencies are where terrorists flourish.

But our question is, why NOW? Whoever devised said forms must be expecting something to happen. What is it? If you go to Ruby Parker, you'll be back to square one, with the added disadvantage of knowing you've alerted her.

I'm at square one now. And I don't care about the forms.

That's why you need to contact Fleming. And I DIDN'T go to see him to warn him off his investigation. The contrary, actually.

Righty-ho. 😊

And BTW, I don't have any friends.

....!?

Get off the tube wherever you like. I'll take care of Braids. I'll do for the others too. After that, I won't follow you. You can trust me.

Mordred put the phone in his pocket and blew a weary flute of air. He was almost past caring now. All this so he could report to Hannah that he'd done what she asked.

But he could already feel another him taking over. He was curious, and growing curiouser and curiouser.

When he got off at London Bridge, Murgatroyd stood and grabbed the braids woman like he was about to assault her and thrust her into a seat. Then he exited the train and stood on the escalator between Mordred and three men who were obviously following him. When they were halfway up, he turned and pushed everyone down – an entire stairway of about twenty people.

He didn't seem to do subtlety. Or public safety. Or legality. Everyone was screaming and roaring. God knows what the nation would think when the whole thing appeared on YouTube. Then on the BBC and ITV.

When Mordred got to the top, he was on his own for the first time since Islington.

He ran.

It was only after three minutes of slaloming between people on their way places that he noticed it. A huge light in the sky.

Wow.

He stopped for a better look. He wasn't the only one. Most people were pointing and asking each other more or less incredulous variants of, 'What on earth is that?'

Because, honestly, it didn't look like anything on earth.

Chapter 12: Quatermass and his Pit

Alec sat in the front seat of the minicab next to the driver, an old man with dyed-blond hair and a tweed sports jacket. Phyllis sat in between Annabel and Tariq in the back. It smelt of upholstery polish. A Feng Shui waving cat mascot hung from the rear-view mirror.

"Mansion House, yeah?" the driver said.

"Please," Alec replied.

"I won't be able to take you all the way. I'll get as close as I can. There are 'disturbances' in and around."

"'Disturbances'?" Phyllis said.

"Probably the wrong word," the driver continued awkwardly. "Lots of people trying to have a big party, that's all. The police are supposed to be moving them on, but they're doing a poor job of it, what I've heard. Probably scared. It's a bit like Trafalgar Square ten-to-midnight, New Year's Eve, if you get the picture. Not 'disturbances' exactly. Not like Arsenal versus Millwall, that sort of thing. Tensions."

"How close can you get?" Alec asked. Annabel was already checking the weather forecast on her phone. It wasn't raining – yet.

"Junction of Moorgate and Lothbury?" the driver said. He glanced into his mirror and pulled out into the traffic. All four passengers had their phones out now, Google maps.

"That's quite a distance from our destination," Phyllis said eventually. "Dressed like this."

"I don't like asking," the driver replied. "But you do have invitations, I suppose? The police are telling us not to bring anyone who's not on the guest-list. How the hell they expect us to check, I don't know. I wouldn't know an official invite from a Sainsbury's bloody Nectar card. Got to ask, though."

"We're bona fide guests," Alec said.

"No need to show me your invitations," the driver said, though no one had offered. "I'll get you as close as I can. May be slow going, though. The police stop me, show them your invites, yeah?"

"Absolutely," Alec said.

After a few moments, Annabel looked out of her window. "What's that?" she asked, pointing into the distance.

Phyllis leaned across to see. "Whoa."

A huge hologram in the sky, white. Hard to work out what it was –a head and shoulders of some sort? But not human. More like a demon of some sort: it had horns, just small ones. Its eyes were slightly crossed, yet penetrating. But as the taxi came closer, it looked more like an insect: a grasshopper perhaps. A devil-insect fusion.

"What the hell's it *advertising?*" Phyllis chuckled.

"Creepy," Alec agreed from the front. He turned to the driver. "How long's it been there?"

"You *sure* you've got invitations?" the driver replied. "How come you don't know anything about that, then?" he answered, in response to Tariq's sigh of impatience. "It's to do with your party," he said finally, in a surly tone.

Phyllis laughed. They didn't want to get into a fight: they needed to keep him sweet if they were to get to the front entrance with dresses and suits intact. "We're just guests. We're not the organisers. Any idea what it is?"

The driver glared irritably in the rear-view. She smiled at him. A flicker of confusion appeared on his face, then he smiled back. "Bit before your time, I'd imagine," he said cheerily. "Any of you heard of *Quatermass and the Pit?*"

"Vaguely," Phyllis said in a way that indicated she wanted him to elaborate. "It's a film, isn't it?"

"Hammer Horror," Alec interposed authoritatively. "They really knew how to make them in those days."

Silence. The extent of Alec's knowledge. Leaving no one any the wiser.

"Right…" Phyllis said in a tone sufficient to indicate she wanted *the driver*, and him alone, to elaborate.

"I can't remember when it was made," the driver obliged. "I saw a black and white version at the end of the '50s, but there was a colour version in the '60s. Much better. They dig up an old spaceship in a tube station called Hobbs End. Millions of years old - the spaceship, obviously, not the tube station. That's quite recent: the tube station, I mean. When they get inside the UFO-thing, there are these big insects, like locusts. That's what the aliens were, see? Well, at the end, they all start coming back to life, controlling the whole human race. In London, anyway. Climax: the boss alien appears in the sky like a glowing phantom. That's what *that's* supposed to be, out of your window. Pretty good likeness, if you ask me. Mind you, I haven't seen it for a long time. It's still on late at night sometimes. They ought to do a remake. Mark Gatiss could do it. You know: that Mycroft. He's big on all that."

All four passengers had their phones out again, YouTube.

"Go to one hour thirty-four minutes and fifty-four seconds," Annabel said.

"What?" the driver said.

Alec showed his phone screen, with a paused phantom alien. The driver swept his eyes from the road for a split second. "Nice. How did you get it up so quickly?"

"The magic of online video," Alec replied.

"I still don't understand," Phyllis said. "It's a very good likeness of the film monster, but what do *either* of them have to do with the party?"

The driver chuckled. "Well, that's why I asked if you had invites. It's supposed to be a *Quatermass themed* party. Even I know that, and I haven't got an invitation. That I know of, ho, ho."

They all fished their invitations out and scanned them.

"It doesn't say anything about that on here," Tariq said indignantly. "It doesn't even say fancy dress!"

"Let's not panic," Phyllis said. "There's probably a perfectly rational explanation." She could feel Annabel beside her, freaking out.

"Maybe they'll have a change of clothes for you when you get there," the driver said. "Chuck them away afterwards. The Lord Mayor's rich enough, so they say. Rich as Croesus, to coin a phrase. 'Coin': hark at me! He owns Square Mile Gold, you know. Immense bank, buys gold for wealthy folk, stores it in enormous underground vaults. Big as Switzerland. Colossal. Mind you, people always exaggerate these things. Bet he's worth a pretty penny, even so. He's done wonders for the office too. I didn't even know there *was* a Lord Mayor until recently. If you'd asked me who the Lord Mayor of London was last year, I'd have said, you know: Sadiq Khan. If you'd said, 'No, the *Lord* Mayor, the *other* one', I'd have gone, 'What are you talking about?' And I've lived in London all my life. Mind you, I'm not saying it's a good thing, him puffing his office up. Too many people nowadays chasing fame for my liking. I had that Joey Essex in the back of my cab once. Nice guy, but too famous. Doesn't deserve it. Not like he's Paul McCartney, or Mick Jagger or John Lydon; Michael Palin, John Cleese, Judi Dench: they're all real. *Really* real. Had her in the back too, one time, Judi Dench. Lovely woman."

They were in the city now, a few minutes away.

"I hope John will be okay," Phyllis said, mainly to kick start more conversation. The driver's monologue seemed to have throttled everyone.

"He'll be fine," Alec said curtly.

"In sum," the driver went on, "Don't worry about clothes. You'll be fine."

"They can hardly turn us away if we've got invitations," Alec said. "And if they do, we'll just go to a pub. We might be a bit overdressed by our usual standards, but we'll fit in. Everyone's in glad rags on Friday night."

Phyllis laughed. "'Glad rags'?"

"It's how we used to refer to glamorous clothing in the days before you were born," Alec replied. "In the nineteen-twenties."

"If they turn us away, I'll be bloody furious," Phyllis said. "I won't take it lying down, I'm telling you."

"It'll be a bunch of bankers, hedge-fund managers, stockbrokers and city chairpersons," Tariq said. "It's not like we'll be missing anything."

Phyllis laughed derisively. "You don't understand! Everybody always thinks that. Like all those guys think about is Armani suits and where their next Ferrari's coming from, ergo they must be really dull and detached from reality. But that's not how it is. Believe me, most of them – men and women – know how to really let their hair down. I mean, have *real fun*. They're living on the edge, a lot of them, most of the time. The decisions they make on a daily basis can bankrupt people, or they can earn them fortunes. If that's your working life, you tend to play pretty hard, believe me. One thing we won't be tonight is bored. *If* we get in. And if we don't, going to a poxy pub for gin and a flaccid slice of lemon isn't going to work. Not for me. Not in the slightest."

They'd reached the junction where the driver originally said he'd drop them, but he gave no sign of expecting them to get out. The road ahead was overflowing with people who'd clearly come to celebrate. The crowds were even denser further ahead. A few moments later, the driver applied the central locking.

"I'll let you out when we arrive," he said. "No telling what some of these people might take it into their heads to do, so be careful getting out. Smashed out of their heads, one or two. Always the case."

They drove at a sedate one mile per hour until the crowds were so thick, progress was impossible. Someone banged hard on the roof. Two men put their faces up against Annabel's window and opened their mouths to put their tongues on the glass.

"I'm going to have to let you out here," the driver said apologetically. "Still about three hundred yards to the front door. Really sorry."

"I've been in the army," Alec said. "Assault courses are my thing."

Phyllis's phone rang. *Unknown caller*. She picked up.

"Henry Greysonwell here," a cheery upper-class voice said. "I hope you don't mind me cold-calling you, Ms Robinson, but it occurred to me that you might have a little difficulty getting in. You are on your way, I assume? Or have I been terribly presumptuous?"

"Not at all," Phyllis said. She was so taken aback – an overwhelming mixture of gratitude and relief - she almost went into hyper-sycophantic mode. *Thank you so much, I'm so honoured, please call me Phyllis, how could you possibly think -*

"Where are you now?" he broke in.

"According to our driver, about three hundred yards from the front door of Mansion House."

"With your three fellow guests, I presume. Which road?"

"Princes Street. About halfway down maybe. Towards Moorgate."

"Perfect. I'll send a few locusts to pick you up." He chuckled genially. "Try not to be too alarmed. It's all good fun."

He hung up. She smiled beatifically.

"I take it that was John," Alec said.

"Henry Greysonwell," she said.

Before she could explain, there was a polite tap at Annabel's window. Four figures in rubber locust masks stood outside, holding long staffs. From the neck down, they wore evening suits.

Phyllis gave the driver fifty pounds and issued the order to evacuate. The locusts unmasked to reveal four smiling men in their late thirties. Handshakes were exchanged like this was a rescue mission, then they re-masked. The crowds parted for them out of curiosity, would-be gate-crashers standing back to size up four *actual guests* and their minders. When they reached the entrance to Mansion House, climbing the side-steps onto its raised base, Henry Greysonwell was waiting to welcome them. They'd been told he was in his early thirties, but he looked about a decade younger, guileless face, clean shaven, brown hair fashionably flattened, blue eyes, strong jawline, a little like a 1940s movie star. He wore a day suit and tie, both obviously expensive. He called a waiter over with glasses of champagne on a tray. A servant took their coats. Greysonwell led them up one flight of stairs, along a landing and up an improvised ladder to the roof to show them the view.

Above them, the huge phantom hologram. Below, a huge throng of people, obviously having a good time, in amongst which strings of people wearing locust masks were conga-ing. Bank tube station had been re-labelled 'Hobbs End'. Police personnel stood around, or rode horses, watching, but making no attempt to interfere. Searchlights in different colours strafed the whole area. Pop music blared: Barns Courtney and, before that, Rag 'n' Bone Man.

"I think everyone's having a good time," Greysonwell said.

Phyllis had never seen anything like it. But when she turned to ask her host the question still uppermost in her mind – why *Quatermass and the Pit?* – he'd already gone. She wondered what was so urgent.

Then she saw. Several yards away, a middle-aged woman in a tight-fitting dress, looking unhappy.

His mother maybe.

Anyway, it didn't matter. They'd catch up with each other later.

Annabel linked arms with her. "This is slightly better than I expected," she said.

Chapter 13: Brent the Paranoid

P-5, L-8, P-6, L7, P-5, L-3.

403068. Because, even today, Mordred tended to do whatever Hannah told him - not just the letter but the spirit - he'd actually memorised the code to the pad in the box whose key was to be handed over in The Frederick and Elizabeth pub. Shades of a Cold War novel, when you thought about it. On one level, he felt like a complete idiot; on another, like the hero in a Cold War novel.

The Halloween face-in-the-sky was directly above his destination. Police officers stood at the end of Princes Street, cordoning off its entrance and directing people to turn back and then keep moving. Others diverted traffic away. A senior officer with a loudhailer ordered people to disperse. Mounted police clip-clopped in wide circles, looking grim.

In these sorts of cases, it was often the police who initiated real trouble. What happened at those times was the BBC and ITV came along, the Met organised an impromptu press conference, and the crowds got the entire blame. He'd seen it happen. The police had a difficult job, true, but sometimes, they took themselves too seriously. Then they got jumpy, and the kettling began.

He avoided the cordon with ease. Inside, EC4 was more packed than it had probably been in its entire history before. God knows who'd invited everyone. You didn't get a crowd this size somewhere normally this gloomy unless someone, somewhere had issued an invitation on multiple social media. Greysonwell's reputation, that was the draw.

So perhaps the press were behind it. Something like this could play for days in the newspapers, especially if it all went belly-up. Make a change from the usual guff on pages

1 through 50. Although, to be fair, the *Metro* and the *Standard* were free. And they weren't usually that bad.

Alternatively, Greysonwell himself might be responsible. That would be consistent with everything the media said about him. One of those people who saw themselves as the World's No. 1 *enfant terrible*. Unfortunately, he had a lot of competition. People in that mould always did. Something ostentatious like this might give him the edge.

The crowd was getting denser. In places, you could hardly move. A person might easily lose control of their intended direction. If that happened on a sufficiently large scale, simultaneously enough, mass panic wasn't impossible. No wonder the police were organising diversions. But from the way things looked, they weren't trying hard enough. It might already be too late anyway.

Yet the crowds seemed happy enough. None of the too-much-alcohol moodiness yet, although that was always inevitable in the long run. A teenage boy with a nose piercing tried to grab Mordred's hat, but only in a friendly way. There wasn't room for a serious thief to operate here.

Mordred kept his eyes on Mansion House as a means of keeping his bearings. But then he passed the entrance to tube station.

Hobbs End? What the - ? For a split second, the weird sensation of dreaming. He was being carried past it, almost despite himself, by the crowd. But no, someone had replaced the real station's banner.

Why?

And why all these people with rubber insect masks?

With his beanie and aviators, he must look something like them. Funny ha-ha, on one level, and maybe it helped him blend in, but if the police came on hard, it might make him an early target.

Another question; how the hell were Phyllis and the others going to get through this?

Maybe it hadn't been this bad a few hours ago, when they'd set off. And she hadn't rung him.

Mind you, that might mean she was sitting at home, waiting for him. *Where have you been, John?*

If she asked him that, he'd have to tell her the truth. Probably. Depending on what he found at the end of his journey.

His *quest*. That was a bit like how it felt now. Like pushing through a dense forest towards a far-flung building sheltering a mysterious keeper of an enchanted key. And a doubly locked room at the end, revealing... who knew what?

The Frederick and Elizabeth was Georgian, part of a long block of buildings, all trying for a distinctive antique style underneath the sky-excluding office blocks. It had a series of windows built into arches, four columns and an oak door beneath a classical portico. Getting inside was going to pose a problem, especially now the police were fencing the area off. Alcohol was currently at a premium.

Not that he had a choice. Ten minutes' of small advances accompanied by polite apologies and grunted excuses, and he emerged at the bar. Ornate, gilt-framed mirrors, a proud array of spirits and liqueurs at the rear just above eye-level, everything lit like an upmarket Christmas advert, beiges, golds, silvers. The conversational noise was deafening. Most people were shouting.

"I'm looking for Brent!" he told the barman, a straggly haired biker-type with a beard, lean, middle-aged and hard-looking.

"What?" the barman yelled, putting his ear closer. *"You'll have to shout louder!"*

"I'm looking for Brent! I'm John! Hannah sent me!

"You're in luck then! I'm Brent!

Brent walked away and stopped behind a pair of wooden saloon doors a bit further up. He beckoned

Mordred over and stood patiently while he made his way laboriously over, trying not to spill the pints of those who were lucky enough to have been served. A crowd this size, you'd think the beer would be close to running out now.

Brent unlatched a plastic chain, beckoned Mordred through, and led him into the back. They entered a small room with a bare light bulb, a single armchair, and a poster of an RAF helicopter on the wall. Brent shut the door behind them. Yet more shades of a Cold War novel.

"You're John?" Brent said.

"Hannah told me you'd give me a key."

Brent removed a key from his pocket. "You mean this?"

Mordred shrugged. "I don't know what it's supposed to look like. I've never seen it before."

"How do I know you're not an undercover policeman?"

"What?"

"How do I know you're really this, um… 'John' person?"

"Why don't you ask me something about her? Something only you know, perhaps."

"We're not that close." He sighed, and gave Mordred the key. "Look, okay, my position is, I don't know what goes on in that room, and I don't want to. I'm happy to keep the key for Hannah because I like her, the lady's heart's in the right place, and she's as cool as a Union Jack cucumber. But she owns the lease to it, so it's her responsibility. Not mine. I just keep the key, and I do it because she's a friend, yeah? *Not my property, not my business,*" he said, as if it was a marketing slogan. "Have a look round in there, do what you need to, bring back the key when you go, but *don't* tell me anything. I don't want to know what's happening in there, or what she's doing, even if it's perfectly innocent, which I'm sure it is. I take it you've got the code – *DON'T* tell me it! Just: yes or no?"

"Yes," Mordred said.

"Brilliant. Go out the way you came, then. Turn left when you leave the bar. There's a door to the toilets at the end. Ignore it. Keep going round. Another says 'no entry'. Go through. Up three flights of stairs. Door at the top. Security box on the left. Unlock using key. Type in code, enter apartment-stroke-broom-cupboard-stroke-mini-office, switch on light, close door behind you, do whatever you're here for, close door on exit, lock security box, come downstairs, find me, return key, go home. Got it?"

"Yes."

"Even if there's a dead body in there, I don't want to know. Officially, that key doesn't exist, so I couldn't have known, get it? Repeat: not my property, not my business. That's why we're in here. In this room, alone together. So no one can see me give you the key."

"Got it."

"It doesn't exist."

"Right."

The way things were going, he half-expected a written test. *1. What metallic item of around 6cm in length is NOT currently present in the real world? 2. What six-digit number -*

"Off you go then," Brent said. "I won't say, 'I hope you find what you're looking for', because that would be completely meaningless, given I've no idea why you're here."

Mordred sighed.

"Hey, I'm just looking after number one," Brent said. "Nothing personal. Okay: you win: *I hope you find what you're looking for.*"

"Thanks."

"Although it is a bit disturbing that I had to do that. I'm already thinking, 'What *is* he looking for?' Anyway, I'm going to stay in here and count to ten after you've gone. When I come out, I expect you to have disappeared."

"Gotcha."

"Pardon?"

"Gotcha. That is, I get what you mean."

Brent put his hand on his chest, wheezed slightly and grinned. "Bloody hell, I thought you were arresting me! Did you do that deliberately, or what?"

"Sorry, no, it was an accident."

"Okay. Apology accepted. Off you go." He flopped down on the armchair as if the whole thing had been a ten-hour ordeal at the hands of practised sadists. A mental light seemed to go out and his lips began to count to ten.

Mordred let himself out. Through to the toilets, then the No Entry door, then the stairs. At the top, a small landing with a single door at the end. By now, what little light there was came from downstairs. He'd brought a small torch, but given a few seconds, his eyes would probably adjust. Best leave it till it was absolutely necessary.

What if someone was waiting for him, inside? He hadn't thought about that before, but the way Brent behaved – like he was expecting something bad to happen – hadn't exactly been confidence boosting.

Well, if it was a trap – which, when he thought about it, seemed unlikely - so be it. He unlocked the box, keyed in the code, and the door popped ajar. He pushed it open and stepped inside.

Light switch to his left, but he wasn't going to flick it yet. On his right, a window. In closing the door, he'd extinguished all illumination from lower levels of the pub, but the light from the Mayor's party outside more than compensated. And he didn't want to alert anyone below to his presence.

The general layout of the room was adequately visible through the gloom, and it was already obvious there'd been some sort of struggle in here. A PC lay with its side-panel removed on a desk and someone had pushed a shelf over. The floor was strewn with what looked like a collection of small ornaments. The room's sole chair was overturned and one of its legs snapped.

Mordred inspected the PC. Missing hard drive. He went down on his haunches and examined the carpet with his torch. Stains, hard and crusty. He pressed his finger down into one and looked more carefully. Then smelt it.

Blood? Could be. If so, it had been here a while.

He tried the desk drawers. All locked.

The same nagging question he'd formulated on Monday. Could the occupant have been the same person who'd been killed that night when he was stabbed? The lack of a hard drive was pretty compelling in that regard.

If so, Hannah's 'she' was a man.

And could well be the same person as 'Guanyin' into the bargain. His sister's mysterious female, Murgatroyd's missing blogger, the Square Mile's murder victim. Talk about three birds with one stone.

No, that would be too good – or bad – to be true. Wouldn't it?

This stuff had to be blood. What else could it be? Someone had been attacked here. Everything indicated a violent struggle.

But then, whoever it was, it couldn't be the murder victim. If *he'd* been attacked here, then how did he then get out of the pub, return the key to Brent – Brent was so paranoid he'd definitely have noticed it missing – and run across EC4 before anyone caught up with him? There'd been five pursuers, according to the CCTV. Five against one in this room would have ended right here. Even two against one.

Back to the first indubitable fact: that someone had been attacked here.

The second was that this was the base where Hannah's semi-anonymous friend posted 'her' blogs.

So the question was, how did the victim of a major assault get out of the pub, return the key to Brent, and not excite comment? Normally, when you were attacked – especially when you were bleeding – you were flustered. People noticed.

And how did the *attackers* get in and out without Brent's involvement?

Well, maybe Brent was in league with them.

No, that wouldn't make sense either. Brent was adamant about not wanting anything to do with what went on in here, and he wasn't putting it on.

None of it made sense.

Or rather - yes it did. *Yes, it did!*

Whoa.

There hadn't been an attack in here. Rather, the occupant had *staged* an attack in a hurried attempt to cover his tracks, and because he knew he wasn't coming back. Because it *was* a 'him'. It was the murder victim.

The post-mortem report would reveal whether he'd been cut before being killed, and assess the probability of any such cuts being self-inflicted. If this *was* blood on the floor – and it almost certainly was – its DNA could be matched to the victim. All in all, it was almost certainly the breakthrough the police were looking for.

But it wouldn't lead to any arrests. Mordred had already worked out that Blue or Grey were behind the killing.

Which meant they must have something against the blogger.

Which by extension meant they had something against Hannah – even if they hadn't made the connection yet.

When they examined the tenancy agreement, what would they find? Links to her.

And of course, somebody would have to answer for the Square Mile murder, especially with so much evidence potentially pointing at the British secret service.

And, from their point of view, where better to divert the blame than to an anti-authoritarian trouble-stirrer with a global following?

It wouldn't even serve her PR-wise. People tended to warm to rebels, but not when they were implicated in murder. Doubly not when the victim was probably a blogging left-leaner. Grey department could make the whole thing look very sordid indeed. Their speciality: framing people and adding precisely the right ingredients to ensure each target became a pariah.

The occupant had almost certainly left fingerprints, strands of hair, and a whole chocolate box of additional forensic evidence. The police would find this place sooner or later, and they'd identify the victim. Then they'd identify him as a blogger. Finally, they'd discover his links to Hannah.

Leaned on roughly enough, Brent would almost certainly crack.

Actually, the leaning wouldn't even have to be that rough. It could be relatively gentle. *Not my property, not my business,* he'd tell the police, blubbering like a baby, then he'd spill everything else, just by way of putting himself a million miles in the clear. *There was this bloke called John came in to look around, blond hair, tall…*

Bloody hell, it was a serious mess, all ways up.

He needed to think. He had to come up with some sort of action-plan before he left here. He might not get a second entry.

And there wasn't even a chair to sit down on.

He put his fingertips on his forehead and closed his eyes. But nothing came. He and Hannah were trapped. His coming here tonight hadn't achieved anything, nor could it have. All that had happened was he'd been given an insight how events would now unfold. He couldn't do anything about them. Catastrophe would engulf them both, and soon. She wouldn't even see it coming.

Could he go on the offensive? Strike some sort of bargain with the devil? Contact Blue or Grey - ?

But he didn't even know which of the two it was. Could even be White, come to that. They were three very different entities, even though he'd lumped them together for the purposes of all this. Going to the wrong one... Even if you knew *how* and *where* to 'go to' them...

Could he make an appeal to Murgatroyd? *I've found your blogger, I'll do everything you're asking, if you keep my sister out of it.*

But he didn't know where to find Murgatroyd, either. And he didn't trust him.

Gears turned gears, cogs ground cogs, and his brain seized up. He couldn't even think any more, let alone formulate a plan.

Suddenly, a three-inch high Sister Wendy appeared floating in the corner, like a medieval vision. She had her *Story of Painting* under her left arm. Her right finger was raised in admonition. She said, "Why don't you go to the window and have a look out, John?"

Why he should think of Sister Wendy Beckett *now* was beyond him. Obviously, his subconscious had taken over. Crazy. With all due respect, it wasn't even like she was a saint. To the best of his knowledge, she was alive and well and living in Norfolk.

Maybe the drugs again, although he'd lowered his dose since the crazy library-euphoria experience a few days ago.

Mind you, that hadn't exactly been inconsequential. A few minutes afterwards, Hannah on the phone telling him to go to the library.

Spooky.

Synchronicity, maybe. Whatever that was.

He went to the window, as commanded. It was covered by a net curtain so he didn't have to worry about keeping out of view.

Bloody hell, you could see Mansion House from here. Not a bad view either.

No sign of Phyllis and the gang, but then anything else would have been a miracle. Of sorts. He took out his phone. *No messages.*

Which probably meant she was in there, partying. She'd definitely have phoned him otherwise.

He was about to turn away when something caught his attention. On the roof of the building, just within its perimeter balustrade, four men of about his own age – City trader boys, looked to be - horsing about with masks, swapping them, trying them on, laughing. Obviously on their way to a skinful.

But these weren't locust masks.

They were griffin masks. Like those on the CCTV.

He tried for a closer look. But the men moved back out of his sight line and didn't return.

Bloody hell - in a fairly good way! This changed everything. It would mean that the murderers weren't secret servicemen.

At least, not necessarily.

Suddenly, he had a flashback. For the first time since waking up in hospital, he remembered something. A chase, him riving one of the masks off someone, putting it on; the victim cowering against the wall, his face the epitome of horror. The knife, the helplessness, the –

Whoa. Powerful! He couldn't afford to get carried away, not right now.

And actually, a few masks didn't change anything, not really. They might be readily available in every tourist kiosk in London, for all he knew. And he hadn't primarily inferred the involvement of British intelligence from the masks. They hadn't even been close to his deductive starting point.

But hang on. Even if they *were* on sale everywhere, the occurrence of a murder within a stone's throw of here should at least have endowed them with negative connotations. Vendors might well have removed them from their shelves, made way for something a bit less currently objectionable. If you were still messing about with them now, and happily, might that not mean you'd…

He didn't know. Seeds of ideas were germinating, but they'd take time.

All except for one.

He couldn't contact Murgatroyd. But he could do the next best thing. DCI Fleming. Maybe Fleming would be open to some sort of deal. They could even agree to split the investigation, keep the criminal and intelligence aspects separate. Discreetly get the police to the real culprits, keep the innocent rock impresario out of it. After all, he had information Fleming didn't. And Fleming had met Murgatroyd. He'd probably cooperate.

He took out the phone Murgatroyd had given him. As he expected, Fleming's phone number was in there. He used it to make the call, keep his own identity under wraps, just in case it all went wrong.

But when Fleming picked up, he spoke before Mordred had uttered a word. "Hello, John," he said. "Nice to finally hear from you."

Chapter 14: A Nice Surprise for Faris

Phyllis and Annabel began their visit to Mansion House with a self-guided tour, just for curiosity's sake. After thirty minutes' looking round the palatial rooms, admiring the art and the wallpaper and the chandeliers and the fabrics and the height of the ceilings, they found themselves gravitating towards the room set aside for the party. Alec and Tariq followed three steps behind, then they regrouped and linked arms to go in: Tariq and Annabel, Phyllis and Alec.

At the front of a hall big enough to hold two hundred people, a DJ worked a set of turntables. Multi-coloured lights swept the floor, wide-beamed and intense. The music was mainly hip-hop, funk and soul. A projector threw stills from *Quatermass and the Pit* onto the ceiling: Andrew Keir looking earnest, Barbara Shelley looking shocked, Julian Glover looking autocratic, the buried spaceship, the war of the locusts, the demon-headed finale. Most people here were ordinary-looking men and women in expensive suits and dresses, but, as usual, a coterie of models – male and female – had been engaged to dance non-stop, like slaves, for the enthralment of the bona fide guests. In the case of six or seven, the ordeal was exacerbated by rubber locust masks. There was a bar at the back with liveried waiters. Ten fabric recliner sofas had been placed against the walls and were mostly occupied, yet even so, the dance floor was full. God knows what the 'Keeper' – the head of staff here – thought. The walls were decorated with *Domine Dirige Nos* plaques, two griffins supporting a shield with the cross of Saint George and a sword, surmounted by a knight's helmet: the ancient coat of arms of the City of London.

"Let's get seats and drinks," Phyllis said. She'd long since learned that the hallmark of a memorable good time was a mix of emotions, not in themselves unfamiliar, but unusual to find together at the same time and likely, therefore, to be slightly confused. In this case, wonderment at the beauty of the décor, a mild aversion to the science-fiction theme (a pinch of revulsion always helped the mix), vague respect for the Mayoral institution, all the usual excitement of familiar music played at loud volume, of a celebratory atmosphere and of unfamiliar, possibly exciting, strangers, and finally, the (now rapidly dissipating) intoxication of alcohol. This was going to be an outstanding night.

"You'll have to excuse me a moment," Alec said. "Nature calls."

"Could you get us some drinks on the way back?" Phyllis asked.

"Absolutely," he said. "What would you like? I believe everything's free, so don't hold back. Although yes, do, if you don't want to be ill."

She laughed. "Dreary man."

"I'll get you home in one piece whatever," he said. "Just remember, you're probably going to be meeting Greysonwell for a *tête-à-tête* later. And of course, it's not a normal Saturday tomorrow. Work in the morning."

She stuck her lower lip out. "Forgot about that." She laughed. "White wine, small then."

"Annabel? Tariq?"

"Any kind of fruit juice for me," Tariq said.

"Surprise me," Annabel said. "A glass of white wine. I don't care what sort of grape. Or what year, providing it's not before 2010."

Alec laughed. "Innovative use of the word, 'surprise'."

She shrugged. "Moscato 2013, then."

"Right."

"There are some pretty good looking women here, Alec," Phyllis said. "Why not ask one of them to dance? Some of them don't even look like they're with anyone."

He smiled thinly. "If it looks too good to be true, it probably is. That's why I'm relying on you to protect me." He pointed at Phyllis, Tariq, then Annabel. "Indeterminate white wine, fruit juice, Moscato."

"Would you like any help carrying, Alec?" Tariq called. But it was too noisy, and he'd already set off.

"He won't have to bring the drinks himself," Annabel said. "I think the waiters will take care of that."

"They'll have a difficult job with all these bodies gyrating," Tariq replied.

"That's precisely why they won't trust it to an inexperienced guest like Alec," Phyllis told him. "No, I'm pretty sure it's just a question of placing your order. They probably won't even *allow* you to take your own. Anyway, let's not talk about that. Far be it from me to state the obvious, but it's boring. Who wants to dance?"

Annabel and Tariq looked at her as if she was mad.

"I don't know how to," Annabel said, turning away slightly. "And the great thing is, I've no inclination to learn."

"I retired from the world of dance when I got married," Tariq said.

Phyllis rolled her eyes. "Brilliant," she said. "Let's just talk about the fascinating question of how Alec's going to get back from the bar with four drinks, then. Maybe we'll be proved right. Maybe the waiters *will* bring them. Or maybe not. The tension mounts. Maybe later, he'll go for more drinks, maybe in bigger glasses, and - "

"Dancing doesn't make you interesting," Annabel said.

"If you want to blend in somewhere like this, you probably need a complete skill-set," Phyllis replied. "I wonder how Ruby Parker will take it when she learns about your refusal to participate in its most prominent social activity."

Tariq laughed.

"Will you mention that in your report?" Annabel asked.

"Sure will."

Annabel didn't respond straight away. Anyone else would have cursed. They'd have raged against the attempted blackmail and the injustice of being forced to ignore their natural aversion. Instead, she looked blankly into the middle distance and made a decision.

"You're right," she said. "I have to learn. Tariq, you stay here. Keep our seats."

Faris Meadows began the evening determined to spook the spooks. He hadn't met, or even seen them yet, although he knew they were two women. Probably self-important middle-aged Tracey-and-Trish-from-the-office types with high heels and legs like elephants'. Fun to be had.

The plan was to nobble their partners: spike their drinks or even physically knock them unconscious. See how the women coped when they realised something was wrong. Freak them out a bit before their chat with Greysonwell. Show them MI5 wasn't invincible. Send them home seriously embarrassed. All that.

Cooking something up wasn't difficult when you had a loyal gang to call on. Paul, at 25 the youngest of them, jet black hair, Roman nose, big blue eyes; Hilldy, little over 30, muscular, boxer's face really: pug nose, deep set eyes; Michael, suave and thin, wet-look gel, slouching walk, knowing smile, the oldest at 35; Raymond, long red locks, disingenuous expression, fluffy beard. All tall and well-constructed and handsome. And rich. And soon to be famous. What a posse.

Then Raymond had a better idea. Spook them with the masks. MI5 had probably heard all about the murder. A kind of *You've seen the CCTV, now here's real life!* sort of thing.

The idea had appealed for a while, and they'd actually rehearsed a few scenarios on the roof, behind the water tank, where no one could see them. But in the end, Paul wasn't keen. And he was right: it was too risky.

They stood against the eastern balustrade, just a few feet from the stairs down to the top floor. It was cold, but you could almost see the stars, despite all the light pollution down in the square. Hundreds, maybe thousands of people at one point, but beginning to thin out now. Probably fed up. They couldn't get in through the front door, the pubs round here weren't exactly spectacular, and the police were doing a good job of moving them on.

"I can't see any point in provoking them," Paul said. He handed his mask to Faris. "I don't mind pissing them about, but we've got big things to lose here. MI5's not like the police. They don't have to play by the rules, and they don't even have to get results. We could end up in big trouble. And for what?"

"It's not like these are the *actual masks, Paul*," Hilldy said. "But... yeah, you're right."

One hundred per cent true. Paul had a massive point, he really did. Meadows collected the remaining masks, lifted the lid on one of the temporary rubbish bins and dropped them in. "Fair enough," he said. "Five of us, we're in the vicinity, and we're wearing these. It does kind of draw attention."

Obviously. But they'd had too much to drink. They'd never have considered it, sober. But that's what alcohol did. It compromised your sense of what was risky. Best go the other way. Be *too* cautious.

"I think we ought to split up," Meadows said. "Even without the masks, we're five guys of similar height and build to what they'll have seen in the CCTV, and we're slap bang in the same locality. Where's Raymond?"

"'Split *up*'?" Michael said. "What, like it's an SAS training course? No way! Lighten up, Faris. This is a party. We're here to have a good time."

"Where's Raymond?" Faris repeated.

"Gone to check out Tracey and Trish," Paul said. "Let's get another drink. I'm desiccating here. If I don't get another shot of alcohol in the next ten minutes, I'll be back to sober again. And it's freezing."

"And boring," Michael said.

They put their hands in their pockets and shuffled towards the exit.

Raymond was coming upstairs to meet them at speed. He wore a wide grin.

"You're not going to believe this, guys," he said. "I've just seen the actual Tracey and Trish. They're *hot*. I'm not joking. Really. Like the-two-biggest-babes-in-the-building hot."

You could read Raymond like a book. He wasn't making it up, that was for sure, and he probably wasn't mistaken. Good taste in women, even if he hardly ever got to indulge it because he was such a weirdo.

But Paul, Hilldy and Michael were already on their way downstairs, like they knew where to find them.

Michael paused and turned back. "Where are they?"

Raymond shrugged. "Touring the rooms last I saw them."

"How do you know they were Tracey and Trish?" Faris said.

"Mummy pointed them out," Raymond said.

Faris nodded. That clinched it.

'Mummy': Lady Julia, Greysonwell's formidable mother. God help all five of them, probably the only woman they'd ever really love. And one of the main things that bound them together as a gang.

He looked into the sky where the luminous head still hovered, and stood absolutely still. Dark energy suffused him in increasingly strong pulses. He could, if he wanted, cause a riot down in the square simply by waving his hand

120

over it. Or chaos throughout the city. Or anarchy across the globe.

But he didn't want to, not yet. Mummy, in her infinite oddity, had once claimed Mansion House was built on the ruins of where Satan had shown Christ the world's kingdoms. A night as perfect as this, you could almost believe it. A night for sucking the life out of the whole universe and kicking its sorry remnants into the gutter.

Tracey and Trish had better watch out. He was coming for them.

"Let me through!" he called after his friends, laughing. "They're mine! *They're mine!*" He squeezed Michael's shoulder affectionately. "Back to the original plan," he whispered. "You and Raymond take care of the partners. Probably not both guys, don't want to scare the ladies too much. Wait till one of them goes to the gents'. Don't hit him too hard. And don't tell Mummy."

"Why should you always get the best pickings?" Raymond said. "I found them!"

"Because I'm the best hunter," Faris replied. "Come on, you know that's true. I'm master of the *I truly respect your integrity as a woman* spiel. And it's not as if I don't let you in afterwards. Too early, you'll only mess it up. Get yourselves some of the free drink. And I'm sure you're wrong, anyway. Trish and bloody Tracey can't be *that* much better than all the other women here tonight. Come *on*, guys! Greysonwell's actually got a bunch of *models* on site. Actual *models*: famed for their faces and waistlines and, in some cases, their gigantic breasts! Give *one* of them a chance, at least. *Pity* them, if nothing else. And leave the spies to your esteemed leader."

The way the four looked at him – smiling, but not entirely convinced – made him half doubt their loyalty. In the long run, it didn't matter. Nothing did. They loved each other, but the end of the world was coming, and things were going to change more than anyone knew. Who could say whether they'd survive?

In the meantime, *Carpe diem.* The spies were his.

Chapter 15: The Valley of Humiliation

"How did you know it was me?" Mordred asked, though he already knew.

"I think you already know," Fleming replied.

Mordred sighed and looked out of the window again. No return of the griffin maskers, and the party looked to be in full swing. His mind felt like this room - upturned and a bit wrecked – and he wasn't in the mood to exchange *bon mots* with Fleming. Still, he couldn't afford to alienate him.

Could he? He might need DCI Fleming, but on the other hand, the situation was undoubtedly mutual. The timbre of Fleming's voice strongly suggested he'd been awaiting Mordred's call, and that he was relieved to finally pick up. He'd made a mistake in not at least affecting hesitation.

"I can probably give you the breakthrough you're looking for," Mordred said. "But I need something from you."

"Go ahead."

"I think someone is trying to frame someone. I need you to make sure said framing won't happen."

"I'd need to know the name of each party before committing myself."

"What I thought you'd say. Bye." He hung up.

He put the phone on the computer desk and looked at the ornaments on the floor. A ceramic Buddha figurine – Amida not Siddhartha – and a small wooden Thai dancer. An eight-spoked wheel on a metal base. A picture of a beatific looking ancient East Asian figure sitting on a low wall, with his - or her - leg raised and resting on the wall.

Guanyin. That's right, yes. The Goddess of Mercy? Revered by both Buddhists and Taoists. But thought to have originated in a male god whose long name Mordred couldn't remember. The male-female thing might not be as clear cut in this case as it seemed, then. The waters were clearing.

His phone rang. He left it a moment, then picked up. "Hello, Nicholas," he said. "Nice to finally hear from you."

"I could have you arrested for obstructing the course of justice."

"But you won't."

"Really? Why not?"

"Because you know I won't care," Mordred said. "And because, deep down, you realise we're both on the same side. Besides, I'm not obstructing the course of justice. Potentially, I'm all that's stopping it flowing into the lake of iniquity."

"You obviously don't trust me."

"Untrue. I just happen to know there are people who are already ahead of you, and are looking to see what next step you'll make."

"So they can divert it into – what was it? 'The lake of iniquity'?"

"Yep."

Fleming chuckled. "In the normal course of things, I'd probably say you were paranoid, but I've had a visit from Mr Murgatroyd too, so I'm willing to cede the benefit of the doubt."

"I need more than that."

"How do you know I'm not having this phone call recorded?"

"Are you?"

"… No. But maybe I should be. These 'people' of yours who are 'already ahead of me', I take it you're talking about MI7? Your department, or one of the others?"

"One of the others. Take your pick."

"You mean: you don't know."

"That's how the different departments thing works."

"Who is this person you're trying to protect? No, scrap that question. Obviously, you're not going to tell me. But I'm guessing it's a family member."

Mordred recoiled slightly. "What makes you say that?"

"Your sister, Hannah."

"Good try." Lucky this interview wasn't face to face. Fleming would have noticed the blood drain from his face. As it was, he almost heard the DCI punch the air in triumph.

"It is a *very* good try," Fleming continued. "A murder in the heart of London's financial district. A woman who's famed for her antipathy to corporate tax avoidance. Her brother who supposedly has crucial information, but who wants a mysterious 'someone' kept out of it? Come on." He laughed. "Listen, John, I've got news. You're out of time. I've been waiting for this call. CID techs have just triangulated it. You're bang in the middle of London's financial district."

Mordred blinked slowly and put his free hand to his forehead. My God. Of course. He'd been a complete idiot. All this Q&A had just been a ruse to keep him on the line. For the second time that night, his world unravelled before his eyes.

He'd badly underestimated his interlocutor. Unconsciously, he'd considered him your stereotypical PC Plod, dogged and unimaginative. He should have known better. At one time, Fleming had been a key member of Ruby Parker's team, and she only ever went with the best.

Himself excepted, obviously, now.

He was caught like a rat in a trap. His one remaining card was a stubborn insistence on not talking. But that was worthless now they knew where he was.

"You win," he said in a monotone.

"Surrender?"

Mordred shrugged. Pathetic really, how he'd let himself be led by the nose. "Bye," he said, and hung up.

He tossed the phone on the desk. Nothing to do now, but sit and wait for the Black Maria.

Probably better go out front, make it easier for them. Only good manners, really.

The phone rang.

Fleming, obviously. Not very nice. One thing to win, another to toy with your victim.

He picked up. "What do you want?"

"I was joking," Fleming said.

"Er – what?"

"Obviously, I could have arranged all that, but I didn't. I need you to trust me, that's all. I didn't - "

"Um, wait a minute…" His head reeled. "How did you know I was in Reykjavík on Thames then?"

"Educated guesswork. Hannah, your sister, and the murder victim intersect there. You acknowledged as much when you gave me just enough time to laugh after deducing it. You've just come across some kind of diamond mine of information. You couldn't have got that at home, lying in bed, thinking. It's a fair assumption you're located somewhere at the intersection."

"Bloody hell, you're good."

"Are you at Greysonwell's party?"

"No. Cross my heart and hope to die. Look, you win, okay. I trust you."

"I know what you're probably thinking. That I imagine I've got things on you, and I can use them to apply the thumbscrews. But that's not how I work. I need you to get your head together now. Go home and we'll talk tomorrow. I want to discover the truth as much as you do, and I accept your assertion that there are people out there who can lead me into your so-called lake of whatever. So we need to cooperate. But I'm not making any promises. If your sister is implicated in murder in any way, I will pursue that."

"Understood."

"Cheer up, John. Like you say, we're on the same side."

God, he was receiving all the concessions. He suddenly had an idea. "What do you know about the deaths of five financiers in a traffic collision on the M23?"

"Pardon?"

"Murgatroyd said it was connected to the murder."

"It's more than he told me. I'll look into it. But I need to think now, so I'm going to say good night."

He hung up.

Mordred wasn't used to being completely and utterly outflanked. Certainly not by someone who then pardoned him on the gallows.

Bloody hell. The weirdest feeling ever. He didn't know whether he was in the depths of despair or at the pinnacle of elation.

Time to get downstairs. Brent would be getting worried.

Chapter 16: Dancing with the Devil

Phyllis turned to Annabel and laughed. "You do realise that if we dance with each *other*, some men see that as an invitation to cut in?"

But Annabel was already on her way. She took up position on the edge of the dancing crowd and began to imitate the closest person, a man of about her age opposite an older woman with a ponytail. Phyllis had no alternative but to follow suit. As she'd anticipated, they ended up dancing with each other. The crowd adjusted to include them, then gobbled them up.

"We can just say we're a same sex couple!" Annabel called over the din of Fully Magic Coal Tar Lounge. She looked annoyed. On one level, she probably did 'want to learn', as she'd put it; on another she resented being forced.

"That won't stop men cutting in!" Phyllis replied.

"Just say 'no', then!"

A long-haired man of about thirty came up and started dancing next to them. Phyllis had talked about 'cutting in' as if it was a Regency ball, but this was the way it happened nowadays. Someone sidled up pointing his body at you and trying to make eye-contact as if to say, 'Let me in'. Mostly, it was too noisy to *ask* for inclusion, or to exchange anything much verbal at all. The way he was looking at them, it was obviously Annabel he was after.

"I'm Roland!" he shouted. "Can I get you a drink?"

"I'm married!" Annabel replied.

He grinned. He was already attempting to interpose himself between the two women. "I'm not offering adultery! I'm just trying to be friendly! You dance really well, by the way!"

The classic pick-up at its most disagreeable: edge the friend out and make her feel like she doesn't exist. Try to take her place. Leave her to make her own way home. Unfortunately, Annabel had said she was married, so 'we're a same sex couple' wasn't an option any more.

"Excuse me," Phyllis yelled indignantly to Roland, pointing to herself and Annabel. "We're trying to dance!"

Roland looked at her as if she was on the other side of a thick pane of glass, then turned back to Annabel. "You're very beautiful! Have you got a name at all?"

"Mrs al-Banna Gould!" she replied.

"Is your husband here tonight? I'd really like to meet him!"

Annabel finally snapped. "Please get out of the way! I'm here with my friend!"

Roland laughed. "So your husband's *not* here? Does he actually exist?"

Annabel stopped dancing. She looked like she was about to hit him, but he was already moving backwards into the crowd, holding his palms up. "Hey, all I'm saying, *Mrs al-Banna Gould*, is that you're totally gorgeous and I'm totally available! This isn't over! I've got a villa in Sardinia and another in Corfu! I can buy you luxury cars and diamond rings! I can take you all over the world! I can introduce you to incredible people! I can even make you famous! You name it, I can do it! I can make you my *queen!* I'm not finished with you yet!" He blew her a kiss, skipped on his heel, and turned and disappeared.

Annabel emitted a weary sigh then started dancing again as if nothing had happened.

Phyllis did a double-take. She hooted and resumed swaying. "I don't get it. Didn't that *faze* you?"

"It used to happen a lot. I'm sure you've had the same thing. It's pathetic, but it's over now."

"If he'd been a little less objectionable, I'd have said play along. We could have had some fun with him."

"I love Tariq," she said, as if the subject was closed.

Phyllis rolled her eyes. "I don't doubt that! But because of what we do for a living, it pays to make ourselves amenable every so often."

"Not like prostitutes, though."

"The word 'amenable' suggests a spectrum of possibilities," Phyllis replied drily. "So no, not that way."

"And not to potential stalkers with no conceivable information to impart."

"As I said, if he'd been a little less objectionable... We're here to have fun!"

Something seemed to register in Annabel, although she wasn't happy with it. She nodded. "I see. What you're trying to say is, *flirting* is fun."

"It is! Or it can be, with the right guy! It doesn't have to end in anything! It definitely wouldn't, now I've got John in the frame. But that's what men and women of our age expect at things like this: a good old flirt. No more than that!"

"How do you know when to stop? Especially with all the drinking we're doing?"

"You've got to trust yourself. Obviously, you don't drink enough to get blotto, just sufficient to lose some of your inhibitions. Come on, Annabel: men and women know hardly anything about each other, even today. This is a way of meeting across the gender divide at a point where we're both having maximum fun. How often does that happen?"

"It sounds suspiciously like nonsense," Annabel said. "You presented this to Ruby Parker as if you were going to chaperone me in some way. I feel like it's going to end up the other way round. How do you know the exact point at which you've lost enough of your inhibitions?"

"Most people, you and I included, learn that by the time they're twenty-three. The rest are probably doomed to alcoholism."

"It may be different in a situation like this."

Phyllis scowled. "You're making an excellent argument for teetotalism. Even James Bond has a Martini when he's working. Thirty-seven per cent proof, before you ask."

"A single glass, that's all."

"We only *see* him drink one. There's a difference."

"So how many do *you* think he has then? Three? Six? Ten? Before you answer, let's just remind ourselves: he's a fictional character."

"You're being over-cautious. It's not like you haven't had anything to drink. Where do *you* think the limit is?"

"Somewhere well before the flirting-with-strangers starts. What if you're flirting with a rapist?"

"Annabel, it's not like you're expected to leave the building alone with them. We're together. We stick together. You don't go off flirting *on your own*, for God's sake. You do it in company with your *friends*. And when your friends start peeling off, it's time to call it a night."

Annabel nodded. "I'm still not convinced. But this is a good example of why we're best friends, Phyllis. We can have a serious difference of opinion, and it never becomes personal. We never start flinging vicious generalisations at each other. I can't see the point, personally, but I can appreciate that we'd both be absolutely safe with the other to hand."

"Given that you're a tenth Dan Black Belt, I think you'd be pretty safe whatever. It's also why I never make our arguments personal."

"That's an example of you telling a joke, I assume. You don't mean it?"

"Of course I don't 'mean it'. We're mature adults, that's the real reason. And you're right: we are best friends. I'm not going to jeopardise that."

Talking about your undying loyalty to each other was usually one of the more reliable signs that you'd had enough to drink. So was holding hands so you could dance together better. The crowd had thinned now. People watched them, some overtly, others from the corners of their eyes: mingled envy, admiration, contempt, lust. A waiter approached with two cocktails and a sealed envelope on a tray and stood to attention beside and facing them.

They stopped dancing and disengaged fingers. They took the drinks with bemusement: not the white wines they'd asked for. Suspiciously like -

"I was asked to say, 'shaken not stirred'," the waiter said with an embarrassed shrug as he backed away.

"Bloody hell," Phyllis hissed in Annabel's ear, when he'd gone. "I wonder how many people know. This can't possibly be Alec's idea of a joke. Surely not. Here, hold my glass while I get this envelope open."

"If it's Greysonwell, he's treading on very thin ice," Annabel agreed, accepting her friend's martini. She sipped her own. "Hmm, vodka not gin. Someone here's a 007 fan. So far, so Alec."

"Don't drink it. Not until we know who's responsible."

"Never trust Greeks bearing gifts," Annabel said, as if it might very well have gone straight to her head. "I enjoyed our dance, by the way."

"Good," Phyllis replied, as if she hadn't heard. She tore the envelope open and read. "'*Don't worry, it's our little secret. So far. Best wishes from your not so secret admirer, Faris.*' Who the bloody hell's 'Faris'? What's he mean, 'so far'?"

"Must be connected to Greysonwell," Annabel said. "There's no other explanation."

But Phyllis was uttering, "the slimy little douchenoggin" while scanning the room. 'Faris' would be someone nearby. No one sent a message like this unless they could gauge the recipient's reaction from close quarters. And the way the message was phrased, he probably wouldn't be lying low.

And there he was. An absurdly good-looking douchenoggin of about 30 years old, sitting alone on one of the couches, looking relaxed and making the expected hard eye-contact with a slightly contemptuous come-and-get-me smile. Evening suit, beach blond hair swept across at the top, well-defined eyebrows, firm jaw, film-star eyes, a slight smear of stubble. He didn't flinch as she descended on him, envelope in hand.

"What's this mean?" she demanded.

He shrugged. "I can't hear you from down here. Sit down, please." He grinned. "You're causing a bit of a scene!"

She ignored him. "What does 'so far' mean? *Stand up when I'm talking to you!*"

He was right, though. She was drawing attention. She swallowed and sat down as he got leisurely to his feet. She started to sit down again as he went to stand up. They realised they were see-sawing and stopped midway, and their eyes met. He put his hand gently on her wrist, a subtle indication that they could both go in the same direction, if only she trusted him.

"I'm sorry," he told her, still looking into her pupils. An earnest gaze, in equal parts contrite and serpentine. "It was a joke. I'm a friend of Henry's. He didn't tell me, incidentally. I overheard it. I sincerely apologise. Please don't take it the wrong way."

She'd joined him in sitting down without even noticing.

"I may have overreacted," she said.

He took the envelope and the letter off her. She didn't resist, and, even though it was a small matter, she noticed her own peculiar acquiescence. Should she feel disturbed? He tore and re-tore into shreds, flattened his hand, beamed broadly, and blew the pieces into the air so they fell like confetti. Two landed on her dress. He looked at her. "May I?" he asked.

She was about to say no. But then that conversation with Annabel about flirting.

She smiled. "Okay," she said.

Somehow – though she'd half-foreseen it - his picking two scraps of torn paper off her was electric.

Pathetic, really. But then, that's what she'd said she was here for: a good old flirt. It required you to get back into the teenage mind-set sometimes, as if everything was magical and you'd never even been kissed before.

"Should we dance?" he asked.

His tone indicated he thought her yes was a foregone conclusion. But she liked his 'should' rather than 'shall': like it might be risky, and who knew what consequences might flow, but, well, he was game if she was.

"Okay," she said. She had to stop saying 'okay'. 'All right' was better, or maybe, 'sure'. Women who kept re-peating themselves in situations like this tended to come across as smitten.

She *was* nervous. God help her, she was.

Or maybe she just expected to be.

She was enjoying herself, though. For the first time since she'd walked through the front door, the night was coming alive. She'd had the feeling it was going to be outstanding all along, because potentially, at least, it had the right mix of contradictory emotions. But now something spectacular had been thrown in, and it was hurtling around making mincemeat of the rest.

Dancing with 'Faris' – she still had no idea of his sur-name – was nothing like dancing with Annabel. It was ag-gressive and energetic. He took it for granted that them being dancing partners allowed him to put his arms round her if that facilitated their shared movement. He didn't even ask, much less look as if he considered it might be inappropriate. The weird thing was, it wasn't. It was good, even though once or twice she had the discomfiting sensation of being led somewhere she didn't entirely want to go. He was in charge, and the way his eyes continued to bore into hers underlined it. The best she was expected to manage was to keep up with him, not flag. The sheer energy left her little power to object.

If the crowd had been watching her and Annabel, it was ten times more transfixed by her and 'Faris'. It was late now, and people were tired. Watching a couple who still had vigour to spare was both fascinating and slightly needling.

It only took two minutes for Phyllis's intoxication to wear off, and for 'Faris' to stand revealed for what he probably was: a poseur.

The real world. Always a bit of a disappointment in some ways. In others... well, no one could live life at 100mph, no matter how much they might pretend.

"What's your surname?" she asked. She'd stopped dancing. She pretended to wipe her forehead and grinned. She decided to throw him another bone. "You win! I can't keep up!"

A complete dud would have ignored her question and followed up on her surrender instead. *I've yet to meet the girl who can keep up with me, no offence* like an Alan B'Stard clone.

He stopped dancing, met her smile with his own and offered his hand. "Meadows," he said. "My surname. Faris Meadows."

She saw he wanted to hold hands, but she pretended to interpret it as a proffered handshake. "Phyllis Robinson."

"Shall we sit down? To be honest, I was just about to wave a white flag."

Maybe not such a poseur after all. She was actually beginning to warm to the emerging him-beneath-the-flash-exterior.

"I'm here with friends. I should really be getting back to them."

"I saw you earlier. I hope you don't mind my asking. Is that man with you... your husband? It's just, well, I was hoping to ask you to dinner one night, if you'd like to, that is."

She smiled. "I have a long-term partner, I'm afraid, and I'm simply waiting for him to pop the question."

"With respect, he must be an idiot if he's prevaricating. I mean, going by first impressions. I don't mean to sound over-familiar, but you strike me as intelligent, and good fun, and you're *definitely* attractive. First impressions are, however, important. Don't you agree?"

"Sometimes, they can be deceptive. But yes, even then, they're still important. As for him keeping me waiting, he isn't. He asked me once, but I declined. Now I've changed my mind."

"Well done him for not upping sticks and moving on. No reflection on you, but if a man wants to settle down and have children, he'll tend to prefer someone who shares that ambition, however dowdy, to someone who doesn't, however beautiful. Is he the man who is with you tonight? Maybe I could have a word with him."

"My partner's my age. He's not here tonight because he's recovering from a knife wound. He was stabbed in the chest, a stone's throw from here, about six weeks ago."

She noticed him flinch slightly. Mansion House probably hadn't relished the bad publicity. "He was *that* guy? Bloody hell. I hope they catch the gang that did it."

"Indeed."

"It would just be dinner," he persisted. "We could be friends."

She bit her lip and hesitated long enough to realise she wasn't actually averse. John was going to America, leaving her to be bored senseless. Maybe dinner with Faris wasn't such a bad idea, after all.

"I'll give you my phone number," she said. "But it wouldn't be a date as such. It'd be purely platonic. And we'd share the bill. If you can live with that - "

"It sounds perfect," he said, before she could finish.

He took his phone out and keyed her number in. She went back to Annabel and Tariq and sat down.

Annabel laughed. "Had a satisfying flirt? I saw you exchanging phone numbers."

"A dinner invitation. Just while John's in the USA, to keep me sane. Nothing more."

Tariq smirked. "It always starts that way. And he's very handsome, whoever he is. Makes John look quite the Mr Homely."

"I will *tell* John," Phyllis said. "About the dinner thing."

"It's none of our business anyway," Annabel said. "You've got to live your own life."

Phyllis rolled her eyes. Then something hit her. "Where's Alec?"

"He met someone, apparently," Tariq replied. "I went to look for him. No sign. Some guy I met saw him on his way outside, arm in arm with one of the models."

Phyllis frowned. "That doesn't sound like him. How long ago?"

"After he left to get the drinks," Annabel said. "Stranger things have happened."

"I'd say it figures," Tariq said. "I'm not judging him, but he does buy pretty heavily into the whole sex and guns and fast cars baloney. In any case, what else could it be? He's unlikely to have got into a fight. We'd have heard. And there can't be that many assassination-minded Alec-stalking foreign agents on the premises."

"I only hope he's back in time to meet the Lord Mayor," Annabel said. "It's going to be pretty embarrassing if he isn't."

A commotion began. As had happened several times before tonight, the dancers parted to watch some kind of spectacle. Because there were relatively few people left in here, what stood revealed was fully visible from where Phyllis sat. But it took her a few seconds to comprehend what she was seeing.

Greysonwell – definitely the man who'd introduced himself as such when they'd arrived – was dancing alone. If you could call it that. There was nothing elegant about his movements, rather it looked like he was making fun of himself. His arms and legs jerked as if they were on strings, and resolutely against the rhythm of the music, and he looked at the floor.

The faces in his audience were stamped with anxiety and distaste. It was late now, people's body clocks reminding them it was deep night outside, all the atavistic fears of nameless vague horrors seeming to break through.

In the background, Lady Julia stood with her arms folded looking mortified. For roughly a minute she watched her son without intervening, or even moving. Her expression changed from embarrassment to boredom. Then she turned and left at speed.

As soon as she'd gone, he seemed to come to his senses. He stood up straight, looked around the hall, and staggered after her.

"What the hell - ?" Tariq said.

"Drunk, obviously," Annabel said.

No one returned to the dance floor. It seemed to have emptied for good, as surely as if whatever had just happened had invoked some sort of evil eye. Even the paid models looked like they'd had their fill. A definite feeling of the party being over hung in the air.

Phyllis chuckled. "Well, one thing's pretty much certain. There'll be no meeting with the Lord Mayor tonight. I suppose we'd better find Alec and get our coats."

They stood up just as a middle-aged servant came over. He said "excuse me", and they all turned to face him, expecting some sort of despatch from Alec. *Sorry, something came up...*

"The Lord Mayor would be delighted if you'd join him in his private study for tea," he said. "Please follow me."

Chapter 17: Hannah's Rage

Fleming poured himself another coffee and switched off his computer. Midnight at the Yard, and time to go home. The office still bustled with officers on internal errands that didn't look terribly urgent, or working at desks piled with paperwork, or threading between colleagues' workstations, stopping occasionally for a chat or a solemn exchange of information. The smell of mingled sweat and coffee, the harshness of the fluorescent strip lights, the anonymity of the hardwood fire-doors. Not somewhere you'd choose to be if you could avoid it, but Fleming's wife was on a week-long conference in Stockholm. He was catching up on paperwork, and since he had his own office, he could work relatively undisturbed. His was the neatest desk in SW1. Flat-screen PC, congruent papers in both In and Out trays, a gilt-framed photo of his wife and three children, and the latest document in the centre, waiting to be signed.

He put on his coat, switched off the lights, left his office and made his way across the floor to DS Bach. She noticed him coming, threw a smile, then went back to work at her PC. He knelt down so he could talk confidentially at the same level.

"I need you to look into something for me," he said. "A pile-up on the M23. Five fatalities. Financiers of some kind."

"Recently?" she asked.

"I don't know. It was a very vague tip-off. Something to do with the murder in Princes Street, that was the suggestion."

"Really? Well, I suppose we should take whatever we can get. Give me a few hours."

"I'm going home now. Let me know tomorrow morning, first thing."

"Yes, sir. Good night."

He took the lift to the ground floor and retrieved his car from the parking bay. He drove across the bridge and turned right towards Lambeth. The night was clear and not too cold. The roads were relatively empty.

How long would it be before Mordred worked out that he *must* have been bluffing? An entire technical department on standby to triangulate his phone when there was no knowing when, or even if, he'd call, and he wasn't actually under suspicion of anything to begin with? *We've located the caller, sir. As you anticipated, he's at home in bed.*

On the other hand, Mordred probably had no idea how badly the investigation had stalled. From his point of view, that guess about his sister might not have been so speculative. If they were already after her – and he didn't know they weren't – then he'd have been identified as a possible lead, and Murgatroyd's phone would have amassed correspondingly high value.

Still, it had worked. Even if Mordred was to have a change of heart now and refuse to cooperate, he'd revealed new leads. Firstly, it had something to do with Hannah Lexingwood; secondly, there was a location, some actual *place*, in the heart of London's financial district, with clues to yield. CCTV might show where Mordred had gone tonight, assuming his disguise wasn't too expert and the crowds weren't too dense.

Although the former seemed unlikely.

The best way forward might be to put Mordred to work in some kind of unofficial capacity. They needed to split the investigation. Presumably, it had two separable aspects: intelligence and criminal. If they could agree to divide it realistically and respect each other's parameters, they could make progress.

But that would mean taking the whole thing off-road. Launching an unauthorised investigation alongside the real one, like in a two-star crime film.

Yet however corny it sounded, it might be the only hope. Whatever else this was, it was deep. Deeper probably than he could deal with.

Also like a two-star crime film.

Meanwhile, he'd be interested to find out what Bach had discovered, tomorrow.

Mordred got on the northbound train at Bank. He was exhausted now, and in no mood to look out for White agents sent to track him down. Anyway, he had other things to worry about. White didn't figure in his list of major concerns. He wasn't even that concerned about Fleming, although he saw now that the triangulation claim couldn't have withstood prolonged scrutiny. Top of his list of apprehensions was Hannah. Because it was clear there was no way he could go to America any more, not with this hanging over both their heads. At the very least, he needed to be here to keep an eye on Fleming. At best, their cooperation might actually help. Being in Connecticut wasn't an option.

The carriage was virtually empty. He sat opposite two men in suits, and next to an elderly woman in a gabardine who smelt of alcohol and looked like she was asleep.

He'd have to ring her, but what to say?

He couldn't tell her he'd had any kind of medical relapse. She'd phone Charlotte and possibly their parents and he'd be trapped again. She might even take it upon herself to fly back to Britain.

But the horrifying thing was, there were very few excuses he could give that *wouldn't* provoke that reaction. The only alternative to *I'm ill* seemed to be *I don't feel like it*, and that sounded nasty. But worse than that, it was mysterious. Likely it too would end in a solicitous visit from the folks.

Telling her the truth was an obvious non-starter. *Your blogger wasn't at home, but there were signs of a violent struggle* would have her on the first plane to Heathrow wearing a deerstalker and smoking a briar.

On the other hand, she might be just too busy with Fully Magic Coal Tar Lounge in the USA. Nothing on earth might budge her. You had to stay visible to remain top of the charts, that's what she thought.

But he couldn't count on it. She was an archetypal Social Justice Warrior. Given the choice, she might well prefer a spot of sleuthing.

To make matters even worse, it needn't be either/or. She didn't actually have to leave America. She could hire a bunch of private detectives. There'd definitely be PD's out there she trusted. Who knew what they'd turn up? If Blue or Grey started putting phoney evidence in their way, and it started mounting, and it pointed to her as some kind of felon, at what point would they feel compelled to go to the police?

Whatever he told her, she'd almost certainly blow her top. He might as well make himself look bad. Anything to stop her turning up on his doorstep. The only realistic alternative was to tell her he'd entered the flat, found signs of a struggle, and immediately informed the police. And the police were looking in to it.

That way, she couldn't do anything. At worst, she'd make the connection between the man killed alongside Mordred that night in Princes Street, and her blogger, and she'd know she couldn't afford to draw attention to herself with unscheduled international travel. She'd be scared, and she'd hit the roof. But she'd stay put in the USA.

Probably.

Angel station. Time to get off, go home and make the phone call, get it out of the way. Quarter to one now. Five hours behind in Connecticut would make it 7.45 over there.

When he got in, he went straight to the sofa and pressed Call. It rang three times, and Hannah picked up.

"Hi, John. I'm busy right now. Concert's just about to kick off. Is it urgent? Are you okay?"

"Fine. Listen, I went to visit your mysterious female, as instructed. Bit of a disaster, I'm afraid. There were signs of a struggle. Things had been knocked over. There was blood on the floor. I called the police. They're looking into it."

Pause.

"Sorry," she said, "could you say all that again?"

He repeated himself in almost identical words. When he'd finished speaking, there was a long silence.

"I hardly know what to say," she told him, almost in a whisper.

"I hope I did the right thing," he replied. Looked at in the right way – from a hundred miles away, ten years in the future, maybe – this exchange was actually shaping up to be reasonably humorous.

"You told the police."

"I thought I'd better, yes. There was blood."

In a voice that didn't sound like hers: "You didn't think to ring me first?"

"How would that have looked? I hate to say this, but Brent seemed pretty jumpy. *Not my property, not my business*: those were his actual words. Sooner or later, he'd have discovered the - "

"You didn't think to contact me first." This time, she expressed it as a statement –albeit an incredulous one - rather than a question.

"Well, no. And I can explain why not. Because what could you have done? If you'd come back from America - "

"For God's sake, John! You've just dropped me in a twenty thousand gallon vat of SHIT!"

"I was trying to look out for you. If you'd come back from America - "

"Have you ANY idea what you've just done? ANY idea at ALL? My God, I can't believe you're so GORMLESS! Forget about the twenty thousand gallon shit-vat; you've more or less put me in front of a bloody FIRING SQUAD, John! I can't – I can't actually believe what you've just told me! Oh my God! OH MY GOD! I'm FINISHED! This is the END! OH MY GOD!"

"Well, I'm very sorry. Honestly. But if you'd come back from America - "

She rang off. She'd probably thrown her phone on the floor and stamped on it, or hurled it against a wall, or launched it into the air and shot it like a clay pigeon, only with a machine gun. He didn't expect her to ring back.

He should probably ring her. He'd get more of the same, true, but at least it would look like he cared. The value of such a thing, at a time like this, shouldn't be underestimated.

As he expected, it went straight to voicemail. "Hi, John here," he said. "Look, I'm really sorry. I didn't call you first because Brent would have found out sooner or later, then he'd go running to the police, then what? Well, they'd ask him all sorts of questions, and he'd crack. He'd say, 'Hannah Lexingwood's brother was here on such-and-such a date.' And they'd arrest me, and they'd take my mobile phone and they'd look at my record of calls. They always do. They'd discover that I'd rung you from inside the flat *at the very time I'd gone up there and discovered it had been wrecked*. Then said nothing to the police. How would that look? This way, I kept my nerve. They'll know I'm ringing you now, sure, but it could be about America since I'm at home. Unfortunately, that's off, by the way. The police have asked me to hang around for a little while, and I've said I'm happy to. We don't want to make it look too suspicious. I told them it's a flat you bought for me to live in. I said I didn't know it had been occupied. You can tell them you took on a lodger because I didn't want it. It can all be explained. You kept it secret from Brent because you didn't want to look like you were flouting London's strict accommodation and housing rules. Something like that. I love you, by the way. Speak to you soon. I hope. Cheer up. Bye."

He had to make it look like he was a simpleton. It was what she understood. And it made her ten times more likely to forgive him.

Time for bed.

Chapter 18: Interview with Greysonwell

"The Lord Mayor would be delighted if you'd join him in his private study for tea," the middle-aged servant said. "Please follow me."

Tariq, Annabel and Phyllis were already standing. They subliminally elected Phyllis as their spokesperson. "It's very kind of him to make time for us," she said in response.

"Excuse me for asking," the servant continued - they hadn't begun to move yet - "but shouldn't there be four of you?"

Phyllis smiled awkwardly. "We don't know where our companion has gone. He left to go to the toilet earlier. He didn't come back."

"We were told he'd, er... met someone," Tariq offered.

The servant's expression darkened in the manner of someone who vaguely knew what was wrong, and that it could be something in which he was implicated, but that some subordinate person would be made to pay. "Excuse me a moment," he said. He turned, tugged a little hands-free microphone down over his mouth and began walking away and talking.

"That doesn't look good," Phyllis said, exchanging ominous glances with the others. "Do you think Alec's had some sort of an accident?"

"Possibly something a little sordid," Annabel said. "Notice how the footman's face changed when Tariq said he might have met someone. As if it might ring a bell."

"*Where casual relationships go wrong,*" Tariq said.

"I don't share your cynicism," Phyllis said. "Alec's not actually here with me in that capacity, but he wouldn't just abandon me for someone else. Not without saying something first. I hadn't thought about it before, but now I do, I'm worried."

Five minutes later, the servant returned, trailing a grim-looking Alec as if he'd found him illegally skateboarding in the local park. He stopped a few paces away from Phyllis's group, stood patiently waiting, and let Alec proceed on his own. Then he walked away again.

"Where are our drinks?" Annabel said sardonically.

"Someone knocked me unconscious and dumped me outside the building," he replied.

"Oh my God," Phyllis said.

"When I recovered I was being stretchered into an ambulance. I managed to persuade the medics to release me. I didn't manage to persuade the bouncers to let me back into the building. And none of the people I met along the way were serving cocktails, so terribly sorry about that."

"Tariq came looking for you," Annabel said. "A man said he thought you'd met someone."

"'A man'," Alec said. "That you can describe?"

Tariq's demeanour had altered to reflect the seriousness of the situation. "Male, about thirty, gelled hair, tall, thin, deep voice, possibly Yorkshire accent."

"What about your wallet?" Phyllis asked.

"Curiously, I've had nothing taken. Not to say nothing's been tampered with, obviously, credit cards scanned, etcetera. I've already called the bank, just to be on the safe side. Can I just get this straight? Even though I came here tonight for the express purpose of chaperoning Phyllis on John's behalf, you all assumed I would abandon that at the drop of a hat because I'd identified a feasible sexual conquest?"

"It wouldn't have been a major crime," Annabel said.

Alec scowled. "So yes, essentially."

"The answer's no," Phyllis said. "Some of the time you were away, I was dancing. First with Annabel, then with one of Greysonwell's eccentric friends. Then we chatted. I didn't feel 'abandoned'. Maybe that'd have been different if you and I had come alone, but I had Annabel and Tariq. I - "

"The Lord Mayor will see you all now," the servant interjected. Like Jeeves, he seemed to have shimmered into proximity from nowhere.

They followed him upstairs and past designer wallpaper and portraits of previous Lord Mayors. Most of the guests had gone now. It already felt like the morning after. In a sense, it was.

They came to a mezzanine landing, running the length of the building. On their left, a series of closed doors as anonymous as a hotel's; on their right, a view down into a huge carpeted hall. After about twenty paces, they stopped before a white door with nothing to distinguish it from the others. The servant knocked, preceded them into the room, and then exited, closing himself out.

They found themselves in a large darkened study with two large bookcases, and three sofas arranged around a coffee table bearing a tea set and cakes on a set of tiered plates. The walls were dotted with landscapes, and a huge mullioned window in the opposite wall was flanked by sky-blue curtains. Greysonwell stood with his back to the room, staring out of the window. One of the sofas was occupied by Faris Meadows and Lady Julia, sitting at opposite ends. Both remained seated when the guests came in. They didn't look pleased to see them. Their attention was fixed entirely on the Lord Mayor. Phyllis got the immediate feeling – and she sensed the others felt it too – that there had just been a raging argument, and a truce had been called entirely for their benefit. But that it was fragile.

"Please sit down," Greysonwell said in a neutral tone.

"We don't have to stay if it's inconvenient," Phyllis ventured. "We could even meet again on a different day. We thoroughly enjoyed your party, by the way. Thank you once more for inviting us."

"I need to talk to you as a matter of urgency," Greyson-well continued, turning to face them. "It can't wait, I'm afraid. Sit down, please, and have some tea."

He gestured to one of the two vacant sofas. He poured the tea and distributed it, completely ignoring his mother and Meadows, who sat as still as statues. Finally, he sat in the middle, and on the edge, of the last empty sofa, leaning forward with his forearms on his thighs.

"Everyone wants to be *urbane*," he said in a mumble. He didn't look at anyone. "Dressing their stupidity up as a heroic loyalty to science and a connoisseur's taste for TV game-show satire. No one dare think the unthinkable any more. And if you break ranks, doing so only because otherwise you'd go mad, they make damn sure you become a laughing-stock."

Phyllis and Annabel exchanged furtive looks. How to respond?

Somehow, the light in the room had diminished even since they came in. They were sitting in near darkness. The atmosphere suddenly seemed not so much acrimonious as eerie, as if none of the original three occupants was truly alive. Greysonwell sat looking at his feet, then raised his head. He looked at Phyllis, then Alec, then Annabel, then Tariq. Then he looked down again.

"Have any of you ever seen *Quatermass and the Pit?*" he asked.

It wasn't the starter for ten they'd been expecting, though they'd have been hard pressed to say, even vaguely, what that was.

"Clips, yes," Phyllis replied. "On YouTube."

"Do you think anything similar could ever happen in reality?" he asked.

Alec took over. "I'd say it's unlikely."

"But not impossible," Greysonwell returned.

"As far as I know, things are only impossible if they involve some sort of self-contradiction," Alec said. "To answer your question: not far off impossible, though."

Greysonwell looked at the floor again. A car without silencers roared past outside. An emergency siren sounded in the distance and faded away. They sipped their tea. Alec took a cake. A minute passed. This was horror-house stuff, like they were being softened up for a session with the local vampire. Normally, you'd make small talk – 'nice cakes', maybe - but that didn't seem appropriate here. Too frivolous, somehow.

"I wonder how you'd react," Greysonwell said, "if I was to tell you that the universe is teeming with life, that some of that life is here among us, and that I've actually been in contact with it for a considerable time."

A long pause. Phyllis could hear her own breathing.

"You're talking about extra-terrestrials," Alec said eventually, in a tone of barely concealed incredulity.

Greysonwell continued to stare at the floor. "Physicists tell us that nothing can travel faster than the speed of light, and that the inconceivable distances involved in interstellar travel would conclusively rule out visitors from elsewhere in the galaxy, even assuming – what, from their point of view, is highly speculative - the existence of intelligent life there. However, that's a reflection of the current state of our scientific knowledge. It isn't an accurate assessment of objective reality. I can tell you that for a fact, because I happen to know that several distinct alien races have already made that journey. Their representatives live among us, and, as a species, we've no way of knowing how benign they are. My own contact with them has been limited, so I'm in no way an expert, but I know enough to realise we're on the cusp of a new and terrible age. One when people will remember the second decade of the twenty-first century as our last period of blissful ignorance, a time when we could still think that

UFO's were the harmless fantasies of cranks and conspiracy theorists."

"Why are you telling us this?" Annabel asked, after another silence. "Do you want us to do something about it? I'm not sure - "

"There won't be a war," he went on. "No one will even know what's happened, except that the global financial system's broken down. Some people will lose all their money, there will be runs on banks, inflation will rocket, all that sort of thing. In historical terms, nothing unheard-of. And it'll all be mended. Afterwards, things will carry on roughly as they did before, only with one major difference. *They'll* be fully in charge." He sighed miserably, paused to recollect his self-composure, then continued: "They'll rule, so I understand, via a kind of global political elite: effectively a privileged clientele of co-opted humans comprising a world government, probably IMF-based. We'll get used to seeing spacecraft in the sky. And other things. Officially, they still won't exist. The conspiracy of silence will continue as before, in other words, only this time brazenly. I wanted to be part of their setup for a while. I actually sought the Lord Mayorship because I wanted entry. But I can't. I can't go on." His voice broke with emotion. "I have to tell the truth."

"Can I ask what you want us to do?" Phyllis said gently. Shock was beginning to give way to curiosity, but only just.

"There's nothing you *can* do," Greysonwell replied. "It may even be in humanity's best interests to be ruled from millions of light years away. We'd have long since destroyed ourselves with nuclear weapons if they hadn't continually intervened. Not that they did it out of compassion for us, of course. Even so, we owe our continued existence on Earth entirely to them. I'm only telling you, firstly, because I want someone to remember me when I'm gone. Someone truly good, who can see the goodness in me. I'm going on TV tomorrow night. I'm going to tell the whole world what I know. Between now and then, my life will be in danger. So the second reason for my telling you is, as a kind of insurance policy. My mother and my so-called 'best friends' are in league with them, of course. Now that they know you know, they'll have to be very careful how they deal with me. But that's not all."

Lady Julia leapt to her feet. *"For God's sake, Henry!"*

"Please sit down, mother," he said.

She strode out of the room, slamming the door behind her.

"There's something they've been looking for since long before the dawn of humankind," he continued. "And it's buried directly beneath this building. When you hear that Mansion House is going to be demolished – sometime within the next few years – you'll know I was right. Because no reason they can conceivably give could justify such a thing under any normal circumstances. I don't know whether any of you pass through this part of the city on a regular basis, but if you do, you may have noticed a series of identical yellow shapes on the pavements. They're myriagons, ten thousand-sided polygons. To us, of course, they just look like circles. Only they can see them as they really are. They can detect them from anywhere in outer space. It's just like using a search-engine. And of course, they're the X that marks the spot. Where they came from, I don't know. They disappeared a few days ago."

"If you don't know where they came from," Alec said, "How do you know they're connected to the… aliens?" He was on his fourth cake.

"I can't tell you that," Greysonwell replied. "I've told you all I realistically can. I take it you're John."

Alec pointed to himself. "Alec. Sorry, we should have introduced ourselves. Alec, Phyllis, Annabel, Tariq."

"My apologies," Phyllis added. "We introduced ourselves when we arrived at the party. But that was hours ago, and you had a huge guest-list. We should have - "

"So where's John?" Greysonwell interrupted.

Pause.

"Are we speaking about the same person?" Annabel asked.

"John Mordred," Greysonwell said. "He was here when William Chester was Lord Mayor. I've heard about him from other sources too. Enough to know he's like me. He's not urbane. Where is he?"

"Getting ready to leave for America," Phyllis said. "He's been absent from work for a few weeks. A nearly fatal stabbing, not far from here. He's going to America to aid the recuperation process."

Greysonwell's eyes widened. He seemed to suddenly grasp something. "Of *course*," he said bitterly. "*Naturally* they'd have taken steps to get John out of the way, stop us meeting. Because that's what's really happened. *Mother, you can come back in now!*" He turned to Phyllis. "Thank you for agreeing to meet me. I'll get someone to show you out. Next time, bring John." He laughed. "Although what am I saying? There won't be a 'next time'. Obviously not."

He got up and went to the window with his back to them like he was on automatic rewind. Meadows continued to sit immobile. Phyllis seemed to realise the interview was over first; at least, she was first on her feet. Alec, Annabel and Tariq followed suit. No one came to show them out, and they didn't want to wait.

On the other side of the door, Lady Julia was waiting, apparently to meet them. She still wore her party dress and heels. Her face showed no trace of her earlier outburst. Her hair was dark, and styled in a 60's-inspired coif. Her face was classically beautiful: wide apart eyes, small nose, well-proportioned mouth, with chin, cheekbones, ears and jawline in perfectly positioned support. She had the figure of a twenty-year-old model, but somehow, despite all this, she looked her age – when you looked closely. She led them silently into another room, this one well lit by a central chandelier. It was bare apart from a chaise longue in the centre, and obviously never used. She closed the door behind them and leaned on the frame.

"Allow me to apologise for my son," she said. "I'll cut a long story short. He shouldn't be in this job. I've made him what he is. Or rather, there is no 'him', not in the sense that people think there is." She wiped a tear away. "It's all me, and I bitterly regret it. I drove him to run for the Lord Mayorship. I thought a little responsibility would be good for him. Make him respectable by surrounding him with respectable people. I had no idea it would be the undoing of him. Now I can't stop him. He's going to self-destruct."

There was something about this speech that felt rehearsed, as if she thought it was what her audience wanted, and expected, to hear.

Phyllis felt obliged to say something. "You mean, on television, tomorrow night? That was what he said."

"Probably best," Lady Julia said, not directly answering the question. "The road to recovery begins with honesty. The TV stations aren't coming because they think it'll be interesting. They're only coming to keep a toe in the door, a kind of goodwill gesture to the Mayoral institution. Mind you, given the number of high-profile parties Henry's thrown since he got the job, some of them probably think it's worth sending a crew for other reasons; put it at the fag-end of London Local News, something like that. But when they actually hear what he has to say, I wouldn't be surprised if they clear the main bulletins and give it top billing." She hooted. *"Aliens!* And he truly believes it! He's going to be carried out of here in a straitjacket!"

"We'll keep what we've heard tonight entirely to ourselves," Phyllis said. "I mean, within the organisation."

She heaved a mildly relieved sigh. "That was what I was going to ask you. Thank you. I'm not holding out much hope, but I may be able to dissuade him. Get him to resign instead, maybe. That might be ideal. The trouble with Henry, though, is, he's obstinate. Once he gets an idea in his head, he's very unlikely to be deflected. Which is often the way with the severely mentally ill, so I understand. In my defence, I've only recently come to realise how unwell he is. Once again, my apologies. I won't detain you. I'd better get back to him, and I'm sure you're tired. Thank you again for coming. Mr Lincoln will get you your coats."

She opened the door and preceded them out. She went back into the room where her son was.

As they walked along the landing, it was as if they'd awoken from an unpleasant dream. They didn't look at each other and they didn't speak.

The middle-aged servant who'd ushered them into Greysonwell's company thirty minutes earlier was on his way upstairs at speed. He slowed when his eyes met Phyllis's. "I'm here to fetch your coats," he said breathlessly. "On the Lord Mayor's behalf, can I just say, thank you for coming and add, I hope you've had an enjoyable evening? Would you like me to order you a taxi?"

"Could I have a word in private?" Alec asked.

The servant looked almost as if he'd anticipated this question, but that, even so, it annoyed him. He scowled. "This way, sir," he said.

He led Alec downstairs at a plod. They disappeared along a corridor.

"What's going on?" Annabel said.

Phyllis shook her head. "I'm not sure tonight can get any weirder. I don't know. But I definitely think we ought to talk about what happened. I'm not keen on going home, and I won't sleep even if I do. My head's whirling like a tub full of muddy water going down too small a plughole."

"Presumably caused by the thing that's buried beneath the building," Tariq quipped.

She and Phyllis both turned an identical glare on him. *Not funny.*

"Hampstead Heath," Annabel said. "I need lots and lots of fresh air."

Alec re-appeared, coming towards them with the servant, who looked much happier, even though he was carrying all the coats. Alec had an expensive carrier bag full of what appeared to be bottles.

"I don't know about you," he said, when they were ready to go and the servant had discreetly left them to make their own way out, "but I'm far from ready for bedtime. I told Mr Lincoln, the *khansama*, that I'd forget all about tonight's little incident if he let me have a few left-over bottles of wine and whisky. And a set of glasses. He was delighted, although, of course, I was never really going to sue. If you want to share it, you can come back to mine. I did say I'd get you all a drink, after all. Or I can get smashed alone. Either way, I'm going to spend the next few hours wide awake and mentally re-running scenes from the X-Files. In extreme reluctance."

"How about Hampstead Heath?" Phyllis said. "Annabel's choice."

"Won't it be cold?" he said.

"True," she replied, "but it's private, and hey, it's X-Files-y."

"That's why I chose it," Annabel said.

An hour later, they sat huddled side by side on a bench, beneath a plane tree, with glasses of wine. The city shimmered in the distance like a party. Above, the sky was moonless and strewn with stars. Planes crisscrossed it at regular intervals, flashing their lights. Tariq pointed out a meteorite. They talked about the Lord Mayor for twenty minutes – they quickly agreed it wasn't a prank: Greysonwell was too obviously sincere, his story too complex – and then marvelled at the eternity of space for ten minutes, like teenagers.

Alec sighed. "The Lord Mayor of London's about to make himself into the world's biggest laughing stock. He'll probably be stripped of his title."

"I'm not sure they'll go that far," Phyllis said. "It only lasts a year, and it's largely ceremonial anyway. They'll probably let him see it out and make sure someone takes his place on overseas ambassadorial gigs. It might even be good for the image, in some ways. Give the institution a touch of badly-needed colour."

Alec hooted. "A touch of *colour?* Have you ever *been* to the Lord Mayor's parade?"

"I'm normally washing my hair that day," she replied. "What I mean is, the incumbent. How many can you name?"

"I thought that was partly the point," Annabel said. "I thought the City of London was supposed to be a secrecy jurisdiction."

"You've been taking too much notice of John," Phyllis told her. "Much as I love him, some of his views are distinctly kooky."

"Greysonwell didn't seem to think so," Annabel replied. "And he would know. The deeper question is, what should we actually tell John? Part of me thinks it would be nice to share the 'joke' with him, if that's the right word for it; the other part says, no, he might take it the wrong way."

"And by 'wrong way'," Alec said, "you mean: what?"

"I can't say precisely," Annabel replied. "On the other hand, neither do I believe those two words don't set alarm bells ringing for each one of us. We all know what I mean, though we'd be hard pressed to put it into words."

Alec considered this and nodded. "Granted."

Phyllis looked up at the stars again. "Maybe what Greysonwell said wasn't too far from the truth."

Alec laughed. "Really?"

"I know it's a funny thing to say," she went on, "especially since I just described John's views – some of them - as off-beam. But it seemed odd that Greysonwell should think John was prevented from attending his party by forces within MI7."

"Classic conspiracy-theory guff," Alec replied. "There's nothing 'odd' about it. And obviously, it's tripe."

"John doesn't think so," Phyllis said. "And I agree with him."

Alec turned to face her. "This, I've got to hear. Go on."

"Three things," Phyllis said. "Firstly, how professional the whole thing was. Secondly that, despite the apparent proficiency, they left John alive, the knife sticking out: which must have been deliberate. Thirdly, a 'John Murgatroyd' appeared to the investigating DCI shortly after the event. Murgatroyd, you may remember, interviewed John regarding radicalisation, two years ago, top floor of Thames House. He's someone within the organisation, in other words; someone senior enough, and distinct enough from Red Department, to interrogate someone of John's rank. And do so alone."

"You say he 'appeared'," Annabel said. "For what purpose?"

"None, as far as we know," Phyllis replied. "John thinks the idea was to make an impression on the DCI, such that the DCI would communicate it to John. It was a kind of oblique message in other words: *your own organisation did this to you. We spared you, but now, forget all about it.* And of course, as far as I know, the investigation's made no head-way whatsoever from that day to this. Which fits."

Alec shook his head. "They were after the other guy. They killed him and dumped a quart of acid on the corpse. This wasn't about keeping John from going to tonight's party. I love the guy, but why does he always have to make everything about him?"

"He doesn't," Phyllis said. "The party thing's my theory, remember, not his. And I'm not saying what you think. I'm just saying Greysonwell thought MI7 was responsible for keeping John away from his party, and *by coincidence*, per-haps that's true."

Annabel chuckled. "I think what you're actually saying, Phyllis, is, let's not tell John anything about tonight. The po-tential for misunderstanding is just too great, and he might take it 'the wrong way'."

"There's nothing to suggest he *needs* to know," Alec said, after a while.

"He's going to America tomorrow," Phyllis said. "If he asks about the party, I'll just say I can't tell him anything till I've been debriefed by Ruby Parker. He'll get that. Anyway, it'll be a transatlantic phone call. We'll have other things to talk about."

"The spy who was left out in the cold," Alec said.

"I'm ready to go home now," Annabel said. "I think we've actually addressed the problem that was troubling me all along. I've achieved catharsis."

They all got to their feet. Annabel was right. John was the real reason they'd been sitting here. They wrapped their coats tightly about them – it seemed colder when they stood up – and shuffled towards the lights of the suburb.

John. It was always bloody John.

Chapter 19: Soraya's Magic Money Machine

Time for bed, but there was no way Mordred's conscience was going to let him go to sleep. Yes, he'd expected his sister to be upset. *That* upset? Well, maybe. Difficult to put a score on it, but it was probably ten. What she was doing now didn't bear thinking about. She definitely wouldn't be listening to his voicemail and nodding sagely in a *that sounds quite reasonable after all* kind of way.

In her mind, the only thing he probably had going for him now was his utter fecklessness. He remembered last New Year; he and his sisters watching *To Walk Invisible*, Sally Wainwright's biopic of the Brontës. The way they kept exchanging furtive glances whenever Branwell, the useless brother, appeared onscreen.

In some ways, he ought to be gratified: an entire adult-hood pretending he was a pointless arse had actually paid off. They'd never, ever believe he was a spy. He'd tried to tell Julia once. She'd cut him off contemptuously in mid-sentence.

Occasionally, he wondered if he might have gone too far. What if, one day, he actually needed them to trust him?

But that would never happen. The truth was, they actually *were* cleverer than him, just in different areas. They'd never require his help, or, if they did, they'd never admit it. All things considered, it was a miracle they hadn't long since ganged up and smothered him with a pillow.

But of course, they couldn't. Any more than Charlotte, Emily and Anne could. It wasn't the liberal way.

He lay in darkness for an indeterminate time, drifting in and out of a restless sleep that couldn't really be called sleep because it wasn't prolonged enough. More like a series of hallucinations loosely connected to a low-grade slumber. He had one of his recurring dreams about meeting the Queen, then another about Ruby Parker in West Africa in the 1990s. Odd how he often dreamed about the Queen, Ruby Parker and his mum, and they were always more or less interchangeable.

What would happen tomorrow morning: Hannah would conclude she'd overreacted, and she'd call him and apologise. She'd do it not because she thought she was wrong, but because she felt sorry for him. She'd be torturing herself, right now; sitting in a hard wicker chair with her bare heels on the seat and her knees up to her nose. *Yes, he's sabotaged everything, but it's pointless being angry with him. It's like being angry with a penguin. He's probably really upset about me yelling at him. He's probably hurt, confused and uncertain where to turn. Imagine how a penguin would feel if you yelled at it.* Eventually, she'd listen to his voicemail. But not the actual words, just his earnest, eager-to-help tone of voice. She'd loathe herself.

From one point of view, it was utterly hilarious, real Laurel and Hardy slapstick stuff. The way they'd spent ages painstakingly cross-referencing *Sister Wendy's Story of Painting* so as to obviate the slightest possibility of mishap. But she'd still torpedoed head-first into a twenty-thousand gallon vat of shit.

My God, he couldn't stop thinking about her! All the other things he had to worry about, and the fact that he'd upset Hannah was paramount. What was he going to do about Fleming? What about those guys in the masks, on the roof of Mansion House? What about Phyllis? What about Murgatroyd? What about the flat behind The Frederick and Elizabeth? What about the poor guy who'd been murdered? Not to mention the murderers?

He needed her to ring him quickly, so he could start thinking about the important stuff again.

He looked at his clock. 3am. It'd be – what time in Connecticut?

Didn't matter. If she wasn't sticking pins in a him-doll, she'd be fussing over stage management issues. All he could do now was try to sleep.

When they were kids. How she was their dad's favourite – or that's how it seemed – and father and daughter would spend hours listening to his collection of 60's and 70's rock and pop in the front room, especially the obscure material. Nowadays, she was better at spotting, nurturing and directing talent than Simon Cowell.

That Christmas, two years ago. When they'd both been drinking, and she showed him her bank statement to prove she'd hadn't overspent on his present. *I can easily afford it, John!* How he'd looked down the list of expenditures, and it was almost identical to his own: Amnesty, Christian Aid, Greenpeace, Whale and Dolphin Conservation, the whole shebang, right down to the exact same greyhound rescue-centre in Bury St Edmunds. One of those *wow* moments, as they called them nowadays. Not an ecstatic one, though; more of a weird, uncanny, science-fiction-y one, like he'd found his twin, but she was four years older than him.

He stopped dreaming and remembering after a while and fell asleep. When he awoke, it was 8am. He got out of bed, made himself some breakfast, and watched the news. The Tory party was tearing itself apart, so Donald Trump wasn't on much any more. But everything was sordid and a bit depressing. He switched over and watched cookery.

His phone rang. *Hannah.* In his eagerness to pick up, he spilt Weetabix on his T-shirt. "Hello?"

"Is this John?" a peculiar squeaky voice said. "This is baby Lek, your niece. Mummy says she's very sorry. Shall I put her on?"

Lek wasn't old enough to form sentences yet. He'd never worked out whether this was something Hannah did as a way of gently poking fun at mothers who pretended to be their pre-cognitive children, or whether she actually bought it. Disturbing if the latter, but not too much, since she was hardly alone nowadays.

"Hi, Hannah," he said.

"Sorry I exploded. I listened to your voicemail. Your plan could do with a few tweaks, but it's essentially sound. You've obviously thought things through a bit more than me. I don't know what I'd have done. I suppose I should expect a visit from the police at some stage."

"Make them come to you."

"Obviously, I'm not going to hand myself in. I'm not a criminal. I expect MI5 will try to make something of it, though."

He sighed. "I know this might sound complacent, but I'm not sure the security services are in the business of tarring public figures any more. With all the information out there, it's too risky. If you're doing something morally dubious, you've got to be pretty bloody certain the next Edward Snowden's not sitting across the office from you. If he is, you might find your little frame-Hannah-Lexingwood bomb blows up in your face."

Good argument. It didn't cover the likes of Blue and Grey, some of whose subsections could be pretty sure the next Snowden wasn't anywhere nearby, but it sounded impressive.

"None of these people have faces to blow up in," she said. "That's why they call them spooks. Because they're freewheeling and insubstantial. They can't be identified, so they don't have to take responsibility. Anyway, no point in crying over spilt milk, and it's not like you were responsible. You just discovered the mess."

"Given that you think they're trying to stop you launch another global campaign against tax avoidance, why don't you just launch it? Get it over with? I'm often being asked when you're going to strike next. I never know what to say."

"You could tell the questioners to mind their own business."

"I do."

She sighed. "But now *you're* asking, right?"

"I might as well. While we're on the subject."

"Even though you know as well as I do that this conversation's almost certainly being recorded?"

"Sadly, I put my Christmas present in the book bank, as instructed, so telling me that way's not an option."

Her tone changed. She addressed her supposed listeners-in. "Actually, no. While we're all on the line together, you, me and MI5, let me tell you the truth. Because no. No, we're not planning World War Offshore 2.0, not anytime within the next century, anyway. I've got Lek to look after now."

"MI5 says it doesn't believe you," Mordred replied. "Sorry, I'm just trying to get into the paranoid spirit of things. You'll have to be a bit more persuasive than that."

"All right, Smiley - "

"*George* Smiley?"

He heard her sigh irritably.

"Sorry," he said. "I meant: cool."

"There's going to be a global financial crash - 2026 at the absolute latest. It won't be like anything we've seen before. It'll make 2008 look like a storm in a teacup. So what's the point in warring against the multinationals? Why put yourself in danger when what you want's going to happen soon anyway? The worst offenders will be swept away like rotten lumber after a dam bursts. And when the world's governments finally get round to remedying the situation – which they'll have to eventually, although they're as much to blame as anyone, maybe more - they'll realise we were right all along. They'll close every loophole in town. By that time, things will be very different."

"I see."

"No, you don't. I can tell by your tone of voice. You think I've turned into a crackpot conspiracy theorist. I can hear your brain. It's going: 'what the hell's she been reading?'"

"You deduced all that from 'I see'."

"You can't fool me, John. Look, it's called a 'black swan event'. An event no one can foresee because we're biologically programmed to think things will always continue as they have in the past. But earthquakes happen."

"If a black swan event's something no one can foresee, how come you can foresee this one?"

"Because I'm ahead of the curve, John. It's my blessing and my curse. How did I know Christine and the Queens were going to make it? I just did. Yes, I know it's not the same thing."

"So it doesn't answer the question."

"I've read things, okay. Irrefutable things. Like how all the biggest governments in the world are spending vastly more than they collect in tax – giving too many big businesses a free ride in order to 'incentivise' them - and printing money to cover the difference. And they can't rein it in. It's gone way too far. But it's got to stop somewhere. Which means the limits of the process itself will stop it. It's a Ponzi scheme and it's out of control. Sooner or later, it's got to cross the frontiers of its utility, and when it does, it'll come crashing down. Banks will collapse. ATM's will stop dispensing cash. Inflation will go crazy. There will be riots. People are going to get killed."

"How did the concert go last night?"

She scoffed. "Is that your way of accusing me of not caring?"

"I only - "

"I do care. But in addition to being ahead of the curve, I'm also Cassandra. Doomed to prophesy truly with no one to believe me. More knowledgeable people than me have written carefully-argued books about it, John. If they're not believed, what chance have I got? Not even you think I'm right, and you're my brother."

"I didn't mean - "

"And actually, I *am* doing something about it. I'm buying cryptocurrencies and gold. And that's what you'd be doing if you had any sense. Did you keep that digital wallet I gave you two years ago?"

"I put it in a safe place, like you told me."

"By 'safe place', I really hope you don't mean what people usually mean: that for all practical purposes, it's lost. Tell me that's not true."

"It's not true."

"Cross your heart and hope to die?"

"I just don't want George Smiley to think, 'Well, that's one thing I've got out of listening to this conversation. At least I know where John keeps his digital wallet. I might go round there while he's out and swipe it.'"

He heard her take a breath. "Yes, I see. But *you* know where it is, right?"

"It's under the mattress."

"That bloody well better be a joke. Anyway, even if Smiley did steal it, it wouldn't be any good without the code words."

"Just in case he really is listening."

"There are ten Bitcoins in there, John. When I bought them, they were about a hundred pounds a pop."

"Yes, I remember you saying," he replied. "Funnily enough, I was thinking about it last night. And you showed me your bank statement, to prove you could afford it."

"God, I don't remember that. Anyway, they're worth over four thousand pounds each now."

"Four thousand?"

"I'm ahead of the curve, John. Like I just told you. Let me give you some advice. Buy more. Soraya's actually got a machine that mines them. I say 'machine': a humongous stack of interconnected computers and a few part-time guys to look after the whole thing. Buy Ethereum. Fill your boots. *Ethereum,* John: Google it. And sign up for Bitnation. Susanne Tarkowski Tempelhof. One of the greatest intellectuals of the 21st century, and she's a woman. The blockchain's the future of everything that's going to happen on this planet, John. You want to say you had the foresight to get there first, don't you?"

She'd lost him. "Just out of interest, how many Bitcoins have *you* got?"

"I haven't counted them lately. Between the two of us – Soraya and me - probably more than anyone else in existence. Look, John, we're not intending to *keep* them. We're going to wait till my prediction's come true and the world's turned to shit, then we're going to use them to buy food and clothes for kids and poor people. Every last coin."

"Where does Tim come into this? Your husband?"

"I know who Tim is. He hasn't time to mine Bitcoins. He's busy with medical stuff. And for all I love him, he's one of the people who doesn't believe me. He thinks it's a bubble. Anyway, we've agreed to differ because I know that, in the long term, he'll have to eat his words. That's what I love about our family. We can differ wildly in evaluating the facts and still get on. Tim's to me like Phyllis is to you."

"Probably. Anyway, sorry about telling the police."

"Er, what?"

"About the flat. Last night."

She laughed. "Oh, *right!* Yes, you mean: the reason I called in the first place. I'm only sorry you can't come to America. I was really, really looking forward to it. Couldn't you just tell them you had a holiday booked, and you'll stay in touch?"

"Looks suspicious. A bit too coincidental, for a start. And three thousand miles is a long way away. Difficult for them to keep tabs."

"I suppose so. Anyway, although you probably think I've wasted your morning blabbing about financial doom, I haven't actually. It's all connected. My big worry now is what happened to my friend. You say there was blood on the carpet. I've thought about that. Whoever attacked her must have done so inside the flat, and somehow – assuming the worst – have lowered the body out of the window. Sorry if that sounds a bit clinical. I didn't know her personally. I don't even know why she wanted that flat. Close to work, probably, and of course close to the cesspit that is the City of London Corporation. I've a feeling she may have worked in the Stock Exchange. And of course, free w-fi, secure, private, totally deniable. I've called Brent. If she'd been attacked there and run through the pub, he'd have seen it. Presumably, someone would have been chasing her. But he's pretty sure there was nothing like that. She had her own key, incidentally. Brent just kept a spare, for me. There's no reason they should ever have met. The police will interview Brent, of course. But they won't get anything. Because he doesn't know anything."

"A mystery."

"They've probably put a forensics team in. They'll soon figure out roughly what happened. They'll have their work cut out linking it to either of us though. Which might not stop them trying to frame me, of course, especially now that I've stupidly given away how many Bitcoins I've got. I'm a person of potential influence now, a competitor. I think we'd better stop talking, while I've still got secrets left. Plus, I've left Soraya holding Lek."

"I'll keep you informed of any developments."

"We should really be using the dark net for all this. Next time we meet, I'll train you up in the use of Tor."

"I thought that was just for the bad guys."

She scoffed. "Shows how little you know."

"I know we've nothing to hide and we're better off talking in the open. If Smiley's listening, he's probably fallen asleep."

"I'll try not to take that the wrong way."

"We're interesting to each other. I'm not sure we're that interesting to anyone who hasn't actually met us."

"Speak for yourself," she said. "Read the latest *Rolling Stone*. Four exclusive pages of me, me, me. How's your stab wound getting along?"

"Nearly better now."

"Take care, then." Her voice dropped a semitone. "Oh shit, I've just had a thought. How are we going to explain this to Mum and Dad? I mean, that you're not coming to America? We'll have to come up with some sort of excuse, and we can't tell them about the flat. Firstly, it's too complicated. But also, they might get the wrong end of the stick."

"Well spotted."

"Thank you," she said.

"Always ahead of the curve. We'll think of something, I suppose. But they probably won't get in touch. We could just both pretend I'm in America."

"Yes! Simple but brilliant. Write a few lines of 'wish you were here' guff then, photograph what you've written and send me the picture. I'll try and forge your handwriting. If you send them a postcard, they won't think to question us. Do it now, before you forget."

"But I wouldn't even be on the plane yet," he said.

"I'm not saying I'll send it *now*, dummy. I'd just like to have it ready. And I'll probably need a few tries to get it right. I might as well start practising."

"A postcard may be over-egging the pudding a bit. What if we're caught out?"

"We won't be. Look, you've just been stabbed in the chest. Who knows how it affected your handwriting?"

"Fair point, but - "

"If, by some disastrous mischance they *do* discover you're in Britain, we could just say you had to come back. You came out here, you didn't like it, you flew home. You got food poisoning, maybe. Something like that."

"Okay," he said.

"Think positive. I've really got to go now. Bye, John. Love you. Look after yourself."

She hung up.

Might as well do it while the imperative was still fresh in his mind. He went into the kitchen, took out a pad and pen and wrote, *Dear Mum and Dad, It's really great here in Connecticut. The scenery is fantastic, very American. Yesterday, Hannah and I went to one of the cafés from Man Versus Food!!! We had a huge veggie burger. Well, I did. Hannah had scampi. :) Hope you're both okay. Speak to you soon. Love John. xxx.* He photographed it and pressed 'send'. A few minutes later Hannah sent him an acknowledgement: 'Boring and sad, but tragically authentic-sounding.'

The next thing was to call Phyllis, let her know he wasn't flying out, after all. He wasn't sure what to tell her about last night – all or nothing? Because there wasn't an in between. And if he told her everything, how to explain that he hadn't told her before?

He could say Hannah called just after they'd left for the party, last night. He didn't have to have been planning it for days. Tell a lie, in other words, albeit not a corrosive one.

He could already hear Sister Wendy: *all lies are corrosive, John, even the smallest.*

He swatted her away. He went to his Contacts and pressed Call.

Phyllis was at work, so, as he expected, it went straight to voicemail. She'd probably return his call at lunchtime, or perhaps this evening, depending on how busy she was.

"Hi, John here. There's been a change of plan. Hannah's cancelled. Unforeseen circumstances. I'm staying in Britain now, after all. Call me sometime today. I need to talk to you about last night. Love you. Bye."

It suddenly occurred to him that she might have seen the men in the griffin masks.

No, she'd have said something. Texted, because she thought he was asleep.

His flashback. Good God, in all the muddle with Hannah and Fleming, he'd completely forgotten about it. It might mean the difference between future outcomes. He sat down on the sofa, closed his eyes and put his fingertips on his temples.

A chase, him riving one of the masks off someone, putting it on, the victim cowering against the wall, his face the epitome of horror. The knife, the helplessness, the –

The victim. He replayed it like it was video. Rarely could you do that with your memory, despite what people thought.

The petrified face rang a bell. Had he seen it somewhere before? Or was that what you always thought with an involuntary flashback? Maybe the part of your brain programmed to recognise previous sightings was falsely activated by the fact that you actually *had* seen the person before – in the original experience – but with the intervening trauma causing an affective breach, essentially a malfunction. So in reality, your 'seeing before' was a strictly literal thing, with no useful informational content.

Where else *could* he have seen the victim's face?

What he wouldn't give now for a police artist to hand. He was already beginning to forget the outlines. Maybe he should call Fleming.

But it might already be too late.

He tried to replay everything in his memory again.

It wasn't anyone at work. But he didn't go out that much, and his circle of friends was entirely confined to Thames House associates.

Family, then? Friends of family?

No, not that he could think of.

A celebrity of some sort, or at least a public figure. That would be least promising, because the likeliest outcome was that the victim looked like someone he clearly wasn't and couldn't be. Louis Theroux, say, or Matt Damon, both of whom, to the best of his knowledge, were still walking about minding their own business.

It might take him all day to mentally scan the faces of all the famous people he'd seen. Ultimately, for one purpose: to eliminate an illusory lead.

Still, if he could find out who he looked like, he could at least tell someone else. He might not *be* Louis Theroux or Matt Damon, but if he *looked* like them, that would be worth knowing.

If it didn't do more harm than good. Finding out that he looked like X might cause his memory to morph into an ever increasing resemblance to X. Maybe he should have done with the amateur psychology, and just call Fleming, get a qualified sketch artist over. It might even make them quits. If that was what he wanted. Did he?

Suddenly, he had a Eureka moment. It came all at once, like a ten ton information dump.

He knew who it was.

He'd have to confirm before he told anyone, but, sadly – it being this particular person and no other - there was no urgency.

And he already knew he was right. Because he had seen him before. Elsewhere. Both before his murder in Princes Street and afterwards.

173

My God, the plot thickened!

Chapter 20: Fleming is Ambushed

Phyllis awoke with roughly the headache she expected. She poured herself a beaker of milk and dressed for work: smart-casual white blouse, tank-top, jeans and ankle-boots. No need to go formal, it was only a de-brief. A short discussion with Ruby Parker, probably in one of the seminar offices on the top floor, a report to write – probably two hours tops; then she'd go in town, do a bit of shopping, get something to eat, head back home.

Then what? John hadn't asked her to go to the airport with him for very good reasons. It might be seen as rubbing in the fact that he was going on holiday, while she was staying here. But she wouldn't have minded. Perhaps she should ring him and suggest it.

Her parents were due a visit from her. Or maybe her brother. One or two ex-army friends she hadn't seen for a while? Or Jill or Sally from *Vogue*? Talk about old times. And if none of those were available, a solo trip to the cinema, or even the theatre. Bit sad, but *c'est*.

As usual, the moment she started playing off her parents against other possibilities, guilt set in. She couldn't spend the weekend feeling blameworthy. Bad enough John going away.

And at least she'd be looked after. She could sleep in, take Buster, her mother's two-year-old Labradoodle, out, eat in country pubs, drink endless cups of Earl Grey, read books in bed, go to 8am communion, help her dad in the garden.

She called a taxi to take her to Thames House. On the way, she browsed the *Telegraph* on her phone, then the *Spectator*. Outside, it rained so hard that, at one point, the car slowed to a crawl because the wipers couldn't cope.

The driver laughed. "Wouldn't like to be out there in that!" He nodded at a few men in *djellabas*, running frantically to shelter. "Look at them! Don't bother, my friends," he told them solemnly. "You're already drenched."

"The forecast's good for this afternoon," Phyllis replied, simply for something to say.

The driver hmm-ed, like that would be the day.

Time to bite the bullet. She went to her Contacts and phoned home. "Hello, Mummy, it's Phyllis."

"What a lovely surprise. How are you? When are we going to see you again? I'm beginning to forget what my own daughter looks like."

"I was hoping, this afternoon. I know it's a bit short notice - "

She heard her mother gasp. "Oh, no it's *not!* Oh, my! It's absolutely *lovely!* I'll book us a table at The Three Crowns for tonight! And you will stay tomorrow, won't you? Have a sleep in. I'll get you some *pains au chocolat* for breakfast. Or anything, you can have anything! Is, er… is - "

"John's going to America to see his sister."

"Oh, dear. Without *you?* And how did you know I was going to ask about John?"

"We're not splitting up. It's just - "

"I don't want you to split up. I didn't mean it like that. I mean, I don't necessarily want you *not* to split up. I want what you want. I want you to be happy."

"We can talk about it this afternoon. Not that there's anything to talk about. I should be there about two or three."

"I'll tell Buster you're coming. He'll be over the moon!"

They said bye, and Phyllis laughed. Buster barely knew her. They went walking together once every six weeks or so, otherwise he regarded her as a nonentity who arrived suddenly, at random intervals, and stole most of the limelight.

Her mind went to last night. Meadows: she rather hoped he wouldn't ring now. She hadn't had a chance to tell John about him, and she didn't really want any additional friends, especially ones with connections in the City. At parties, those sort of people were the life and soul. Elsewhere, they were too often puerile know-alls. She'd been through all that with Toby, her last boyfriend. Switching to John had been progress.

Not that Meadows was after her in that sense. Or so he claimed.

But then, they always said that. Sometimes, they were probably telling the truth. But you couldn't usually tell in advance. Which made it best to steer clear.

Was she being boring? Or was she growing up? Or were the two things one and the same? Bloody hell, she couldn't concentrate on her *Spectator*. That, and Greysonwell's UFO spiel.

Still, it had been entertaining. She had to hand it to him. Not what she'd been expecting, but enough to furnish her with lasting memories.

Would Greysonwell go on TV tonight, or would his mother put a stop to it? Did she even have that sort of influence over him?

She'd find out soon enough. If the news channels elected to broadcast it, that was. There might be too many other things happening in the world.

How big an event was the meltdown of a London Lord Mayor, in current affairs terms? Difficult to say off hand. It wasn't the world's highest-profile post, but it was a long way from nothing. Again, she'd find out presently. Stop thinking, just read.

The taxi stopped on the double red lines outside Thames House. Phyllis paid and got out in an adept single gesture, and walked up the steps and through the front door. 9.40. She wasn't due in till ten, but twenty minutes early was normal. You couldn't predict the traffic, so you tended to overcompensate.

Colin Bale, Thames House's bald, stout, young-ish receptionist, stood behind his desk. "Ms Parker will meet you in H4, top floor," he said. "You're not due there till ten, so feel free to grab yourself something from the canteen. She said to let you know it should only take an hour."

"Have the others arrived yet?" she asked. "Annabel, Tariq, Alec?"

"In the canteen, I believe."

Fleming got into work early. He wanted to catch DS Bach before she clocked off to go home after her night shift. He found her sitting at her computer, more or less just as he'd left her several hours ago. They exchanged good mornings. She picked up a sheaf of papers and followed him into his office. He closed the door and sat behind his desk. "How did you get on with the motorway crash?" he asked.

She handed him the papers. "I can't find any evidence that there was one, sir. There was a long holdup on the M23 seven weeks ago, but it was eventually cleared. Before that, nothing for over a year, and, on that occasion, it was a well-documented case of an escaped horse running into the southbound carriageway. The cause of the seven-weeks-ago holdup isn't reported in any of the traffic officers' reports. As regards the media, only two local papers mention it. *The Maidenbower Chronicle* attributes it to an overturned lorry, no casualties. *The Redhill Gazette* says it was a jack-knifed HGV, again no casualties. Both concentrate almost exclusively on the duration of the holdup and the length of the tailback. They mention the cause only in passing."

"The officers' reports don't mention it?"

"Seems odd, I know. And there were no addenda that I could find."

"That would indicate a cascade failure, maybe."

"A...?"

"When a traffic jam's caused by lots of sudden braking incidents, all independent and random, one after the other. They have a cumulative knock-on effect, and eventually stall the natural flow. The officers involved wouldn't mention it because it would be speculative, and possibly take them outside their expertise."

"Seems odd that the papers thought there was an overturned vehicle then. Where would they get that from?"

"Leave it with me. You're about to head home, aren't you?"

"I'm here for another hour, sir."

"Okay, good. See if you can track down the journalists then. Maybe they'll be able to answer your question. I'll try to arrange an informal interview with the traffic officers. And before you say anything, I agree: it's beginning to look very like a wild goose chase. True, it's anomalous: no causes mentioned in the official report, and that's at variance with what the papers say – the media usually knows at least something – but it's difficult to see how it can have any bearing on the Princes Street murder."

"Very good, sir. I'll get back to you before I leave."

She returned to her desk. Fleming picked up the papers she'd left and glanced through them. He noted the names of the police officers and put a call through to Surrey Police Traffic Division, requesting an informal meeting for the purposes of gathering information regarding a separate ongoing inquiry. He arranged to be in Guildford at noon.

Forty-five minutes later, Bach returned to his office to let him know she was heading home. "I managed to track both journalists down," she said. "Neither saw anything first hand. They got their information from the local radio station. A public-spirited motorist had called the traffic alert line to say there was a queue due to an overturned lorry, and could they let other drivers know? Later, they also cross-checked with each other, 'just to be on the safe side'.

179

Of course, they had the same story. It was never going to be front page, so of course they just went with it. In their words, 'No one's ever come back with a contradictory account, but why would they'?"

When she'd left, he went to his pigeonhole, took another pile of documents back to his desk, then had a coffee from the machine. Afterwards, he went to get in his car.

As he was crossing the forecourt, Sergeant Green emerged from the building behind him. "Sir!"

Fleming turned round. Green smiled apologetically. "Super wants to see you, sir. Didn't say what about."

"Now?"

"That's what he said, sir."

Fleming ground his teeth and headed back inside. Green peeled off at the lift, and Fleming ascended to Floor 4 alone. He strode briskly along the corridor and knocked on the superintendent's door.

"Come!"

Superintendent Dale Brighouse was going bald, so had decided to shave the top of his head, grow a smattering of beard and buy a chunky pair of glasses. He spoke with a faint Cornish accent. He didn't get to his feet.

"Sit down, Nick," he said tetchily. "What's all this I hear about you being interested in a traffic accident on the M23?"

"I was just heading out to Surrey now, sir. See what I can dig up. I admit - "

"I can't see what it has to do with your investigation, that's all."

Fleming had prepared for such a question. He didn't want to give Mordred away. "I received an anonymous tip-off claiming the two things are connected."

"Connected how?"

Fleming shrugged. "That's what I aim to find out. I'm trying to follow all leads right now, even the slenderest."

"This 'anonymous source': have you ever had dealings with him or her before?"

"It's a 'him'. No."

"So you don't know whether he's reliable."

"No."

"Potentially a huge waste of petrol, then." He flashed an avuncular smile and leaned forward. "Genuine question. What are you actually thinking, Nicholas?"

"I was told it was a pile-up involving five financiers connected to the City of London somehow," Fleming said. "Which is where the murder took place, obviously."

Brighouse's mouth popped open. He appeared to sit up, but continued the trajectory and flopped back in his chair. For an uncomfortable several seconds, silence smothered the room.

"I see," he said coldly.

More silence. Brighouse appeared to be wrestling with something. He focussed on a series of different objects around the room, but weirdly, without seeming to see them. All his attention was directed introspectively.

"In what manner did this 'anonymous source' come to you?" he asked at last.

"Phone," Fleming said. "I was sent a cheap mobile and told to keep it. The source used it to call me."

Brighouse was writing now. "This was when?"

"A day ago."

"And you included it in a report, yes?"

"Not yet. I was going to. Like I say, I've only had it a day, and I haven't had contact with this source before. When it arrived, I had no reason to think it would provide information leading to an arrest."

"I will need you to get me that phone, Nicholas. I mean, get it for me and *put it on my desk*. Like *right now*."

"Didn't we just agree that the 'information' it supposedly provided was 'a huge waste of petrol'?"

Brighouse fixed him with narrowed eyes. "I'm beginning to think you know more about this than you're letting on, Nick."

"With respect, sir, I'm beginning to get the same feeling about you."

"Get me the phone," he replied. "Put it on my desk. Then forget about Surrey. Finished. Finito. *Kaput*. And if this 'source' tries to contact you again, you come straight to me, understand?"

Fleming got up, went downstairs, retrieved the phone and took it into the gents' for privacy. He switched it on, copied the only number in the Contacts list onto a scrap of paper and thrust it into his pocket. He took the phone to Brighouse's office and put it on his desk. Brighouse made a point of pretending to be absorbed in paperwork, and only acknowledged him to the extent of muttering, "And close the door on your way out".

Fleming went downstairs and left the building. Presumably, at some point, Brighouse would realise it was probably in 'their' interests – whoever 'they' were, but they definitely existed – to have him followed. Luckily, he hadn't reached that point yet. Typically slow on the uptake.

No point taking his car, it would be the best indicator that he'd gone somewhere. He walked across the road, took a left turn and kept walking north until he came to a phone shop. He bought another cheap mobile and called Mordred from the second floor of Selfridges where he was certain he wasn't being observed.

"You need to ditch the phone Murgatroyd gave you," he said. "Long story. I was forced to surrender mine, and they'll use it to find you. Can you meet me in Hyde Park tomorrow afternoon, one in the afternoon? I'd say today, but it'll arouse suspicion if I'm away from my desk too long."

"Glad to," Mordred said. "Whereabouts?"

"The Serpentine Bar?"

"I've new information. Something that could get you promoted."

"Looking forward to it." He hung up. No point asking what it was. The way Brighouse had just behaved, nothing representing progress in this case was likely to earn praise from the Met.

Still, it must be worth hearing. Mordred sounded excited.

Ruby Parker listened to the four different accounts of Greysonwell's party while Stella, her erstwhile secretary, took notes in shorthand. She said little until all were complete. She shook her head disbelievingly.

"Under normal circumstances, I'd suggest we get back to Greysonwell and request an investigation into what happened to you, Alec, but it sounds as if the Lord Mayor has more than enough problems."

"I've had a fresh thought regarding what might lie behind it," Alec said.

"Go on," Ruby Parker said.

"It didn't occur to me until now, but this is the first time I've heard Phyllis's account in detail. There wasn't time last night, and after we came out, we were all thinking about Greysonwell's alien story."

Phyllis pointed to herself. "*My* account?"

He turned to her. "Faris Meadows seems to have been very interested in you. No fault of yours, obviously. But given how close he is to Greysonwell, it's conceivable he knew you were with me from the outset. He certainly didn't look surprised when I turned up with you in Greysonwell's study. And yet it must have been obvious we were two couples: Tariq and Annabel, you and I."

"I see," Ruby Parker said. "You're suggesting he may have arranged for you to be out of the way so he could introduce himself to Phyllis."

"I'm just saying it's a possibility," Alec said.

They all nodded. Phyllis felt herself flush slightly. Why hadn't she thought of that? Simple, yet obvious.

Ruby Parker turned to her. "Phyllis?"

"In retrospect, it's plausible," she said. "I'm sorry I didn't see it earlier."

"I'll make a few discreet enquiries," Ruby Parker said. "Someone must have seen something happen to you, Alec. Maybe not who knocked you unconscious, but it's difficult to see how you could have ended up outside the building without someone noticing something."

"Alternatively, if *no one* saw," Annabel put in, "that could indicate that the culprit, or culprits, were very familiar with the ins and outs of Mansion House. Which might again point to associates of Meadows."

Ruby Parker nodded. "I take it none of you have spoken to anyone else whatsoever about what happened last night?"

They all shook their heads.

"Please keep it that way," she said, "until I explicitly authorise anything to the contrary. Now, if there are no questions, you're free to go. Have a pleasant weekend, and I'll see you all on Monday."

They got to their feet and made their way separately to the exit. Phyllis decided to walk into the city centre. She'd get a few presents for her family, then hop on the train at Waterloo.

On her way across Lambeth Bridge, she switched her phone on and saw she had a Voicemail.

"Hi, John here," it said." There's been a change of plan. Hannah's cancelled. Unforeseen circumstances. I'm staying in Britain now, after all. Call me sometime today. I need to talk to you about last night. Love you. Bye."

She rolled her eyes. Typical. She'd made plans now; she couldn't change them.

Still, maybe it was for the best. She wasn't allowed to talk about the very thing John was apparently so interested in. Which serendipitously chimed with Annabel's conclusion on Hampstead Heath. *We shouldn't tell him, he might take it the wrong way.* A weekend apart from him meant she wouldn't be tempted.

Not that she'd give in, even if she was. But John had this uncanny power of asking discreet questions and being able to read the answer in your body-language.

Might as well strike while the iron was hot. Pointless putting it off. She pressed 'Call'.

"How did the de-brief go?" he asked when he picked up.

"Fine, but I'm not allowed to talk about anything connected with it. Look, I'm really sorry, John, but if I'd known beforehand, we could have arranged to do something together. As it is, I promised Mum I'd spend the weekend in Berkshire. A little Brit Family Robinson time. I'm just off to pick up a few presents, then it's straight for the train."

"Certainly no need to apologise. I'm the one who should be sorry."

"What for?"

"Not going to America. I don't know. Look, it's good that you're going to spend time with your parents."

She laughed. "I know it is. What happened to America?"

"Something to do with the Billboard Hot 100. I won't bore you with the details. It was me who cried off."

"You're feeling okay, aren't you? It wasn't health related?"

"I'm tip-top. But I want to be ready to go back to work. The way things were about to pan out over there, it might not have been as restful as I thought."

"Join me in Berkshire if you like. Mum won't mind. And Buster's always pleased to see you."

"Thanks, but no thanks. I think your mum's probably expecting a lone Phyllis. And Buster's inclined to casual violence."

"Don't think I'm not on to him. I'll probably be back late Sunday, you know what Mum's like. I'll give you a call on Monday."

"Has Alec been sworn to *omerta* too, by the way? Just in case I get the urge to call him."

"Me, Alec, Annabel, Tariq. Sorry, John, it looks like you might have a lonely weekend."

"I'll live. I might go home to Hexham. See my own parents. Have a good time."

They exchanged I love yous and hung up.

Chapter 21: The Press Conference

Faris Meadows had just returned from the gym. He sat alone on a threadbare chaise longue, the sole piece of furniture in a small windowless room on the top floor of Mansion House. He wore a track suit and trainers and had a towel around his neck. A chandelier directly above him bathed the room in a hard, unforgiving light. He lowered his head into his hands.

Tragedy was like a machine. At some point in the narrative, the cogs would start turning and the intended victim would be caught in the gears. From then on, everything, large and small, was decided. Meadows wasn't much into Greek tragedy. Biblical tragedy was more his style, and it usually began with a small act of mercy. When Joshua's men couldn't carry on slaughtering the Canaanites; when Saul spared the Amalekites. Trying to do the right thing, but at the wrong moment. That was when the cog caught your sleeve.

Like when they'd all chased the blogger down that night, and they'd decided not to finish the accompanying have-a-go hero, never thinking he might come back in the guise of Death. Never imagining he was an MI7 agent, a bloody good one, by all accounts, someone who'd now fully recovered, and was probably about to swoop.

My God, they'd been utter *idiots! Always* err on the side of caution, especially in that sort of scenario!

And Phyllis. He'd let himself imagine she was his quarry, not once stopping to consider it might be the other way round. The way she'd gradually drip-dripped information about 'John'. She obviously knew what was going on. *Keep it up, Faris,* that's what she was saying: *the trap's almost sprung.*

187

Which of course was why 'John' hadn't been there. He'd selected a different means of making his grand appearance.

He chuckled at his own paranoia. Worst case scenario, that's all *that* was.

But by no means impossible. Quite the contrary. When tragedy hooked you, it didn't let go. And because tragedy was tragedy – it had to have intelligent protagonists – you knew when you were ensnared. You had to. Otherwise, it'd be melodrama – or farce.

The trap's almost sprung. How right that was, actually! With or without 'John', the end of the world was about to arrive. John's victory – if that was how it panned out – could only be pyrrhic, because they were the only sort of victories left.

So let Greysonwell do his thing. Let him go through the process of warning the world about his 'aliens'. Let him humiliate himself on the national – and probably the international – stage. Let him lose his job. Let *Have I Got News for You* and *Mock the Week* lampoon him on primetime TV. Let him be chased out of Mansion House by crowds hurling turnips. Let him wander the inhabited earth with the mark of Cain on his forehead. It didn't matter.

'Phyllis'. Probably not her real name. 'John': nor that his. And 'Annabel', 'Tariq' and 'Alec' might not even have been secret agents, just bit-part actors, hired at the last minute to beef up the finale. *The Fall of Faris Meadows* starring Shia LaBeouf.

So what to do now? He had to fight back, even though he couldn't win. *Especially* because of that. It wasn't tragedy if you lay down and died when things started to sour. You had to keep struggling till you were speared through the heart. And then the Chorus. *Lo, he is fallen, and around great storms and the outreaching sea.*

To begin with, he needed to find out everything he possibly could about this 'John'. If possible, kill him – repay him for his smugness, make amends for what should have, but hadn't, happened the night the blogger died. *Murder* him, even if he had to do it in plain sight. Michael, Paul, Hilldy, Raymond: they were all listed in the *dramatis personae*, so they'd all have to do their bit. And for no other reason than that.

If 'John' died, they'd probably all go down a bit faster – they were taking more and more risks now - but then the crisis would hit and eventually they'd be restored. With luck, within a decade, they'd rule the Earth. They were young. Men of their class, wealth, connections and obvious talent didn't stay in prison for long. Only sexual crimes really put you beyond the pale nowadays, and none of them were guilty on that count.

The main thing that mattered to all of them now was that Julia should emerge unscathed. Anything else was unthinkable. In order to guarantee it, he had to get proactive.

So where could he find out about 'John'? Well, 'John' had been to visit Mansion House during the previous administration, under William Chester, so there was that to investigate. Then the CCTV footage from the killing of the blogger, presumably on YouTube. Never thought he'd want to see that again. And there was also the fact that 'John' and the City of London had some sort of history pre-dating Chester. That might yield a gold mine of information.

Room for optimism. He could begin by staking out Thames House, where 'Phyllis' worked. She'd probably be at work Monday morning. He could hide somewhere and watch her go in, then meet her on her way out with flowers. What could be more natural than that? She'd probably try to give him the brush off, yes, but he could have her followed home. Probably a professional PI for that. No good getting any of the gang to do it. She'd be trained to recognise a shadow.

She and 'John' might not be lovers, but they were almost certainly closely linked. All that stuff about 'John' going to America was likely bullshit, designed to augment his – from her point of view - false sense of security.

But she had a surprise coming. She and 'John' both.

The Fates wouldn't be surprised, though. From one point of view 'John' and 'Phyllis' represented conventional moral justice. The script actually *required* their deaths, in any case before Faris Meadows got his final comeuppance.

He heard footsteps approaching outside. His heart leapt because he knew instantly who it was.

The door opened and Julia stepped inside. She wore a heavy winter coat, heeled boots and a fur hat. She came over and kissed him lightly on the lips.

"Get ready," she said. "We're about to leave. Get the others together and tell them to wear coats, and not to take them off when we arrive. We've got to appear to be supporting Henry, but also like we're not part of it. As if we're there under protest. Which, of course, we are."

So he was determined to go through with it. Meadows frowned and sighed in an effort to give the impression that he'd expected another, better outcome. He knew Julia loved Henry, but he was a lost cause. There had been about a month, ten years ago, when Meadows and he had been great friends, but from then on it had all been downhill. Not anyone's fault really. You couldn't be friends with Henry. He was too strange. In the end, he didn't even want friends. Except for John Mordred, maybe.

Actually, what did Henry even know about John Mordred? And where had he got the notion he might be some sort of kindred spirit?

Worth looking into. He'd have to ask him. Nicely, to begin with.

He went along the landing to the room where he lived with his four friends. Since Greysonwell's election, they'd converted it into a kind of stopover pad and occasionally, they spent days at a time here. 'The Barracks' they called it, only half-jokingly. Five cots and a long wardrobe, nothing fancy, in an otherwise nondescript room.

Paul and Hilldy sat on their beds, looking at their phones. Raymond stood in the corner, staring into a hand mirror and combing his long red hair. Michael lay gazing at the ceiling and drumming his fingers on the bed-frame. They all stopped what they were doing when Meadows came in. They looked at him dejectedly.

"It's over," Meadows announced. "He won't be swayed. Grab your coats. We're going to Guildhall for the press conference."

They let out disgusted groans in unison.

"What the hell," Paul said, getting to his feet with extreme reluctance, as if the effort might kill him.

"He should never have become Lord Mayor in the first place," Hilldy said. "You should have run, Faris."

"The party's finally over," Raymond said.

"I couldn't have run for Mayor," Meadows said. "The only reason Henry won was because of the family name. I'm not a Viscount. I'm a nobody. And the parties, Raymond, were all Julia's idea, try and drum up friends for him. The only input he ever had was that idea about bloody Quatermass!" He laughed. He'd never even heard of Quatermass before Henry dug it up. He scowled at himself laughing. "And I don't think any of us could have foreseen how that would turn out."

"I still don't know what it is," Raymond said.

"It's a person," Michael told him. "Bernard Quatermass. And a film. Or a series of films. Actually, what *is* it, Faris?"

"Why doesn't anyone in here *listen* to me?" Hilldy burst out, putting his hands in his hair. "We need to take Henry to one side and put the fear of God into him. Julia doesn't have to know. We could put a stop to this now. We don't have to leave any marks on him."

Faris sighed. "For the last time, Henry's not scared of us, or anything we might do."

"I don't think we've been sufficiently imaginative," Hilldy replied.

"I've known him a lot longer than you," Faris said. "Believe me, it only works up to a point, and no further. Nowadays, he's more scared of the aliens."

"If he's so scared of them, why's he holding a press conference with the intention of exposing them to the world?" Michael asked.

It was a good question. Unfortunately, it didn't have an answer. "Because he's Henry," Faris said.

"Because he's a 'good person'," Raymond said bitterly. "Willing to sacrifice himself for the sake of humanity. That's how he sees himself. Not only is he scuppering our futures, and his mother's, and humiliating us all by association, but he's also managed to persuade himself he's on moral high ground."

"Which is how you might see it if you thought you were saving the world from alien invaders," Faris said. "Or do you think he's putting it on?"

"He needs to be properly managed," Raymond said. "Using techniques from the book of degradation and pain."

"We don't *have* a future!" Faris snapped, going back several steps in the discussion. They needed to be getting ready, not standing about talking about done deals as if they were still undecided. "The Lady Julia's our only concern. Get your coats on and get ready."

They snapped out of their reluctance and wordlessly did as he told them. He was their leader, and so effective that a single barked command could dissipate all their disinclinations. They put their coats on, plus ties as dark as they could find, as if they were going to a funeral.

"It might not be as bad as we think," Faris told them, in a voice grim enough to make it clear he wasn't offering a concession. "I had a hand in setting up the press conference. I've invited those sections of the media concerned with entertainment and celebrity gossip, not the serious contingent. With any luck, they'll go away thinking it's just another publicity stunt."

"Perhaps that's why Julia organised all those parties," Hilldy said lethargically. "Maybe she knew it would come to something like this. If she could pass him off from the start as the 'Jester Mayor', anything weird he then did would pass under the radar. Maybe this will too. Mind you, he's never done anything this weird before. No one has." He reached into the wardrobe, took out a half bottle of gin, and swigged it. He passed it to Michael, who replied with a 'no thanks'. Raymond took it and gave a deep pull. "Ready to go," he said.

"He's never done anything weird full stop," Paul said. "Not in the extrovert, fun sense of the word, anyway. That's what gets me. To read the freebie press, you'd think he was the most exciting man on the planet. In reality, it'd be difficult to find anyone more lacklustre."

"I don't think a man who's been kidnapped by aliens is necessarily lacklustre," Faris said. "But I see what you mean."

"Do we know he even *was* kidnapped?" Paul asked. "I mean, that that's his story? I thought he was an unthinking collaborator, but then he decided to work against them."

"Like Moses and the Egyptians," Faris said. "Well, I suppose we're about to find out."

There was a knock at the door. He opened it to find Lady Julia still looking devastated.

"The car's waiting," she said. "Hurry up. I don't want Henry starting his revelations without us." She looked them over with satisfaction. "You all look absolutely marvellous, by the way. I knew I could rely on you."

As they left the room, they discreetly vied with each other to walk beside her.

Guildhall was less than half a mile from Mansion House, and a three minute drive. Most times of the year it would have been easier, and nicer, to walk, but the clouds threatened rain and a hard wind blew through the streets. It was 7pm. Lady Julia went in the limousine with Faris and Raymond. Paul, Hilldy and Michael followed immediately behind in a taxi. Henry had apparently left just before them on foot. He'd promised to wait for his mother, once he reached his destination, before he began speaking.

Halfway there, Faris gently nudged Julia and pointed out of the window. Henry, in a smart wool coat, head down, hands in pockets, ploughing through the neon gloom alone.

"Should we offer him a lift?" Faris asked.

"Let him walk," she replied. "It's what he wants."

She gazed pityingly as the car sped up and her son receded. He was the Lord Mayor and he couldn't even muster a few friends to accompany him to what was likely to be the most momentous self-inflicted injury of his life. Things would have changed disastrously for him in a few hours, yet he looked as if his sole concern was arriving without getting out of breath. So sad.

A hundred yards on, the car slowed to a halt for traffic congestion. Henry passed, and turned and looked directly into the car at them. He didn't smile, and somehow, he looked different. Greyer, older.

"*Is* that Henry?" Faris asked. Maybe it wasn't.

"I don't know," Julia said. "I had exactly the same eerie thought." She wrapped her coat more tightly around her. "I could have sworn it was him a moment ago. Maybe the aliens have done something to him." She didn't say it like it was a joke.

Five minutes later, they arrived at Guildhall, went through the necessary formalities with the staff and shuffled reluctantly onto the podium. Henry was already up there, alone beneath the level gaze of Guildhall's effigies of the Biblical giants, Gog and Magog. He had taken his coat off, and wore a grey suit and tie. He had just two microphones to speak into. Facing him, the audience was big enough to occupy the front two rows of seats, and there were two television cameras, but most of those present looked to be interns or even curious laypersons somehow admitted on false pretences. This was a medieval venue, soaked in fable from its inception, and its rigid gothic architecture, high ceiling and apparently bizarre links to *Troia Nova*, ancient Roman blood sports, and mythological British monarchs coalesced to make it feel as uncanny as anything in Quatermass's pit.

Henry waited till his mother was seated, then tapped one of the microphones before him, testing for sound. He began to speak.

"I have waited a long time to say what I'm - "

"Excuse me, Lord Mayor," a cameraman interrupted from the floor. "Could you just wait a *minute* till we give you the countdown? Sorry for the delay. Just give us two ticks."

Henry looked at the table and flushed. No point in holding a press conference without the press. They held all the cards. They didn't even have to show respect. So presumably, he'd have to wait till they were ready. His humiliation fanned out and encompassed all those on the podium with him. For the first time that evening, Faris felt truly angry.

"All finished!" the cameraman announced. "You ready, Lord Mayor?"

"Absolutely," Henry replied in a monotone.

"Three, two, one…"

Henry was sweating. He shook. For a moment, he didn't speak. He reached into his jacket pocket and took out a piece of paper and read in a trembling voice:

"No one would have believed in the last years of the twentieth century that this world was being watched keenly and closely by intelligences greater than man's and yet as mortal as his own; that as men busied themselves about their various concerns they were scrutinised and studied, perhaps almost as narrowly as a man with a microscope might scrutinise the transient creatures that swarm and multiply in a drop of water. With infinite complacency men went to and fro over this globe about their little affairs, serene in their assurance of their empire over matter."

He folded the paper up – silence for two seconds – and put it back in his pocket. He interlaced his fingers in front of him.

"The words of HG Wells," he said. "Only I changed 'nineteenth' to 'twentieth'. The age of aliens is upon us, and within a decade – 2026 is the far limit – we'll all know it."

He cleared his throat. He focussed on the microphones.

"I have been associated with the extra-terrestrial project for some time," he continued, still shakily. "I haven't exactly been working against the human race, but neither have I been cooperating with it - my own species - as much as I ought to have been. That, I regret. Not all of the aliens currently on our planet are prepared to work with us. Some would prefer to enslave us. But I'm confident that, as things stand, we have a relatively bright future. Only, it's not ours. Of course, should the balance of power in the universe one day change…"

He trailed off, and rubbed his forehead. "I love humanity," he continued. "Although I've said that some of the aliens want to work with us, I don't know why, or to what ultimate purpose. Their minds are vastly superior to ours. I want us to go forward in full knowledge. In many ways, it's even possible that the notion of holding this press confer-ence, right now, this very evening, wasn't *my* idea at all, but one that was *given* to me, *made* mine. Through lots of little forewarnings, like this, humanity gradually becomes accli-matised to its unavoidable fate. Oh, the earliest messengers, like me, get ridiculed, but over time, it comes to look not so bad..."

Suddenly, he started to cry. He took a handkerchief from his pocket and wiped his eyes, then blew his nose.

"You might well say, 'What is he telling us this for? Is he calling us to arms? Should we rush out and get guns to re-pel the alien invaders? Is that what he wants?' Well, the an-swer's no. There's no way of fending them off, even if that were desirable, which it probably isn't. They're here. They've been here a long time, and they know all about us. They can manipulate the laws of physics in ways we can't even begin to imagine. We can't fight them off. We can't even begin to fight them off. There will be no resistance, be-cause, well, for a start, our weapons won't work on them. Our guns won't fire, our bombs won't explode. Not that we should want them to. They can guide us to a good future. They can probably breed with us..."

The audience had begun to talk amongst themselves, quietly at first, but with mounting excitement and mirth. Suddenly, Henry was struggling to make himself heard, even with two microphones. Just as earlier, a wave of humi-liation had spread across those on the podium, now a wave of alarm hit them.

"I simply want to exonerate myself," Henry said. He wiped his eyes again, harder. "I don't want to be re-membered as the traitor, but as the foreshadower. Yes, be-fore I finish: the circles on the pavements outside Mansion House, and across the City, are proof they've come. Al-though they've all gone now – the circles, I mean, not the ali-ens: of course *they* haven't gone, the aliens, they're... I'm ..."

The rest of his speech was drowned out. Julia blinked slowly, as if she was in physical pain, and nodded to Faris. He gestured to Raymond and Paul, and they stood up and got Henry to his feet. It wasn't difficult, because he didn't struggle. He didn't seem to know what he wanted any more, except he clearly had no preference for staying put.

They escorted him off the stage and behind the scenes without relinquishing their grip. Lady Julia was the last to get to her feet. She followed the others off the stage without making eye-contact with anyone in the audience.

When Henry was out of sight of the cameras, and when he saw his mother coming, he shook himself free of his re-strainers and ran out of the exit door. No one said anything or made the slightest effort to go after him.

Chapter 22: Conference in Hyde Park

Sunday, 12.15pm. Mordred changed for his appointment with Fleming – chinos, brogues, oxford shirt, crew-neck sweater, sports jacket – then grabbed a tiny notepad and a pencil, and went down into the Islington streets. Everything brown and drippy, a typical late autumn afternoon. His last contact with the DI: *You need to ditch the phone. I was forced to surrender mine, and they'll use it to find you.* 'They'. Who were 'they'?

Obviously, the same 'they' as always. Powerful people with vendettas, maximally cosseted, and immune to harm.

Mordred had then obeyed Fleming's instructions, leaving his flat in haste and slotting Murgatroyd's phone into a bin at the top of Roden Street. True, 'they' could already have traced him. But since they either had or hadn't, getting rid of it was either pointless or absolutely necessary. In neither case could it hurt him. As far as he knew, no one followed him.

Right now, although half of him was obsessing about Fleming, the other half was concerned with Phyllis. He could tell from her voice that something was wrong. But that could simply be that she wasn't allowed to talk about Greysonwell's party.

Although that in itself was interesting. Something had obviously happened there.

Perhaps he wasn't the only person who'd caught sight of the men in the griffin masks. MI7 had sent four of its best agents. It seemed unlikely all of them would have missed what he'd seen from an overlooking window simply by chance. And he could imagine how Ruby Parker would react when they told her. *Don't breathe a word of this to John. He's too personally involved.*

Bloody hell. Life.

Back to today then. Focus. He bought two pay-as-you-go mobiles in Tesco Express, unwrapped them in the shop and thrust one into each of his jacket side-pockets. He left the wrapping, with the numbers, in the carrier bag. Then he went back onto the street. A bus was better than a taxi for avoiding tails, and, although he couldn't see anyone following him, he couldn't be too careful.

He caught the bus at his usual stop, still looking about to see if he could identify shadows. As usual, the more you did this, the more you felt you were being watched – even when you weren't. He sat on the back seat so he could keep an eye on the other passengers. He pretended to read his phone. If 'they' were following by car, they'd see his blond hair framed in the back window. It would give them a clear indication of when and where he was about to get off. Not for the first time in his life, he wished he'd brought a hat.

Of course, he could also turn his visibility into an advantage. Get up from the back seat and go further up the bus, say. Could work especially well if there was another blond guy aboard, one who was getting off before him.

But 'they' probably weren't following him by car. Because how would that work? They'd see him get on a bus, so they'd flag down a taxi and bark, *Follow that double decker!*

No way. Getting a taxi to stop for you in London was never so simple. Try stepping out with a folded copy of your daily paper raised, and you were lucky if the driver swerved to avoid running you over. Anything else was as rare as a snow leopard on a unicycle.

But maybe it was just him.

He took the phone wrapping out of the bag, hurriedly copied the number for each into his notepad, put it all away again.

They might follow on bikes, a few of them. You rarely saw that in films, but it happened. Especially if you knew the mark was a confirmed bus-user in a congested urban area. Easy to keep up. Easy to switch to foot when he or she disembarked.

But he couldn't see any bikes. Not the non-suicidal type that didn't whizz past you at any hint of a gap.

He got off at Knightsbridge and crossed and re-crossed the road a few times, twice circumambulating the Wellington Arch to assess the situation.

No one he could see. He wasn't being followed. He ditched the carrier bag and checked the time on his phone. Fleming was probably already in place. He crossed the road and briskly entered Hyde Park.

He found the DCI sitting at one of the tables outside the Serpentine Bar, nursing a cup of coffee. He wore what appeared to be all new clothes: brown suit, matching brogues and a camel coat. He didn't look like a policeman at all. He looked like an advert for Savile Row. An elderly couple sat on the other side of the same table, eating sandwiches. By comparison, they looked like they were dressed in rags, although their attire was well within the socially acceptable limits of contemporary shapelessness.

Fleming got up and came over, apparently unflustered. He had something of the Connery's Bond about him: professional, stylish, free spirited. "I think we should find a bench somewhere we can be sure we're not going to be overheard," he said, gently guiding Mordred by the elbow. "I trust you weren't followed."

"I've done every check in the book," Mordred replied. He didn't want to look complacent.

They walked to the middle of the park and slowed to a stroll, still keeping an eye out for watchers. Mordred discreetly took one of the phones out and slipped it into Fleming's coat pocket, along with the number of the one he'd kept. Trying to keep the transfer out of sight, in case they were being watched.

Fleming's face registered mild surprise, then he felt in his pocket. He nodded as if he'd expected something of the sort, and, don't worry, he wasn't going to give the game away with any sudden gestures. Without saying anything, they'd both abandoned the idea of finding a bench. They needed 360 degree vision.

"I take it you ditched Murgatroyd's phone," Fleming said.

"First thing I did after I spoke to you yesterday. How did you lose yours?"

"Confiscated. After I investigated those five financiers you told me about. M23 collision. Murgatroyd told you about that, right?"

"He didn't make a song and dance about it, but I'm pretty sure he wants us to find 'the truth'. But I don't even know about what."

"All I've been able to discover," Fleming went on, "is that there was a holdup on the M23 about seven weeks ago. None of the duty officers' reports mentioned a cause, and only two local papers reported it, both in matchbox-sized articles. They blamed an overturned lorry. But neither of the journalists actually saw it. They relied on hearsay. I was about to set off for Surrey, do a bit of asking around, when, out of the blue, the superintendent called me in. He demanded to know my original source. I told him it was anonymous and via a phone provided to me by post yesterday. He impounded the phone and told me to forget all about going to Surrey. Which, to be fair, I have."

"I know who the murder victim was, that night I was knifed."

"You mean, the guy with the vandalised hard drive?"

"He was Martin Curzon."

"Martin ...? Should I know him?"

"Apparently, he was 'kidnapped in Venezuela' at about the same time as he was killed in Princes Street."

Fleming stopped walking and turned to face Mordred. "Sorry, I'm not quite sure what you mean. Are you saying that Martin Curzon isn't, and has never been, in Venezuela?"

"Because he was killed in Princes Street. I've no doubt a flight out was booked in his name, possibly even by him. But he never made it to the airport."

They began walking again. "What are you basing this on?" Fleming asked.

"I suddenly remembered his face from that night. Total recall, just for a few moments. But I also happen to know that the murder victim was a blogger who went by the name of Guanyin. In that capacity, he worked out of a semi-secret location in the City, five minutes from where Curzon worked, in the stock market. Everyone agrees Guanyin must have been a trader of some sort. But since he – and it is a 'he' – disappeared, no one's reported any traders missing. With the sole exception of Martin Curzon. But it 'can't' be him, because he was abducted and murdered in Venezuela."

"It certainly looks promising."

"Added to which, let's say he really was kidnapped. Normally, the abductors put out a video of the victim to prove they're holding him. There was none of that in Curzon's case. Just the occasional personal item: a wedding ring, his passport, a photo of his wife. Things that didn't really prove anything. And then, after his killing, no body."

"Yes, I see."

"It can be proved. All you need is a sample of Curzon's DNA. His wife could provide it from his house. Then you need to seal off the semi-secret location I've just mentioned for forensic analysis; then you need the DNA of the murder victim. I'm pretty sure you'll find they're one and the same person."

"I'll get right on it. Only, of course, I won't need the semi-secret location. There'll be other ways of proving he's the blogger."

"I was hoping you'd say that. And I'm not finished yet. These 'five financiers' Murgatroyd spoke about. You might find they weren't on the M23 at all. Or rather, they were – and weren't."

"Sorry, you're speaking in riddles."

"Venezuela again. Of course, I can't prove it. But five IMF officials were kidnapped and killed there just before the supposed abduction of Martin Curzon."

"And you think they're the ones Murgatroyd mentioned? Then why didn't Murgatroyd know about Venezuela?"

"Because they really were killed on the M23."

"That's your theory."

"It would explain the apparent cover up. Someone's taken one maverick financial investigator – Guanyin – killed him in Britain and transferred the action to Latin America. That takes organisation. Assuming Murgatroyd's correct, we've also got five missing financiers, all deceased. If they're the Venezuela ones, then they're IMF officials. What if they were investigating something in Britain? Someone killed them, and then, magically – using the same technique as on Curzon – made it appear they were never here to begin with."

"It's painfully hypothetical. If someone killed five IMF officials in Britain, the IMF itself would launch an investigation. It wouldn't sit on its hands while someone transferred the crime scene to the other side of the world."

"Not if they were killed deliberately. But what if they died accidentally, say in an actual pile-up on the actual M23? And what if they'd actually concluded their investigation and their conclusions were so frightening that it actually suited the IMF, as well as the British government, to hush the whole thing up?"

"That would have to be pretty damn frightening."

"We need to find out what Guanyin was blogging about when he died."

Fleming chuckled. "If this is as big as you're suggesting, we're already stalled. Especially as regards Curzon."

"What do you mean?"

"We might not have discovered the whole reason Curzon – if that's who he was – was doused in acid."

"Go on."

"If I was organising something like what you're suggesting," Fleming said, "I'd douse the corpse in acid to make it unrecognisable. Sometime after the post-mortem, I'd switch it with another, similarly mutilated, corpse. Then, if someone was clever enough to make the connection to Curzon, they'd do the relevant DNA tests, and the results would indicate no match. As a consequence, whoever suggested such a test in the first place would be in deep trouble. Enough, perhaps, to get him a posting and thus remove him permanently from the picture."

Mordred nodded. "We still have a trump card. The semi-secret location. We can establish the connection between Guanyin and Curzon that way."

"True, but connection isn't identity. And unless it links to the murder in Princes Street, we've got nothing."

They stopped walking. "In that case we're at a dead-end," Mordred said.

"Not necessarily. We need to stop looking at it as a murder."

"But isn't that what it is?"

"If you're right," Fleming said, "and my instinct tells me you are, we're missing the bigger picture. There's something here that dwarfs the murder. Something important enough to kill Curzon for, and fraudulently re-stage his killing in Venezuela. Important enough for the IMF to run scared. What's in Venezuela?"

"Oil."

"The IMF doesn't need oil," Fleming replied. "And in any case, oil's cheap as chips nowadays."

"Maybe it's just a good place to hide bad news. A corrupt leadership, a restless population, a proliferation of criminal gangs. For all its faults, the government in Caracas needn't necessarily be in on it."

"Whatever it is, that's what we should be investigating."

Mordred laughed. "I don't think so."

"Er, pardon?"

"It's been an interesting discussion, and I'm flattered that your instinct tells you I'm right – I mean that sincerely – but I think, given that we're roughly agreed, it's time for both of us to walk speedily away and not look back. Put it this way," he went on, noting Fleming's aggrieved expression, but also his speechlessness: "we're not in a film. In a film, two heroic but otherwise average Joes would combine to defeat overwhelming odds. But in real life, *overwhelming odds* aren't called that for no reason. They're called that because they win ninety-nine out of every hundred battles. Statistically, therefore, there's every reason to think they'll win this one, especially since we don't really know what we're up against. Think about it, and imitate what I'm doing right now. Because I'm asking myself, what will happen when I'm killed? Well, first of all, my sister will go into Sherlock Holmes mode, then she'll be killed. My girlfriend might well do the same, only more skilfully, and she'll be killed. Your wife too: she'll be killed. She works for White Department, and she's highly unlikely to take your death lying down. If it was just me and you, I might well say, fine, let's be Batman and Robin. But it isn't. The great thing is, it probably *is* bigger than us. Much, much bigger. And that would mean it can afford to discount us. If we stop now, and make ourselves amenable, it'll forget we irritated it, and we should be safe. Which means, we preserve the lives of those others."

Fleming ground his teeth and sighed. "I get what you mean, but I already know this is one of those look-in-the-mirror-without-feeling-contempt-for-the-rest-of-your-life affairs. They don't come along very often. Some people probably never encounter one. But you recognise one when you see it. Or I do."

"Rubbish."

Fleming did a double take. "I beg your pardon?"

"Why? Only because you've made it like that. It doesn't have to be that way. It's just a melodramatic story you've told yourself."

"Don't you want to get to the bottom of all this? Don't you think truth itself imposes a categorical duty on us to uncover it?"

"I already know the truth. The people at the top are nearly all crooks. You can't fight them all the time. There are too many, and they're too powerful."

"I can't believe what I'm hearing. My wife told me you were an idealist!"

"While she was telling you that, did she also say, *Listen, Nicholas, it's perfectly okay for you to condemn me to death, in my absence, in the course of a long conversation one gloomy after-noon in Hyde Park with said idealist?*"

"Well, if she - "

"*Because so long as the idealist's pursuing his ideals, I don't actually care whether I live or die?*"

"Well, if she - "

"*I don't EVEN care if I'm kept uninformed, and, by the way, it's irrelevant that I'm also a mother, and you're a father, and our children haven't been asked either.*"

"Well, if she - "

"*Or that said idealist's sister and girlfriend will be killed, and his family, and ours, will be cast into unimaginable grief.*"

Silence.

"Have you quite finished?" Fleming asked darkly after a moment.

"*Because, hey, that's what idealism is,*" Mordred said. "There, I'm finished. I hope you've now got some perspective. And I'd just like to commend your wife for her very sensible contribution. *Thank you, John, I did my best.* Your husband's a very stubborn man, though, he probably won't listen. *Oh, I KNOW he's stubborn. You should try being married to him.* No, thanks."

Fleming turned on his heel and strode away.

Yet Mordred could tell he was conflicted. He knew Mordred had a point, only he couldn't shake the notion that he was under a strict moral obligation to something called 'The Truth'. A fundamentalist, really. But letting him go off alone was almost as bad as joining him. Either way, he was probably marching to annihilation. He ran and caught up with him.

"It doesn't have to be all or nothing," he said.

"I can see you're right," Fleming replied quietly. "I'm not stalking off in a childish huff. I just need to think. From here on in, anything I do, I'll do alone. You're right: there's no reason for you and yours to be caught in the fallout. Or mine - so I may do nothing. You're pretty persuasive, I'll give you that."

"Thank you. Listen, it doesn't have to be just us two. Red Department specialises in this sort of thing. So how about I take it to Ruby Parker and make the most impassioned plea of my professional career? Assuming I succeed, then at least whatever happens next, we're backed by a proficient organisation. And it might well follow your agenda without totally exposing us two on its front line."

Fleming looked like he'd just had an unexpected piece of good news. "Yes… Yes, I hadn't considered that."

"Give me seventy-two hours. I can meet you back here on Monday. Say one o'clock, the Serpentine Bar again? Until then, I need you to behave at work as if nothing's happened. No making yourself obstructive. Obey the boss with a smile and a song."

"I'll settle for that," Fleming said. He smiled and nodded, as if still unable to believe that something credible had been proposed. "Good luck."

They parted in opposite directions. As he walked back towards the Wellington Arch, Mordred noticed a lone figure, way over on the other side of the park, watching them through binoculars. When Mordred caught sight of him, he turned and walked hurriedly away.

In less than a second, he'd gone.

Chapter 23: Gloomy is Sunday

Mordred took the bus home. The man with the binoculars had spooked him, enough to worry about whether Fleming was somehow leading him up the garden path; towards something so fearsome that it tried to eliminate anything that even suspected its existence.

On the other hand, it could just have been a perfectly innocent man with a completely innocuous pair of binoculars. A bird-watcher, perhaps.

But there were better places to watch birds than Hyde Park. And in any case, you knew when someone was looking directly at you, didn't you? Scientists might dismiss it, but you had a sixth sense. You *knew*.

On the other hand, what would be the point? If Mr X wanted to check whether Nicholas Fleming was meeting John Mordred in Hyde Park, Mr X could just jog over and have a look. And what could Mr X possibly gain, without some sort of transcript of their conversation?

Which brought Mordred back to the possibility that maybe Fleming was a kind of double-agent. Or maybe he was wearing some sort of wire on his clothes, and didn't even know it. They could make them that tiny nowadays. And he dressed pretty formally, so lots of folds and creases for miniature devices to fit into.

His demeanour hadn't been shifty. That was important.

No, he was no kind of double-agent, not even the modern kind, working for the same country, different organisations, or even for different levels within the same setup. Oh, the world had become exponentially complex since the end of the Cold War. What you wouldn't give sometimes for the old Soviet-West thing. Halcyon days, spy-wise.

He looked out of the bus window. Two seagulls on the pavement alternately pecking a leftover sandwich like they were having a game. A man sitting on the edge of a bench, smoking a cheroot. A teenage boy on a bike several sizes too small for him.

Going in to see Ruby Parker tomorrow would achieve two things. He'd get her help, but he might also gain admittance to the investigation. It was pretty clear Phyllis, Alec, Annabel and Tariq had seen something singular last night. He wanted to know what it was. And he had a lot to offer.

Not that he had much choice as to whether to hand his findings over. His job was his job. It involved keeping secrets, but not from his employers. Once he sat down in Ruby Parker's office, it would have to come out, all of it. He needed her far more than she needed him.

On the other hand, he also knew Phyllis, Alec, Annabel and Tariq had seen something. Even alone, it might not take him long to work out what. And the fact that he'd been attacked by men in griffin masks didn't mean he was involved *personally*. Far from it. He could make a good case for being included in their plans from here on.

He'd need to rehearse his arguments, put an effective spin on it. Yes, he'd have to explain Hannah's part in it, but they probably wouldn't suspect her of anything. They already knew she was a bit of a communist revolutionary, after all. The harmless British type.

Everything considered then, lots of reasons to feel positive. And at least he'd used his sickness leave to do something useful, track down a gang of griffin-mask wearing murderers, not just sit on his bum watching Netflix and BBC iPlayer.

Like he probably should have done. Like anyone normal would have.

The bus turned a corner. All four passengers lurched slightly to the left, then righted as if nothing had happened. Someone stood up and nonchalantly pressed the bell to alight.

The rest of Sunday was going to be hell. Hanging around waiting for Monday to come, just sitting on his hands doing zilch because he probably couldn't concentrate on anything like a book or a magazine, or even TV. Tragically, he'd already done all the housework, so there wasn't even that to fall back on. He'd find himself counting the hours, minutes, seconds. Not that he'd be bored. He wouldn't. He'd be in limbo. He'd probably find himself watching *Songs of Praise* at some point. Then there was the 4-6pm graveyard double-hour, when you were neither at home nor at work, but somehow in the worst of both, sad, sticky and slow as a snail.

It mightn't have been so bad, but he didn't have anyone he could talk to. Alec, Annabel, Tariq and Phyllis were out of bounds. His mum would be better than okay, but she thought he was in America.

It was raining when he disembarked in Islington. Of course it was. He hadn't brought an umbrella, so he simply raised his shoulders, lowered his head and thrust his hands in his trouser pockets. He didn't care if he was being followed any more. Let them watch him if they wanted to, the morons.

He'd do something he'd never done before when he got in. Pour himself a rum. That bottle Annabel and Tariq had given him, at the back of the cupboard, hardly touched.

No, he wouldn't. Stupid idea.

What had Fleming been thinking, wearing that suit? If ever anything was going to make you conspicuous on a Sunday afternoon in Hyde Park, it was flaunting an expensive wardrobe. Idiot.

Or maybe he'd wanted to be seen.

Been through all that, though. Fleming *wasn't* an idiot, and he wasn't working for anyone other than himself. He had to stop thinking about it. He was home now. He keyed in the code for the block, went upstairs and let himself into his flat.

Be nice if there was a dog here. One like Buster, only less sadistic.

Instead of just silence.

He switched the TV on and made himself tea. Nothing on Freeview. He went to Netflix and watched *Jerry Before Seinfeld*.

Time passed, then more time, then a bit more time. Suddenly, it was 6pm: dinner. He warmed himself a can of mushroom soup in his microwave and ate it with a wholemeal baguette. How long till he could reasonably turn in for bed? He hadn't even mentally rehearsed his interview with Ruby Parker yet. Saving it for when he got *really* bored, maybe.

Washing the bowl and the plate and the spoon was almost crushingly daunting, but eventually he did it. He dried them and put them away. He wiped the draining board down. He laid the tea-towel flat on the unit to dry. A tiny glow of satisfaction.

He went to the back of the cupboard, found the rum and poured himself a glass. He'd sit back on the sofa, and drink it like he was an elderly gentleman.

It suddenly occurred to him: St Mary Magdalene Church, just down the road. He could go to Evensong. Why hadn't he thought of that before?

Too late now, probably. And it was still raining. And he'd just poured himself a rum.

Why had Fleming worn a suit? Idiot.

He sat down and switched the TV on. The news. He was about to switch over when he noticed Mansion House in the background. In the foreground, a woman of about forty in a raincoat stood talking to the camera. She looked concerned, but then they always did unless it was some sort of Royal anniversary, when they looked jaunty. He switched it up.

"… is the latest in a growing list of businesses with voting interests in the City of London Corporation to strongly distance itself from the Lord Mayor's remarks, following yesterday evening's claim by Eric Shambles, the CEO of hedge fund Ritchie-Magnus, that the 'so-called press conference' had brought the Mayoral office into 'disrepute'. Lord Agnolis today called it 'exceptionally ill advised' and called on the Secretary of State for International Trade, Charles McMahon, to make a statement censuring Viscount Greysonwell and – I quote - 'encouraging his resignation.' Rita Sivakaran, the Under-Secretary of State for Small Business, Consumers and Corporate Responsibility, described the Lord Mayor's 'irresponsible antics' as a potential catastrophe for the City of London 'at a time when it needs all its reserves of strength to weather the storms of Brexit.'

"There have also been sympathetic voices, though. *Coronation Street*'s Ada Pullman was at the Lord Mayor's party just two nights ago, and is a long-time personal friend."

The screen cut to a pre-recorded clip of a young actress. In the background, a poster for *Oh! What a Lovely War*, and slow-moving couples in evening wear. "People are being far too hard on him," Ada said over a dull conversational roar. "I think anyone can see it wasn't a stunt. He needs to know he's got people's love and support, and that he *can* get through this, whatever it is. And by the way, I think *lots* of us have been somewhere similar in the past. It's okay to be upfront about it nowadays. Pressure's partly what it is. Anyway, he's got lots of friends who don't care a fig about the City and its stuffed suits. We're all there for him."

"What do you think about his claim that he's seen aliens?" the presenter, off screen, asked.

Ada frowned, as if it was a stupid question. "I wouldn't know. I don't prejudge these things. Like I just said, anyone can see it wasn't a stunt."

Cut back to the TV studio. The anchor, an old man called Alan Ferdew, spoke genially. "He is an incredibly popular character outside the City, though, isn't he, Nura? Ordinary Londoners seem to have taken to him in a way previously unseen. And many people would argue that 'Lord Mayor of London' is a title with no political weight nowadays, merely a cosmetic one."

"He has been, and is, very popular with some people," Nura said. "But as Lord Agnolis said, he's not so popular with the residents and businesses of the Square Mile, whose livelihood his conduct directly affects. As for his office being purely ceremonial, as some do indeed claim, I think the extent of the political fallout in the last twenty-four hours very much shows otherwise."

"What about these rumours that the Lord Mayor himself, Viscount Greysonwell, can't be found? That he disappeared after last night's events, and possibly as a direct result of them?"

"It could just be he's lying very low, Alan, taking stock of the situation. Obviously we've heard nothing official to contradict that, otherwise we wouldn't be talking of 'rumours', but you're right: there have been persistent off-the-record reports that he left Guildhall alone immediately after last night's press gathering, and hasn't been seen since."

"Thank you, Nura."

Nura disappeared and Alan turned sombrely to face the camera. "Nura Hussain reporting. We'll come back to that story later, and of course there'll be regular updates on our website. Now, Hurricane Brian - "

Mordred switched channels to YouTube, and did a quick search. The entire press conference had been posted. *4.6M views. 1 day ago.* My God, how come he was only just hearing about it? How could it have gone on for an entire day without him picking up on it?

Irrelevant right now. Presumably, he'd been thinking too hard about things he believed had no chance of making the news, and he'd wanted to screen out all distractions. He'd done it before.

He watched the press conference with increasing incredulity. Bloody hell, here was a man who was seriously ill. Ada Pullman was right: he definitely wasn't faking it.

How could it be Henry Greysonwell, though? Greysonwell wasn't supposed to be like that! The media portrayed him as a hell-raiser, a kind of cross between Lord Byron and Liam Gallagher. This couldn't be the same man, could it?

It obviously was.

Was *this* why Phyllis & co. had been forbidden to speak to him? Maybe he'd been on the wrong track all along. Perhaps it had nothing whatsoever to do with griffin masks. Something like Greysonwell's 'press conference' – the bigwigs were right: you couldn't really dignify it with that sort of term – was a political event, with potentially significant repercussions. Obviously, assuming some sort of advance notice, every step would have been taken to hush it up before it happened, presumably in the hope that it might be averted.

Poor Greysonwell. Maybe he really *had* seen aliens. Perhaps the world really was full of them. The universe was so big that it permitted of virtually every conceivable possibility, including beings who'd overcome the limitations of 21st century science, and who'd scanned their entire sky for signs of life using who-knew-what instruments. Then come here. Then stayed here. It wasn't impossible.

But of course you were a crank if you thought like that. Proof, if any, that modern secularism wasn't about reason, only about shoring up the cheesy contemporary version of common sense: an unimaginative, this-world-is-all-there-is dogma. The triumph of urbanity, in a word. *We're only thinking animals, we're alone in the universe, there are no higher beings, there's no higher reality, and any denial of all that is cowardice.* The ability to produce the suave impression of knowing all answers, especially to metaphysical questions; never being surprised by anything, because anything too surprising was rubbish. Achilles at cocktail parties.

He was surprised at how angry he'd become. He wished he'd gone to Greysonwell's party now, instead of running Hannah's errand. He could have done the errand another time: deliberately missed his plane to America, and caught another a day later. He and Greysonwell were probably two of a kind, deep down.

What now for his tomorrow morning interview with Ruby Parker? Things weren't quite what they'd originally seemed. She might completely wrong-foot him.

But so what if she did? He didn't have any choice in the matter. Caught between Fleming and his sister, a rock and a hard place.

He still had another week of sickness leave. He could use it to track Greysonwell down, or if he reappeared, try and get an interview with him. Maybe Greysonwell knew more than he was letting on.

He was tired now. Sleep probably wouldn't come, though, not with all this hard thinking at 100mph about Greysonwell; and alongside him, Fleming; and alongside him, Hannah; and alongside her, Phyllis and Ruby Parker. Too many permutations.

He made himself a cup of Ovaltine and watched Newcastle versus Southampton on YouTube. He wasn't much of a football fan, not like most men he knew, but it passed the time. Everything was always identical, and at the end, the commentators always spotted the same problems and praised the same moves. A bit like going to the local pub, really, or attending a church service: comfort in stasis.

He undressed, got in bed, switched off the lights, and, once his eyes had got used to the darkness, lay staring at the ceiling for an hour. He got up, switched on the light and re-trieved his e-reader from his bedside drawer. Battery still at 50%, should be okay for several hours yet. *The Magnificent but Slightly Dubious Adventures of Mavis Coldbeam Hackett.* Page 4.

Ten minutes later, he put it back in the drawer and got down again. He fell asleep almost immediately.

Five men, all in masks, shouting encouragement to each other. They herded the guy they were chasing into Princes Street. It was super dark down there, and completely deser-ted. Their voices gave them away. They were intent on murder.

Mordred was coming to the rescue like he was flying. He came up behind the slowest chaser, grabbed his collar and yanked him off his feet. He removed his griffin mask and went to punch him in the face.

Then everything slowed down. Out of the corner of his eye, he saw his fist coming. But the centre of his field of vis-ion was entirely focussed on the confused face of the man he was about to hit.

He woke up and sat up simultaneously.

Good God. He'd seen that face before! Recently!

He swung his feet over the side of the bed and switched the light on. He wrapped a dressing gown round himself, went into the living room and switched the TV on. YouTube again, Greysonwell's press conference. Fast forward.

His pulse sped up. Good God, there he was, sitting in the background. Mid-twenties, jet black hair, Roman nose, large blue eyes. That was the man he'd punched. He was sure.

He put his head in his hands. No, of course he wasn't sure. He couldn't be. *Feeling* sure and *being* sure weren't the same thing. An alternative explanation might be that he'd subliminally registered this man's face while watching the YouTube video first time round, and it had re-surfaced in his dream, somehow pasted, by his subconscious, onto the face of the masked man.

But why *that* face?

And when you looked behind Greysonwell, what did you see? Five men and a rather older woman. *Five* men. Who looked to be exactly the same build as those in the CCTV.

Too much of a coincidence? Maybe not. Perhaps it was that number – five – that his subconscious had picked up on, which in turn had given it the bright idea of copying and pasting into his dream.

Bloody hell, his head was spinning.

But hang on a minute.

It didn't actually matter that he couldn't make a positive identification. He had a *might be,* which was more than he'd had a few hours ago. The important thing was, he couldn't rule it out.

Now for Facebook, Twitter et al.

He began with Ada Pullman's page. Lots of *Coronation Street* posts, but also, as he suspected, lots of tagged photos of the Lord Mayor's party. Lots of links to other guests.

An hour later, he knew the names, and something of the backgrounds of all five men, and he'd seen enough photos of circles on pavements outside Mansion House – posted by sympathetic well-wishers - to last him a lifetime.

Now he really did have something to go to Ruby Parker with. Something he didn't even have to show if his hand collapsed in the first round of play. For the first time in a while, he felt vaguely back in control.

Time to call Fleming again.

Chapter 24: McFarlane ('Sir')

Monday morning, 7am. Meadows got up, washed and dressed casually in a T-shirt, hoodie and jeans, and set off from the Lord Mayor's official residence to do as he'd resolved on Saturday afternoon: stake out Thames House with a view to seeing Phyllis enter. Check she really did work there, for a start. It was possible her desk was actually in the MI6 building on the other side of the river, but he didn't think so. He'd posted Hilldy and Raymond outside, just on the off chance. Paul and Michael were keeping watch in Whitehall, on the remote possibility that she was some kind of intelligence advisor with a more conventional political brief. It wasn't inconceivable, after all, that one or two MP's would want to keep an eye on Greysonwell.

He'd found a lot out about 'John'. Or rather, *John*, because that really was his name. In a way, he was actually a tad famous. The brother of Hannah Lexingwood, the manager of Fully Magic Coal Tar Lounge, and one of the richest women in the UK. He'd been mixed up with the radical politician, Chapman Hill, a few years ago, although personally, not professionally, because his other sister, Julia, a novelist, had been seeing him. All in all, he'd led a complex and colourful life, and he was still only thirty-two. No wonder Greysonwell, Viscount Henry Boring, wanted to meet him. The interest-value might rub off.

Running away from home was about the most exciting thing Greysonwell had ever done. Still now, no one had any idea where he'd gone, which was - whatever else you might say about it - at least sustaining the excitement. All he had to do now was pilot a UFO over Trafalgar Square, waving his arms in the cockpit and yelling, 'I told you so!', and the performance would be complete. Last him a lifetime. Need never do anything interesting again.

Meadows arrived at Thames House at 7.30 and sat down, with a few sandwiches, in the little strip of parkland facing the river, directly in front of the building. He was prepared to wait a long time. Most of the day, at least. First, he wanted to see Phyllis come in, then he wanted to see her leave. He'd arranged for a PI to meet him here at 4.30pm, just in case she did try to shake him off.

He wasn't worried that this was supposed to be the headquarters of British intelligence, and that someone might emerge to shoo him away. The way spies worked nowadays, they probably never looked out of their own front windows. They spent all their time peering into monitors. In any case, if they didn't want people sitting here, they shouldn't have installed a strip of parkland and a row of benches. It was their fault, and he had his rights.

At 8.40 he saw what he was looking for. A taxi pulled up at the entrance and Phyllis got out. Meadows removed his phone from his pocket and sent the agreed code message to his four friends. *The Eagle has landed.*

Phyllis climbed the few steps to Thames House and entered through its heavy front door. As always, Colin, the chief receptionist, stood behind his desk as if he was on guard, stomach out, ears akimbo, as Alec liked to say. Yet something was wrong. She felt it as soon as they made eye-contact. Some days – bad days, mostly - he was like a barometer.

It'd be pointless asking him, though. Even though he adored her, the question would only embarrass him. He'd be forced into an explanation of how he wasn't allowed to say anything.

Best pretend she hadn't noticed. "Morning, Colin," she said, as cheerily as she could.

He smiled. "Good morning, Phyllis."

Whatever it was, perhaps it wasn't too bad. Not as bad as she'd originally thought. Or if it was, he didn't care that much. She signed the register and went upstairs to her workstation. The place was about three-quarters full. Early birds looking comfortably immersed in work. She switched on her PC. Alec was already here in a suit, looking grimly at his own monitor, five desks away. When he saw her, he got up and came over.

"Urgent meeting's been called at nine on the dot," he said. "Check to see you've been invited, would you?"

"Urgent? About what?"

"I don't know. If you have been invited, and Annabel and Tariq have – they're not in yet – I think we can all assume we're in for another Q&A about Greysonwell."

She had a new notification in the top right corner of her monitor. Yes, she was to attend a meeting a nine sharp: Seminar Room H4, top floor. No indication as to the sender, but it had to be Ruby Parker.

"I'm in," she told him. "I suppose it figures. They still haven't found Greysonwell, from what I heard on the news."

"Although of course you didn't hear that announced explicitly, because there's been no 'official' word."

"I wonder if we'll be sent out to look for him."

"I doubt it. That's a job for the police. More likely, we'll be expected to make ourselves available for interview. Or the police might actually be there, in the meeting. Any word from Mordred, incidentally?"

"I can't remember whether I told you: he's not going to America now."

"Bloody hell. You don't think he's going to do a little poking round on his own account, do you? You know what he's like."

"America was cancelled before Greysonwell's press conference. I haven't seen him since before the party, when you did. After Saturday's meeting here, I told him I'd been commanded to keep schtum. I spent the weekend at my parents' house in Donnington."

"That's a bit drastic, isn't it? What did you think he'd do? Tie you to a chair and apply the thumbscrews?"

"It was arranged before all that, dummy. No, thankfully, we're one of those couples that's capable of posting a 'Do Not Broach' notice on a subject and respecting it."

"Still, best be on the safe side, eh? As in, putting fifty odd miles between you and your beloved."

"I've told you. It was coincidental."

"Okay, but are you saying he didn't even call you after the press conference? I would have."

"No, he didn't. And maybe he actually *is* 'poking around', I don't know. My brief was not to speak to him about the party, which I haven't. It wasn't to babysit him, stop him getting into trouble. I love him, but he's an adult."

Alec laughed. "Good luck with that."

Annabel and Tariq arrived at 8.55. Annabel looked at her computer, exchanged ominous glances with her husband. They began drifting towards the meeting. Better follow them. Phyllis saved her work, logged off and got to her feet.

Alec arrived and they took the lift. They didn't speak on the way to the top floor. When they entered H4, a tall, well-groomed man of about forty with a fashionable close-shaved beard, swept back hair and a suit occupied a chair, clearly waiting to meet them. He stood up without introducing himself, and invited them to sit down. He closed the door and went to stand at the front of the room.

"Good morning, everyone," he said. "I'm Jeff McFarlane. I'm standing in for Ruby Parker for a week or so, just until she gets back into work. She was the victim of a minor hit and run while crossing the road in Brixton, last night.

Broken ankle, but it could have been much worse. Before you ask, the police are treating it as a top priority."

Minor shockwaves spread out and passed by. Annabel was the first to speak. She said what they were all thinking. "Could it have been directed at her... in her professional capacity?"

"Currently, we think not," McFarlane replied. "Obviously, we're not ruling that out, though, which is why the Met have been instructed to give it top billing. Normally, when it's an attack by a foreign government, there are warning signs in advance. She personally doesn't think we should read anything into it. Which is irrelevant, of course. We're leaving no stone unturned."

They nodded. What to say? And where on earth had 'Jeff McFarlane' come from? Phyllis had certainly never seen or heard of him before.

"You're probably wondering about my background," McFarlane said, apparently reading her thoughts. "I'm not allowed to divulge any details of that, I'm afraid. Once Ms Parker returns, I'll be gone." He grinned in the manner of someone about to launch a witticism. "Believe me, I wouldn't be here, in Thames House, talking to you now, unless I had full authority. You're just going to have to trust me. Because you have no choice. I'd like us all to have a formal relationship from now on. I'll be *Mr* McFarlane, or 'sir'. I'll call you by your surnames. Don't worry, I already know them."

They smiled politely, but no one said anything. Phyllis already disliked him, just a little. Perhaps she'd get used to him.

"I'm fully authorised to take charge of every aspect of Red for seven days at least," he went on airily. "To begin with, in the light of what's happened since Saturday morning, I'm to de-brief you again about the Lord Mayor's party. And I'm afraid I'm going to have to ask you to stay in the building until the police have interviewed you. It'll be much more convenient, and vastly preferable security-wise, if they can see you here, rather than meeting you in four different, possibly widely-dispersed locations."

They all nodded.

"Item two on the agenda," McFarlane went on. "John Mordred. Where is he today?"

"On leave, sir," Annabel said.

"I haven't yet got fully up to speed," McFarlane replied. "He'll need to be recalled. I can't go into the details, but we've an overseas situation that urgently requires his presence."

"Did Ruby Parker authorise it?" Alec asked. "Sir."

"That's none of your business," McFarlane said gently. "I simply need to know where to contact him."

"You need to call Esther in admin," Phyllis said. "Sir."

McFarlane grimaced. "I was given to understand *you* might be able to get him on the phone. He is a friend of yours, isn't he?"

"I'm not entitled to give him orders, sir," Phyllis replied. "And if I was to put you on the phone, he probably wouldn't acknowledge your authority. He'd have no reason to. As you've already said, it's premised on your being here, in Thames House, talking to us."

"Very clever," McFarlane said. "Fine. Tell me about your enjoyable night out at the Lord Mayor's official residence, then go and sit at your desks, do whatever you normally do for a while, and await further instructions."

They took it in turns to recount their versions of events again, beginning with Alec. McFarlane asked no questions, didn't take notes, and his face registered no emotion, not even when Alec told him he'd been knocked unconscious.

"As I've already intimated, the police will want to speak to you today," he said when they'd finished speaking. "Well, that'll be all. Dismissed."

They scraped their chairs back and exited in silence. They got in the lift. They exchanged wide-eyed looks. They still didn't say anything. Annabel, Phyllis and Alec returned to their desks, Tariq continued down to the basement and the IT hub.

Two hours later, Annabel, Phyllis and Alec met up in the canteen for tea and a Chelsea bun. Tariq had to leave the building for an hour on a software-related errand. He called Annabel to say he'd reconnoitre with them at lunch, share thoughts about the new boss.

"Like David Davis at a Brexit meeting," Alec said. "I particularly admired his complete lack of interest in anything we had to say."

"I'm much more concerned that he wants to send John abroad," Phyllis said. "Ruby Parker never mentioned anything on Saturday."

"That's the nature of international relations," Alec said. "Things just come up. They're not usually in the habit of giving advance notice. McFarlane – sorry, 'sir' – is definitely a creep, but not necessarily an evil one. We're not in *Tinker, Tailor*."

"We don't know that," Phyllis said.

Annabel took a sip of her tea. "You're letting emotion get the better of you, Phyllis. John's a languages expert, reputedly the best MI7's ever had. What could be more natural than an overseas positing, even if it's at short notice and interrupts his leave?"

"I simply don't trust McFarlane," Phyllis said.

"That's completely irrational," Alec said. "Annabel's right: you're succumbing to emotion."

"As 'sir' correctly pointed out," Annabel added, "he wouldn't be here, in Thames House, with us, unless he had full authority. It's not for us to question the legitimacy of that, however much we might want to. And, as a matter of fact, I agree with you, Alec: he's unpleasant."

As usual, Annabel could see things clearly. And she was right, of course.

"I wonder how Ruby Parker's getting on?" Alec said, in obvious attempt to change the subject.

No one replied. In any normal workplace, they'd have clubbed together to buy her a Get Well card, and deputed someone to take it round to her house with some flowers. But you didn't do that sort of thing here, not where your superiors were concerned: any knowledge of where they actually lived, or what their non-work hours involved, was likely to be perceived as inessential at best, then intrusive, and at worst, exposing both you and them to a level of risk above and beyond all the usual hazards in this job. In some ways, it was probably the most frustrating workplace in the world.

Tariq appeared in the canteen doorway, looking confused. He gave them a little wave and came to sit next to Annabel.

"What would you like, Taz?" Alec asked him. "Tea or coffee or American cream soda? I'm paying."

"I thought you were going out for an hour," Annabel said, without concern. "What happened?"

"I didn't know they did American cream soda here," Tariq said.

"Mordred asked for it," Alec replied, as if he didn't necessarily disapprove. "You know how the kitchen staff are with him."

"How they love to mother him," Annabel added drily. Another cuttingly accurate observation.

"I wasn't allowed out of the building," Tariq said, finally answering his wife's question.

She put her teacup in the saucer. "Er, pardon?"

"I'm not joking," he said. He leaned forward conspiratorially. "Two bouncers. Colin says they arrived about an hour ago. They've got specific instructions to stop us four –

just us! – leaving the building. According to Colin, our detention's covered by the COL1 form we signed a few weeks ago. In other words, MI7's legally entitled to hold us here. The bouncers are just an added level of insurance."

Annabel frowned. "And yet, the first thing you do when you sit down is get into a conversation with Alec about American cream soda?"

"I'm in minor shock," Tariq said. "Sorry, I didn't know how to break it to you. I wasn't even sure you'd believe me. Do you think we're under suspicion of something? McFarlane talked about us having to wait for the police, earlier."

"I think we'd better go and see him pronto," Phyllis said. "Find out exactly what's going on."

"I don't think we'll be able to," Tariq said. "He left the building when I was down there. Completely ignored me, even though I was standing right by him. Told Colin he wouldn't be back till tomorrow morning."

"Tomorrow morning?" Alec said.

They all looked at each other. Phyllis had her phone out. "Hello, Colin. Yes, Phyllis Robinson here. Could you just confirm something for me, please? Has Ruby Parker's replacement left the building? ... McFarlane, that's right. He has. And is it correct that Alec, Annabel, Tariq and I are forbidden to leave, on pain of legal penalties?" She looked at her colleagues. "That's also correct. Yes, thank you. You've no idea why? ... No, of course not, I wouldn't expect you to. It's just that Mr McFarlane met with us this morning at nine, and he didn't mention anything about it... You've no idea, I suppose, when it's due to end? ... So it could go through into tomorrow? Thank you, yes, you've been very helpful." She hung up and let out an indignant laugh. "Well, it looks like we could be spending tonight in the basement pods! And possibly tomorrow too!"

"I don't understand," Alec said. "Why would they do that?"

"Who are 'they'?" Annabel asked.

Alec shrugged. He looked like he was surprised by what he was about to divulge. "I don't know," he said. "But I bet they listened to that phone call you just made."

"I'm beginning to realise what may have happened," Phyllis said. She gestured for them to move closer to each other, so she could lower her voice a few notches. "John."

"I'm not sure I follow," Annabel said after a beat.

"You mean you agree with *me* for once," Alec said. "Yes, that would explain a lot. It would explain, for example, the sudden desire to send him abroad." He turned to Annabel. "When I first came in this morning, I had a short conversation with Phyllis. It turns out John hasn't gone to America, like he planned. And she hasn't heard from him all weekend."

"In his defence, I told him I couldn't speak about the party," Phyllis said. "And I did go straight from here to my parents' on Saturday, and didn't get back till late last night."

"That doesn't mean anything," Annabel said. "He loves you. He'd have called to say goodnight, at least. You're saying he didn't?"

"We don't necessarily do that sort of thing," Phyllis said. "Sometimes we go to bed at different times. But I know what you mean. No, I didn't hear from him at all. I was so busy enjoying my family's company, so to speak, I didn't think of it as odd."

"My theory is he's already investigating everything pertaining to Greysonwell," Alec said. "I suggested it only semi-seriously to begin with, but it would explain why they're treating us so oddly. The bouncers are there not just to stop us leaving, but to stop him getting in. They want to prevent us from teaming up with him."

"They won't be there to stop him getting in," Phyllis argued. "No one's *expecting* him to come in. If anyone was, they'd have instructed the bouncers to detain him on sight." She took out her phone again. "Colin, hi, it's me, Phyllis, again. Sorry to keep on about it, but I understand there are some *men* on the door, posted to prevent us leaving?... No, no, I know it wasn't your idea! No need to apologise. I know that. That's not why I'm calling. I simply want to ask, what about John? He's not due to finish his leave … Oh… Wow, right. That's very interesting… Gosh… And they didn't do anything? ... I see, I see. That *is* interesting. Well, I never! Thank you."

She hung up. "John's been in. Don't ask me why, I don't know, and no one was expecting him. He asked to see Ruby Parker. Colin shooed him away without letting anyone know who he was. The bouncers didn't twig. They can't have been properly briefed."

"When was this?" Tariq asked.

"About an hour ago," Phyllis replied.

"He must have discovered something," Alec said.

Phyllis spread her hands. "About *what*? What's even supposed to be going *on*? What the hell are we being imprisoned for? Has *anyone* here any idea?"

No one did, except that it had something to do with Greysonwell, it was huge, and it was probably the reason Ruby Parker had been run down.

"The obvious thing to do now would be to call John," Annabel said. "Only I very much doubt you'll get hold of him. Remember how eager McFarlane was for you to ring him. That probably means he made an attempt, but couldn't get a connection."

"Try," Alec said.

"But if they're listening in to our communications?" Tariq said. "Mind you, they've probably accessed all our phones, looked in every possible contacts list."

"Isn't that your territory, Tariq?" Phyllis asked. "You are our IT manager."

"GCHQ trumps me big time, every time," Tariq said. "Especially something like this. I'm more of a network manager with frills. Sorry to disappoint."

"Try ringing John," Alec told Phyllis again. "If you don't, I will. But it'd be better coming from his girlfriend."

"I've suddenly had a terrifying thought," Annabel said. They turned to look at her. She was paler than usual. "Maybe there really *are* aliens. Maybe that's what all this is about. Think about it: what's *your* theory?"

They looked incredulously at her, then seemed to wake up. She was right. At least, provisionally. Insane though it sounded, right now it was the best explanation in town.

Phyllis called John, took the phone from her ear and looked at it like it was playing up. "Straight to bloody voicemail," she told everyone. She put her elbows on the table and pressed her fingertips hard into her forehead. Suddenly she was really worried. "Now what?"

"We've been in the canteen far too long," Alec said. "We're probably beginning to look suspicious. By that, I mean: as if we're hatching a conspiracy."

"I've just remembered something," Annabel said. "We haven't been formally told that we're subject to a COL1 ruling. If MI7 wants to keep us here as a consequence of our being signatories to that form, it has to inform us through the proper channels in an officially minuted meeting."

"Hang on," Alec said. "You actually read the *small print?*"

She looked at him as if he was an idiot. "Of course. Didn't you?"

"No," he said. "I'd just heard that Ian had died."

"Lucky for you I kept a level head then," she replied, "in spite of my grief. Or are you trying to imply that I somehow didn't care about Ian as much as you? Because I did."

"I'm sorry, I didn't mean that at all," he said, cowed. "I apologise."

"Accepted. The upshot is that, since we haven't been informed in the appropriate manner, we're free to leave whenever we want to, and if those bouncers try to use force to restrain us, we could sue for assault. Presently, the law's entirely on our side. Added to which, we're up against a couple of men who, for all their apparent brawn, probably can't fight their way out of a paper bag."

"How long before they realise they haven't quite locked and bolted the escape hatch?" Alec. "Because my advice is, we get moving asap."

"And go where?" Annabel said. "John's probably long gone. He could be anywhere at all now. And without him, we might as well be here."

Silence. They looked at each other. They were trapped again, this time by the utter lack of a plan. Hell, they didn't even know what was going on, let alone how to talk tactics.

Phyllis's phone rang. She looked at it blankly, lying on the table next to her elbow. *Unknown caller.* She looked at the others. Fear. Somehow, no one thought it would be a call centre. She put it on speakerphone, turned the volume down and picked up. "Phyllis Robinson."

Mordred's voice. "Are you alone?"

Her phone was probably being tapped. Best stick to the formalities. "John, where *are* you? We've an acting head, and he's keen for you to join an investigation abroad, exact location unspecified."

"Effective immediately, I suppose?"

"That's what he implied."

"I'll be quick then. I'm in trouble and I need your help. But you don't have to. It's probably a job loser - "

"For God's sake, John," she burst out. "Of course, I want to help! Stop being an idiot and get to the point!"

"You're probably being watched. Act as if you don't know, and go and stand on the westbound side of Lambeth

Bridge. I'll meet you there. I need to know everything you know about Greysonwell."

The line went dead.

Annabel put her bag on her shoulder. "I'm coming with you," she said. "Tariq, you go downstairs and carry on as if nothing's happened. No point in us both getting fired. Alec, we need you to act as the fall guy."

Alec's phone beeped. He took it out with a sigh. "Sorry," he said. "BBC news alert." He looked at it sombrely, nodded as if he'd been half-expecting it, and put it back in his pocket.

"Greysonwell's dead," he announced.

Chapter 25: Clash of the Titans

Sunday night, Monday morning Mordred dreamed of the same relatively uninteresting thing over and over: going into Thames House and talking to Ruby Parker. He awoke at 8am, feeling exhausted, even though he'd turned in for bed early. Looking back, Sunday had been a busy day: that meeting with Fleming, then the crushing boredom – always a drain on your short-term vitality – then the sudden discovery of the five guys in the video. Yet progress had definitely been achieved. Today, he'd plug everything into the officially approved channels and stand back and see what happened. He didn't know what that would be, except that he and Fleming wouldn't be alone any more. Knowing Ruby Parker, it wouldn't be nothing.

Ten was when he'd show up at work. Nine was too early: everyone else would be arriving, and there'd be things to catch up on from the weekend. They'd probably begin with a big conflab about Greysonwell, review what they'd already reported on Saturday. The police would probably arrive at some point, to do interviews; or they might do those over at their station on the embankment by Waterloo Bridge, where MI7 had authorised contacts. Either way, if he arrived an hour into the working day, a lot of analysis would have happened. They'd probably realise they were at a loss. His offer of new leads would find receptive ears.

He ate two Weetabix in front of the TV, a morning ritual: he'd never felt remotely sceptical when experts said breakfast was the most important meal of the day, and he'd been an early bird Weetabix-eater since 1991, adding the TV element during his teens. Only at weekends did he vary.

He put on his dark suit and tie – best to look as smart as possible when you were ahead of the game; it augmented your advantage for doubters – and polished his shoes with black *Kiwi*. He looked in the mirror. Disappointing, perhaps, but that was his face, neck and hair, what could he do?

The next step was to make a decision: bus, tube or taxi? The first two were risky. Still impossible to discount the possibility that someone might follow him. Possibly with a view to stopping him arriving. Taxi was probably safest.

Phyllis would be there now. With a little luck, they could lunch together. She could tell him about her parents, he could tell her how he'd missed her. Which he had, notwithstanding the weird excitement/boredom alternation of his weekend.

He arrived at Thames House at 9.55. He was suddenly aware of how much time had passed since he was here last, and experienced an odd sensation of revisiting a life not quite his own. As he walked through the entrance, for example, into the relative gloom of the reception area, Colin didn't look exactly pleased to see him, and the two thick-set men on either side of the doorposts were a completely new addition. He'd probably have got used to them now had he not been off work for seven – *was* it seven? – weeks. Thames House had a smell too. Floor polish. Stale upholstery. He hadn't noticed it before, yet, as his nose now told him, it had always been there. Weird.

He tried to get Colin to smile as he approached, but failed. It would be just like Colin to insist on protocol. *Dear me, no, John, I can't let you in today, you're not down on my list of people I can let in today, no, no, no.* In his faint Edinburgh accent.

"Hi," he said, stopping before Colin's desk. "It's me."

"Welcome back, John," Colin said quietly. It was already clear something was wrong. Something more than Mordred's name not being on any list. The way Colin's eyes kept sweeping up, it was something to do with the guys on the door.

"I'd like to make an appointment to see Ruby Parker," Mordred said.

"You should have rung ahead," Colin replied. "You could have saved yourself a journey. Sorry, I didn't mean that to sound sarcastic. I mean, it's literally true."

Mordred felt his heart sink. "So she's not here? When will she be back?"

Colin lowered his voice even further. Clearly, he didn't want the men to overhear. What was going on? "Ruby Parker was involved in a minor hit-and-run last night," he said, "and won't be in to work for the next few days."

"Good God. So - so who's in charge?"

Colin smiled dejectedly. "That's above my pay grade, John, as you know. But I'm afraid I can't let you in. Officially, you're down as 'in America'; she's not here to revise your status, and I doubt the temporary head will have the inclination. I can only advise you to go home."

Like being hit in the sternum with a rock. Nothing for it now but to follow the doctor's orders – the doctor, on this occasion, being Colin.

His mind raced. He'd have to call Phyllis, beg her to tell him what had happened at the party. Plead for her help. Get Annabel, Tariq and Alec on board too. Edna and Ian if he could find them. Perhaps even Suki and Victor.

The two bouncer-y men snarled slightly at him as he passed. He'd been rejected by the chief receptionist, so he obviously wasn't welcome here, and that's what bouncers were paid to do: snarl at your back as you hightailed it. Their job, nothing personal.

Outside, the sun shone. Nearly all the leaves were down on the plane trees by the riverside. Still, people were sitting on the benches. A group of lads, by the look of it, with beer cans and their backs to him. They were probably freezing.

He had to think, and walking was best for that. He'd brought his pay-and-go, in case Fleming wanted to contact him, but he was also beginning to think that if he contacted Phyllis, it'd have to be through that, not his own phone. Because: hit and run. That couldn't be coincidence, could it? *There's something here that dwarfs the murder. Something important enough to kill Curzon for, and fraudulently re-stage his killing in Venezuela. Important enough for the IMF to run scared.* Something big enough to put Ruby Parker out of action for? Just see how naturally that sentence followed from the preceding three.

He was in trouble. Like an idiot, he'd staked all his hopes on Ruby Parker.

Two men were coming towards him from the other side of the bridge. A sixth sense told him they were about to jump him, and they were armed. He did a swift about turn. But two more men had run up from behind, and grabbed him either side, an arm each.

"There, there, John," one of them said, his mouth right up against to Mordred's ear. "We don't want to hurt you. Just follow us. We simply want to talk."

The shock of recognition. Not just any five, but *the* five. Faris Meadows gripped his right arm, and was still speaking mock-reassuringly; Raymond Carvell had hold of his left. They were strongmen, no doubt about it, but they were drunk, which might make escaping easier.

For the time being, though, he didn't want to escape. He wanted to discover what they were up to. He acted as feeble as he knew how, pretending to be in a panic, because that was the best way to ultimately win in a situation like this: make them over-confident. Hilal Al-Ghaith, Michael Cline and Paul Wheen brought up the rear, using their bodies to screen the abduction.

They took him down a set of steps into the strip of parkland where he'd first spotted them. A bulky Sainsbury's carrier bag lay beneath one of the benches. Meadows and Carvell sat him down without releasing their hold and took up position either side of him.

"Get him a drink," Meadows said.

Wheen reached into the bag. He held up two cans: a Special Brew and a Whiskey and Coke. "What do you want?" he asked Mordred.

"I'm not thirsty," he replied.

Al-Gaith punched his stomach. "Wrong answer."

Meadows laughed. "The world's about to end, John, haven't you heard? You might as well have a drinkie-poo. There'll be precious few laughs after the aliens have shown themselves. You saw the press conference, I take it?"

"How do you know my name?" he asked in a feigned croak. Although of course he knew. From the news reports on Princes Street.

"You're famous, John," Meadows said. "By the way, I'm here to see Phyllis. She was great on Friday night. And she agreed to meet me for a date, and 'maybe more', while you were in America. How does *that* make you feel, *eh, John?* How's your *stab wound*, by the way?"

He jabbed Mordred's chest. Mordred yelped in only half-feigned agony.

Wheen pulled the tab from the Special Brew. He held it high, and stood before Mordred. "Prepare for a cleansing shower, Johnny boy."

Meadows chuckled. "Don't think it's *us* that's trying to stop you, John. We're just messengers. But take our advice. Go home and lie down, okay? Because you haven't got *too* long to live."

"And you wouldn't want to worsen your *stab wound!*" Carvell said, making another prod at Mordred's chest.

Mordred gave another yell, but they'd obviously relaxed now, and their grips had loosened. In the pretence of contorting in pain, he leaned forward and raised his feet.

Then brought his heels down hard into their shins. They yowled and doubled and met his elbows going the other way. Then he extended from the bench and kicked Wheen's groin. Then met his down-bound head with the top of his own skull. He felt the crunch of a man's nose, and sensed blood.

In fact, there *was* blood - a lot of it. He'd ruined three faces in under three seconds, and Carvell and Meadows were effectively lame. A personal best. On the minus side, his best suit was probably ruined.

Although it might dry clean.

Seriously embarrassing to hand in at the shop counter, though. *Sorry, I'm a serial killer.*

He stood upright. Apart from a lingering discomfort of Carvell's chest-prod, he was unharmed. Al-Ghaith and Cline looked beaten already. Their expressions showed confusion and terror.

Out of the corner of his eye, Mordred saw an old man on the pavement ten yards above, beyond the railings. He looked intently at them and spoke into his phone. 999, no doubt about it. He was describing a serious breach of the peace.

Al-Ghaith suddenly lunged with a knife. Mordred side-stepped and tripped him into the metal railings. Another crunch. Like a neck this time.

"Lie down," he told Cline breathlessly. He was annoyed now. "Unless you want to run away. But you won't get far. The police will be here soon. In fact, all of you, lie down." He gestured with his palms down, as if he was training dogs.

Al-Ghaith was unconscious. Cline put his hands in the air like a POW, then lay on his stomach. Wheen, Meadows and Carvell sat miserably on the flagstones, holding their faces.

There were CCTV cameras by the million round here, and they'd exonerate him. He need have no fear of the police. But that knife Al-Ghaith brandished, and Meadows's threat - *you haven't got too long to live* - had unnerved him much more than the physical apprehension had.

His life was in danger. No use running away from the fact any more. Someone had knocked Ruby Parker down in a car, but he was probably ten times more of a threat to whatever the hell was going on than she was. He'd nearly met his end here, two minutes ago, and if whoever was behind all this thought they could have him killed by five bozos in broad daylight, he or she or they obviously didn't fear the consequences. Because there probably wouldn't be any. They'd deployed Meadows and his crew twice now – once in Princes Street, once here – but 'they' presumably weren't limited in terms of ways and means. As Meadows himself had just intimated, there were a thousand alternative methods of permanently disposing of someone like John Mordred. If he was to survive, he had to do what Greysonwell had done, possibly for the same reason: make himself invisible.

Which was going to be difficult, given that the police had just arrived in force.

Luckily, he had a plan.

Belgravia Police Station, an anonymous red brick building about three minutes away from Thames House. Mordred gave his name and address to the duty sergeant, and handed over his possessions, including both his phones. Two middle-aged policemen took him to a small windowless room with grey walls for interview. They looked as if this sort of routine usually bored the pants off them, but the fact that Mordred had been one against five, had subsequently passed a breathalyser test and wore an expensive suit with newly-polished shoes, all suggested that today, their pants might stay on for a change. They already grudgingly liked him, he could see. All he had to do was not be too smug. He waived his right to a solicitor as if everything he'd supposedly done could soon be cleared up as, morally, he had nothing to answer for – always a high risk tactic – and asked to see DCI Nicholas Fleming.

"You'll remember I was picked up outside Thames House," he said. "The MI5 building," he added, in case they didn't realise. "I'm currently working with DCI Fleming on a matter of national security, I can't say what, but that was part of it. If you bring him over here, he'll vouch for me in person. I'm pretty certain he'd expect to be present at any interview I might give. I believe he's currently based at Scotland Yard on the Victoria Embankment."

The two men looked at each other and nodded. "Okay," one of them said, "we'll look into it." They already believed him, which was a start.

They removed him from the interview room, and put him in a cell on his own. He sat on the fold out bed and waited.

It didn't take long. The cell door opened and Fleming stood with one of the two policemen. "John," he said warmly, "well done, and I'm so sorry about this. I should have been at our rendezvous this morning, but it looks like the case has developed further complications. Don't worry, Sergeant, I'll take it from here. I hope you weren't too badly hurt," he said, turning back to Mordred.

"I'm pretty intact," Mordred said.

What 'rendezvous'? What 'further complications'?

It was obvious. Only the likelihood that he was still slightly dazed explained why he hadn't twigged immediately. Non-existent ones. A ruse to get him out of here.

"Keep walking," Fleming said under his breath. "We'll pick up your things at reception. Once they discover you're here, they'll use it. They'll throw the book at you. Quite possibly, attempted murder. Guess what? I'm being transferred to Hertfordshire. Out of the blue, as of this morning. With a promotion. Closer to home, I suppose they thought I'd jump at it. I've got the details of the five men you called about last night. They've just been charged with disturbing the peace, so I know where they live."

Mordred retrieved his possessions at reception. As they went out into the street, he called Phyllis.

"Car's down here," Fleming said, picking his pace up.

"Phyllis Robinson?" said an uncertain voice.

"Are you alone?" Mordred asked.

"John, where *are* you? We've got an acting head, and he's keen for you to join an investigation abroad… exact location unspecified."

He chuckled. "Effective immediately, I suppose?"

"That's what he implied."

"I'll be quick. I'm in trouble and I need your help. But you don't have to. It's probably a job loser - "

"For God's sake, John! Of course, I want to help! Stop being an idiot and get to the point!"

"You're probably being watched. Act as if you don't know, and go and stand on the westbound side of Lambeth Bridge. I'll meet you there. I need to know everything you know about Greysonwell."

He hung up.

"Greysonwell's dead," Fleming told him. "They removed his body from the Thames about an hour ago. Suicide's the early verdict, if you can believe that. I'll drive around a bit, give her time to arrive. I've got a hire car, so we should be okay for a while. You should probably have said 'we', incidentally. *We'll* meet you there. Never mind. I've brought you some of my spare clothes. I anticipated we'd both need to change." He looked Mordred up and down as they walked, noting the blood. He smiled. "Not quite this urgently, though."

Chapter 26: Hotels are for Planning

Why did anyone ever decide to go into self-imposed exile? Probably, it was an accumulation of small inconveniences. Each one, in itself, you thought, 'I can just about live with that', until one day you looked out of your window and noticed it wasn't a mere pile: it was a mountain, poised for an avalanche. It'd got that way because each item had arrived individually with no particular fanfare. Now you were in real danger. And not just you, but those around you. And then you told yourself you'd been stupid, you should have left much, much sooner. But *when?* At what point had the pile become something else, something genuinely threatening? As Mordred sat in the passenger seat of Fleming's hire-car on the way to pick up Phyllis, he mentally checked off the items. The stabbing, Murgatroyd in various guises, the shadows on the tube, Hannah, Fleming, all the secrecy surrounding Greysonwell, the watcher in the park, Ruby Parker's 'accident', his proposed posting overseas, Fleming's proposed transfer to the sticks, the attack by Meadows and his gang, Meadows's warning, and now Greysonwell's supposed suicide. Individually, none looked like much, but they added up. *What are you waiting for?* they seemed to say, in a despairing voice, as if the only proof they *hadn't* yet given was his own murder, and why the hell was he waiting for *that?* (Although, by the way, it was already budgeted for.) 'Abroad' in the abstract. A good place to lose someone.

They picked up Phyllis and Annabel on Lambeth Bridge, and drove to Clerkenwell. They left the car in a Tesco car park and made plans to meet up again in three hours' time. They each drew out £300 from an ATM, switched their phones off and separated. When they met at the London Wordsworth Hotel in Southwark, just after 4pm, they were in different clothes. Phyllis had booked a room on the top floor using cash – she had three bank accounts and had managed to accumulate just over £1000 - and the others sneaked past the receptionist and took up temporary residence with her. It was a large room with an en-suite, a king-size bed, a sectional sofa and all the usual dressing and snacking accoutrements. Annabel and Phyllis sat on the sofa and talked. Fleming poured himself a Scotch. They thought about their P45s.

Mordred switched on the TV and went straight to the BBC news channel. The talk was of the lack of progress in the latest round of Brexit talks, but the ticker tape at the bottom kept re-announcing Greysonwell's death. *London Lord Mayor, Viscount Greysonwell, found dead this morning* on a loop with Donald Trump, Harvey Weinstein and Catalan independence.

"How's the new acting head?" Mordred asked Phyllis and Annabel, while he waited.

"We probably wouldn't be here if he was any good," Annabel said drily. "Jeff McFarlane, he's called, but we're expected to call him sir. Old school, but not very bright. Hadn't read the small print on the COL1 form, for example, so didn't realise he hadn't dotted the i's and crossed the t's. Then just left us in the building while he swanned off somewhere."

"I hope you've got some sort of plan," Phyllis told him. "Because Annabel and I haven't had time to come up with anything. We're following your lead right now, and I estimate we've two days until we run out of funds."

"What are we actually up against?" Annabel asked.

"I wish I knew," Mordred replied. "As for my plan: Nicholas has managed to get hold of the home addresses of the five men I think were responsible for my stabbing in Princes

Street. I'll tell you their names later. Their real target was Martin Curzon, aka 'Guanyin', a blogger who's presently supposed to be – but isn't – in Venezuela. Curzon was the man who was killed, then doused in acid. What we need now is to find out why five IMF financiers died in a pile-up on the M23, and why it was covered up, and by whom."

Annabel and Phyllis exchanged impressed looks.

"I'm pleased you haven't dragged us out here for nothing," Annabel said. "I don't yet know quite what you're talking about, but I think we can both see you haven't been sitting on your hands. At least we've got a few reasonably precise questions to answer. I came along because I assumed you might need a burglar. Correct?"

"Yep." He held his hand up slightly. "But you can also be useful in other ways."

The newsreader read out the barest outline of Greysonwell's recovery from the Thames, replayed visual footage of his Saturday night press conference – which she summarised glibly in a voiceover, out of respect - alluded to concerns about his mental health, gave a brief account of his pre-Mayoral career as head of Square Mile Gold, and finished by saying that the police had ruled out foul play.

"Of course, this means Meadows and his gang will walk free," Fleming said. "They'll claim that they heard about the death of their friend – maybe they *did*, for all we know – and they behaved the way they did out of grief. Diminished responsibility. Charging them will be difficult, especially as they came off worst, and there's no one left to press charges. If they're set free, it'll make breaking and entering their houses – if that's what we're planning - more risky."

"They'll go back to Mansion House if they're released," Mordred said. "Not home. My guess is that they're based there for some reason."

"When you say *Meadows*," Phyllis asked. "Who are you talking about? You can't mean…?"

"Faris Meadows," Mordred said. "He was at the party."

"Oh, my God," she said. "Oh, bloody hell. I actually gave him quite a lot of information about you. I didn't know. "

"Just to get you up to speed," Mordred said, "about three hours ago, he and his four friends attacked me outside Thames House. A passer-by called the police, Nicholas rescued me from custody in Belgravia, and that's when I phoned you."

Fleming turned to Mordred. "What makes you say they're based in Mansion House?"

"It explains how they could be waiting for Curzon that night," Mordred replied. "They followed him to the Frederick and Elizabeth pub from work – he was based at the stock exchange, and I guess they are too – and saw him go in. They couldn't find him when they entered, and Brent, the landlord, wasn't very helpful, but they knew he hadn't left. So they staked it out. They couldn't have done so in the street – five guys the same height and build as the attackers loitering about around the scene of the crime several hours before the murder would have shown up on CCTV. Which likely means they each took turns, while the others laid low. And where better to lie low than their friend's official residence? By way of confirmation, I looked at a few photos of Friday night's party on Facebook and Google Plus. They seem to have a 'room' there, or that's the boast. How did Greysonwell conduct himself at the party, by the way?" he asked Phyllis.

She told him what had happened that night, excluding the fact that Greysonwell had wanted to meet him, and that she'd agreed with Annabel, Alec and Tariq not to tell him. She saw Annabel relax slightly.

"And how did McFarlane react when you told him Alec had been knocked unconscious?" Mordred said.

She swept her palm over her head. "Exactly like that."

"Hmm," he said.

"We need a timetable," Annabel said. "Where are the premises to be burgled, when, and what specifically are we looking for?"

Mordred turned to Fleming. "You said you'd got the five guys' details. Does anyone know you've got them?"

"I printed them off from someone else's download," Fleming said. "We've got house addresses, occupations, dates of birth, that sort of thing. But no one knows we've got them."

"Since we don't really know what we're up against," Mordred said, "we're going to use Bayesian statistics. What you do is start with a hypothesis, then you look for evidence to confirm or falsify it. As the data comes in, you look for the relative balance and update the hypothesis appropriately. And you continue that process. Eventually, you should end up with something that's roughly correct."

"What we normally do, in other words," Phyllis said.

"The difficulty is knowing what hypothesis to begin with," he replied. "What do you suggest?"

She shrugged.

"Not so simple, after all," he said.

"What's your hypothesis, smart Alec?" she asked irritably. "And before you answer, don't forget, we've put our careers on the line for you today. I don't think you're entitled to be smug."

"Let's not argue," Fleming interrupted. "All our careers are on the line, and none of them need be, not even John's. We're here because... I don't know."

An awkward silence.

Annabel met his gaze. "Because what shall it profit a man, if he shall gain the whole world, and lose his own soul?" She turned to Phyllis. "It's what Ian would have done."

"Who's Ian?" Fleming asked.

Mordred resisted the obvious James Bond-based joke: *Have you never heard of Ian, Fleming?* despite the once-in-a-lifetime opportunity. He remembered Fleming's own words, just yesterday - *I already know this is one of those look-in-the-mirror-without-feeling-contempt-for-the-rest-of-your-life affairs* – which he'd peremptorily dismissed. He felt slightly ashamed.

"A former colleague of ours," he muttered. "Recently killed fighting ISIS in Syria. Long story."

"Sorry, John," Phyllis said.

"Sorry for sounding smug," he told her. "It happens every time I say, 'Bayesian statistics'. It's got a pretentious twang to it. It's not intentional."

"Never say it again. Describe it, yes, just don't use the term."

"Well, I'm glad we got that sorted," Annabel said. "Can I ask a question now? A few moments ago, John, before we stopped to watch the news – put the TV on mute now, by the way: we need to talk – I asked you if you wanted me to help with a burglary, and you said yes. But then you added something like, 'Not just for that'."

"I'm sending you back to Thames House in about an hour," he told her. "Sorry, not 'sending' you: *asking* you to go back."

"I assume this isn't out of some ill-advised concern for my career," she said.

"It's part of my plan," he told her. "I've known Ruby Parker for long enough to realise she's not going to take a few days off to recover from an ankle injury. Whoever decided it would be a good idea to side-line her seriously misjudged the level of input required. She'll want to get straight back to her desk, especially when she hears about Greysonwell. She'll wonder whether the two things – her accident and his suicide - could conceivably be connected, and because she won't be able to rule it out, wild horses won't stop her coming in. She'll do it because she's got what every good spy's got: sane paranoia. I reckon McFarlane's living on borrowed time."

"So you want me to find out if that's correct," Annabel said, "and if it is, contact you?"

"In a word, yes," Mordred said. "But McFarlane may be ahead of us. The same thought may already have occurred to him, in other words. Which means she may be in danger. Since he left the building well in advance of you, it may be too late to do anything, but my guess is, she'll have anticipated that too. Whatever *we* think *he* might think, *she'll* already have foreseen. That's how good she is. I honestly don't think we need worry about her, but it is possible they've somehow prevented her re-entry to the building, and that McFarlane's still hanging on by his fingernails. That's where your re-appearance is going to be useful."

"Go on," Annabel said.

"They'll naturally assume I co-opted you because I'm planning a burglary, so they'll have those bases covered. Your return will therefore surprise them. Now, don't take this the wrong way, but you're known, and valued, in MI7 for preferring Queen and Country to conscience, personal friendships and autonomous reason."

"I *will* take it the wrong way," Annabel said, "if you don't mind, and I think the fact that I'm here now gives the lie to it. But I'll save my full reaction for when this is all over. Keep going."

"I'm just saying that's how you're viewed. It's not true, obviously."

She sighed. "Get to the point, John, before I lose my temper. This has been a long day."

"You return to Thames House. You demand an interview with McFarlane. You tell him that you infiltrated our little group out of loyalty to the firm. And you tell him we've already committed a burglary, without your involvement, because that's why you cried off. Martin Curzon's house. Where is that again, Nicholas?"

"Forty-three Harrow Square, Belgravia," Fleming replied.

"We stole scores of USB pens, some marked 'IMF', some with 'Top Secret', some 'HM Government' – make it up as you go along – and we're on our way to meet an important Wikileaks guy in Paris. You can explain that we deduced that Curzon is Guanyin, and that he's not in Venezuela, and that he was the man murdered in Princes Street. If I'm right, all of that should turn him to jelly. He'll pull everything away from his they're-going-to-commit-a-burglary projection and hurl it at closing Dover, Folkestone and possibly even Portsmouth. We'll be given a free hand. And since the guys behind all this will panic, it's likely they'll make mistakes."

"So you want me to lie," Annabel said. "Not just a tiny lie, either, but an absolutely gigantic one. What if all this turns out to be a benign cover-up? What if it transpires that *we're* the bad guys? Since we don't actually know what's going on yet, isn't that possible?"

"It's not *im*possible," Mordred said. "But let's remember: we're just trying to find out. If it turns out we *are* the bad guys, we'll stop, no harm done. We're not *really* on our way to give Wikipedia lots of files we haven't even looked at ourselves. That would be wrong."

Fleming held his hand up. "Sorry, John, but none of that's going to work."

They all looked at him.

"Think about it," he continued. "Martin Curzon's death occurred in Venezuela, but he was kidnapped first, and 'negotiations' were prolonged. If you want to transfer the scene of the crime somewhere like that, why not just have the victim abducted and murdered the night he supposedly stepped off the plane? Why string it out with fictitious attempts to bargain?"

Mordred shrugged. "Because whoever arranged it wanted to erase the very possibility of an association between the real killing in Princes Street and the fake one in South America. They began by disrupting the temporal link, putting six or seven weeks between them."

"Wrong," Fleming replied. "They did it so everyone in forty-three Harrow Square, Belgravia, would hurriedly go to Venezuela, leaving the property vacant. Then they take it apart and could go over the pieces with a fine toothcomb, find anything pertaining to Guanyin, and destroy it. They'll have had the floorboards up and the tiles off the walls. That takes time, even more to repair in such a way as looks like it never happened. Six weeks means you don't have to rush too much. The point is, McFarlane will know you're bluffing, but more crucially, he'll suspect Annabel's lying."

Mordred sat back and closed his eyes. He groaned. "How did I miss that?"

"I think you know why," Fleming said.

An extra level of misery. Fleming was right. Because he couldn't face the necessary alternative.

"What's he talking about, John?" Phyllis said. All eyes were suddenly on him. Fleming's out of curiosity; the women's out of a kind of low-level panic.

"The night you all went to the Lord Mayor's party," he began, "I went a few doors down – The Frederick and Elizabeth pub – to case a tiny flat where a mysterious blogger had his base. As a personal favour to Hannah."

"Your *sister* Hannah?" Annabel said.

"The same," he replied. "I went thinking it was a wild goose chase, but when I got there, it wasn't. She actually rents the flat, Curzon aka 'Guanyin' aka 'the blogger' utilised it to publish damning reports concerning certain shady activities in the City of London which eventually got him killed. As far as I know, even now no one suspects he was ever there."

"You did all this without telling *me?*" Phyllis said.

"I didn't want to spoil your night out. I had no idea it might be dangerous. Like I said, it was just a kooky errand for a paranoid relative."

"I'm not sure how I feel about that. It sounds a bit like betrayal."

He smiled. "When Faris Meadows was poking my stab wound a few hours ago, he said you'd agreed to meet him for a date, 'and maybe more', while I was in America. At the time, I thought, 'That sounds a bit like betrayal'. But then I thought, 'No, because, however much it may sound like it, Phyllis wouldn't betray me'."

"I didn't say 'maybe more'," Phyllis replied. "And it wasn't a date."

"You didn't tell me, though."

"I didn't get a *chance!*"

"You had ample chance on Saturday morning, when we spoke on the phone. The real reason you didn't tell me was because you didn't consider it important enough. And you were right. And I didn't consider *this* important enough. And *I* was right. And I don't want to lose you because of some stupid misunderstanding. I love you."

Silence.

"John's right," Annabel said. "You're both in the wrong in a stupid way that isn't remotely worth bickering about."

"Apology accepted," Phyllis told Mordred. "Okay, plausible analysis. Mutual about the love. Couplehood intact."

"I saw several men from the window in Hannah's flat," he went on, "on the roof of Mansion House, wearing masks identical to those used in the attack. I've been having random flashbacks, including one in which I saw the face of the man whose mask I tore off. He's one of Meadows's four friends. I recognised him from the press conference footage. In fact, that's what caused me to have the second flashback. All of this happened over the weekend."

Fleming leaned over. "All right. Now that's out of the way, you've got a major choice to make, John."

"You've lost me again," Annabel said. "And I suspect Phyllis too. What choice?"

"When John first contacted me about all this," Fleming said, "he agreed to give me what information he had on condition that I kept his sister out of it. She can be linked to Guanyin, you see, and therefore she can be framed for his murder, I think that's the idea, isn't it, John?"

"It would deflect attention away from the real culprits," Mordred said miserably, "and get rid of a troublesome woman. Blue or Grey – if it's them – could make it stick, no matter how implausible it might sound right now."

Fleming nodded. "John's wondering if he can send you, Annabel, back to Thames House on roughly the plan he just outlined. But with Hannah's flat, instead of forty-three Harrow Place, as the site of our burglary. The advantage is that it really *would* give them apoplexy. The disadvantage is that it would mean exposing his sister, Hannah."

"They're probably going to find out about it, anyway, to be fair," Mordred said. "We might as well get some use out of it. And they probably won't dare frame Hannah if they think we've got a stick of dynamite beneath them."

Annabel cleared her throat and gestured at the TV. "Switch mute off, John."

They all saw what she saw, and they saw its significance. Footage of Soraya Snow, in London.

"… signing autographs in Leicester Square this morning," the newsreader said. "A concert in Torrington, Connecticut, scheduled for this evening, and another at the weekend, in Rhode Island, have both been mysteriously cancelled, prompting speculation that Fully Magic Coal Tar

Lounge may be about to split up. Its lead singer, the multi award-winning singer, and former *Voice* presenter, this morning strenuously denied the rumours. However, other band members were unavailable for comment. The band's manager, Hannah Lexingwood, is with Ms Snow in London, and, according to undisclosed sources may be seeking to negotiate a solo contract for her. More on that as we get it."

Mordred lowered his head into his hands.

Chapter 27: Say Something, John

Mordred ran his hands over his hair. He felt tempted to put his head between his knees. Bloody, bloody *hell*, just when he thought things couldn't get any worse!

No doubt about it, Hannah's arrival in Britain had added a time-bomb to the mix. It even looked odd to the BBC. God knows what McFarlane and his crew would make of it.

But that was wrong, of course. *If only!* No, it was obvious what they'd make of it. They'd assume she'd got some sort of signal from her brother that he was in trouble, and ridden flamboyantly to the rescue. They'd already have about five people following her.

And what would she do? She'd sneak out of the hotel that night, her and Soraya, and they'd make straight for The Frederick and Elizabeth, see if they could discover for themselves what had happened. MI7 would be right behind them, of course, and probably the police. They'd be apprehended on their way out of the pub, taken into custody, and a whole lot of awkward questions would be asked, culminating in them being charged with conspiracy to murder. *A criminal always returns to the scene of the crime*, that'd be their guiding creative principle. Hannah was about to give them the gift they'd always dreamed of: her head on a platter.

But wait a minute. She couldn't be that stupid, could she? She knew the police were involved. And she was paranoid. In this sort of situation, that was a virtue. Surely, she wouldn't be so crass as to make a bee-line for EC4?

She might be. Sometimes, when you knew the police knew, and you felt it was only a matter of time before they pounced, you went a bit crazy. You set out to provoke the crisis. Bloody hell, you knew it was coming anyway. You stopped caring whether you'd survive. You just wanted it over and done with.

She'd probably been round to her brother's flat, or sent someone there to fetch him, or tried to ring him. What would she conclude from the fact that he was out of contact?

Another level of complexity, that. His head was about to explode.

Oh, my God. What if she'd already *been* to The Frederick and Elizabeth? They wouldn't necessarily stop her on the way out. The CCTV would prove she'd been there, and probably fingerprints, and probably ... just about everything. They could afford to wait, savour their victory.

"Say something, John," Annabel told him tetchily.

"We haven't time for burglaries," Mordred said. "I'm not sure there's time for anything."

"This is what we're going to do," Phyllis said, standing up. "I'm going to switch my mobile back on, ring Hannah, arrange to see her right now, refuse to take no for an answer, and I'm going to give her a written message, penned and signed by you, in a sealed envelope, telling her not to go anywhere near that pub. Then stick to her like glue. Annabel, you're going to go back to Thames House. If McFarlane's there, follow John's plan, only substitute the pub for Curzon's house. John and Nicholas: you stay here. Do something. Figure out what's happened and make a plan, then carry it out. Believe in yourselves."

She stood over Mordred while he wrote, "Don't go anywhere near the Sister Wendy pub" on blank hotel notepaper, then took it off him and folded it in two.

"I thought you said it was called The Frederick and Elizabeth," she said suspiciously.

"It is. Don't make me explain Sister Wendy. Not yet. We'll be here till the end of next week."

She put it in her bag. "I'll buy an envelope on the way," she told him.

"She'll want to know where I am," he said. "What are you going to tell her?"

"That you're in hiding," Phyllis replied. "What better way of letting her know the danger she's putting herself in? If she's got any sense, she'll get straight back on the plane."

"She thinks she's Scott and Soraya's Bailey, that's the problem. I've actually heard them talking about it. That's why they're here."

"Forget about them. Start thinking about the mess you've got yourself and the rest of us - and apparently the whole world - into, and work out what we're going to do. Come on, Annabel."

"Good luck, John," Annabel said.

Phyllis held the door for her, and they left without looking back.

"Greysonwell owns Square Mile Gold," Fleming said. "Or he did. I'm speculating now. But he wasn't the brains behind it, not at any stage. It was set up by Meadows and his crew, and possibly Lady Julia. They needed a name from *Debrett's Peerage & Baronetage* to attract enough depositors of the right quality. Once there was sufficient gold in there, they began removing it, knowing the owner would get the blame. They unbalanced Greysonwell – using drugs, perhaps - to make his culpability look doubly plausible. Or perhaps, out of pity: apprehended, he'd probably never go to jail."

Mordred nodded. "It's a theory. It would fit with what I saw on all five of the faces ranged behind him during that Saturday night press conference. Pleasure at a job well done. Lady Julia, I still don't know. She was unreadable."

"So let's work on the assumption that these five guys have sequestered the gold," Fleming went on. "So far so good, but of course, it doesn't answer the wider questions."

"Why the deaths of five IMF financiers were covered up," Mordred said, "who transferred their deaths to Venezuela, who covered up the murder of Martin Curzon, why you were subsequently told to stop investigating, why you were then transferred, why Ruby Parker was targeted, why I'm being sent abroad. This has much wider ramifications than a robbery. Still, it's a start. It rings true, and I definitely can't think of anything better." He stood up. "Although…" He walked to the window.

"You've had an idea?" Fleming asked, after a minute had passed.

"Who are we going to tell?" Mordred asked.

"What do you mean?"

"I mean, let's say we actually realise what's going on. Let's say we zoom over to Mansion House, where Meadows and his friends probably are, and confront them. Let's say we trick them or provoke them into a confession. Let's say, just to make this story perfect, it's a confession that matches our hypothesis. Just imagine all that for a moment."

"And who are we going to tell," Fleming echoed.

"The police aren't interested, as evidenced by your superintendent. MI7 isn't interested, at least that's what we've got to assume. There are those guys in *Line of Duty*, but we'll probably be eliminated long before it reaches that stage."

"In that case, we've got to do it for its own sake," Fleming said. "Because it's the right thing to do. That's all that's left."

"Like Edward Snowden."

"Because what shall it profit a man. Are we actually in a position to 'zoom over' to Mansion House? Did you have some kind of epiphany, over there by the window?"

"I think so. I probably need twenty minutes' fact-checking. Is that a smart TV, do you think? Can it access the internet? Let's have a look." He switched it on. "Hurrah," he said unenthusiastically.

"I hope you're not going to look for 'Guanyin'," Fleming said. "I've tried. Whatever he put up's been deleted."

"Ditto," Mordred replied.

He searched for 'gold missing from bank vaults' and scanned the results. Then 'Dutch bank ABN Amro'. *In 2013, the bank informed its customers that they could not take receipt of their gold on demand, in apparent contravention of the storage agreement. This led to large withdrawals of gold from other banks, notably Scotiabank and UBS. The Swiss Central bank banned the withdrawal of gold…*

He clicked the 'back' button. Further down the list, other results spoke of 'Paper money bubbles' and 'Planet Ponzi'. At the bottom of page 1, an entry said, *Kondratieff Wave due to hit no later than 2026.* He opened it.

From there, he went to a description of The Fourth Turning, then a series of prognoses by eminent economists to the effect that the developed world was on the brink of economic collapse. The horrendous extent to which government spending just about everywhere was out of control was masked only by the perpetual creation of new money by central banks. Paper money didn't represent anything any more. The entire planet was living on credit. Sooner, rather than later, the charade would become unsustainable. The slightest adverse event could trigger a catastrophe worse than the sub-prime mortgage crisis of 2008. Which was inevitable in the short to medium term, and in any case, no later than 2026.

My God, it was exactly what Hannah had told him in her last phone call! *There's going to be a global financial crash - 2026 at the absolute latest. It won't be like anything we've seen before. It'll make 2008 look like a storm in a teacup. Banks will collapse. ATM's will stop dispensing cash. Inflation will go crazy. There will be riots. People are going to get killed.* Could it be – ?

How could anyone know the future with that degree of precision?

"Cheery reading," Fleming commented. "At least when we're arrested, the government will only have enough cash to keep us in prison for eight years."

"And when we come out, it'll be a dystopian nightmare," Mordred said. "Assuaged only by the spectacle of Hannah and Soraya doling out Bitcoins to ragamuffins."

"So what's your theory?" Fleming said. "Are we ready to go over to Mansion House?"

"I'll explain on the way, as the Americans say."

"I'll ring for a taxi then. How good a theory is it?"

Mordred smiled. "It explains everything. However, on the minus side, it'll require someone else to prove it – although proof *can* be had – and it'll mean we're probably about to get beaten up by Meadows and his gang, then thrown into a prison cell."

"And Hannah?"

He sighed. "I've done my best, but I think she's as doomed as we are."

Chapter 28: A Visit to Mansion House

The black cab turned up ten minutes later. "Remind me again why we're going to Mansion House," Fleming said as they got in.

"Because we can't run away," Mordred said. "Have you ever read Plato's *Crito*?"

"Probably. Who hasn't?"

"If you really want to do the right thing, you've got to stand your ground. Even if it means you'll suffer for it. Anyway, it could be fun."

"We probably won't get anywhere near Meadows. There are five of them, and only two of us - "

"I don't like to blow my own trumpet," Mordred said, "but I severely weakened them. They're probably not up for round two."

"I'm sure there'll be trained staff they can call on. Not to mention the police."

"True."

"We might not even get past the front door."

"We will."

Fleming took a deep breath. "It's not far. I'd like to hear this theory of yours, if that's okay, before we arrive."

"Switch your phone on."

"What? But I thought we - "

"I want the police to know where we are. Let them fasten on to our location. We're done hiding. Remember *Crito*."

"I'll be honest with you: all Plato's dialogues seem a little dull to me. Still." He took his phone out and switched it on. It gave a little tinkle of joy. "Let the countdown begin. Our fates are now sealed. It was nice knowing you, John."

"Let's not be too hasty. We could end up sharing a cell, for all you know."

262

"And yet I'd rather not reach that point without knowing why."

"Meadows and his four friends used Henry Greysonwell in exactly the manner you described in your earlier hypothesis. They set him up as the head of a gold company, watched the bullion roll in, then emptied the coffers. But it wasn't simple robbery. They knew someone would find out, and they calculated it would be the snowflake that would cause the metaphorical avalanche and bring the world financial system down. Because when that happens, paper money will become worthless. The people with gold, land and possibly art and cryptocurrency will survive.

"But they were playing a double game. When the IMF came to do a routine check on the soundness of Square Mile Gold – something they'd fully anticipated - it discovered a horribly gaping hole. That could have been the end of the story, except it wasn't, because Meadows and his gang had already decided to stop the news from getting out. The five officials responsible for the inspection probably died as the result of that, although it needn't have been on Meadows's orders, because by this time, HM government had also become embroiled. IMF headquarters wanted it covered up because it was too soon – its contingency plan for a global financial collapse wouldn't be fully up and running till much closer to 2026 - and the Treasury wanted it covered up because the City of London is supposed to be one of Britain's greatest economic assets. The idea that its top gold storage facility, run by the Lord Mayor himself, was out-and-out toxic, would cause confidence to collapse. No one dared touch Greysonwell, much less have him arrested, because that would also have sounded the fire alarm. But he was a renegade. He had to go. Meadows and his four companions, having sequestered the gold and pinned the blame elsewhere, made a show of wanting to assist in the cover up. In this way, they placed both the IMF and the British government in their debt. Come the actual financial crisis, they'd have powerful friends in all the highest places, and gold in abundance. Money and connections. Those two things together are sufficient to ensure that, sometime within the next forty years, they get as close to ruling the world as is possible. Guanyin worked out what they were up to, and was probably in a position to prove it. He was an investigator, like us. Where's the gold they've stolen? Simple, it's buried deep beneath Mansion House. Greysonwell had an inkling of that, but of course he thought it was Quatermass's spaceship down there. God knows what they did to get him into that state, but it can't have been nice."

"And that's why you say it's provable?"

"Anyone with a metal detector can verify it."

"Why hide it beneath Mansion House?"

"Mainly, the usual reason. It's the last place anyone would think to look. But also because gold's quite heavy and it's conveniently round the corner from the vaults of Capital Gold, and, sometime in the next twenty years – sooner, rather than later – Meadows anticipates running for Lord Mayor himself. And with his abundance of connections, he'll likely be a shoo-in. Him, or one of his friends. Then he'll retrieve it."

Fleming folded his hands in his lap. "Well, it's a theory."

"It fits all the facts. I can't think of another that does. Unless there really are aliens from the other side of the universe. But Ockham's Razor says we should prefer the simpler hypothesis. At least, for now."

"I'm much closer to believing in aliens now than I was six weeks ago."

Mordred hmm-ed.

"What if Meadows has a gun?" Fleming asked.

Mordred laughed. "I expect he'll shoot us, or try to. But we're probably going to die anyway. We might as well go down fighting."

"Nearly there now."

Mordred's phone rang. *Phyllis.* He probably should have called her to say goodbye or something. But she'd only rush round to Mansion House, get herself tangled up in his spectacular demise. If she was elsewhere in London, she could plausibly deny being truly allied with him, even now.

"Hi," he said.

"John, you're never going to *believe* this. Where are you?"

"In a taxicab with Nicholas. We're on our way to see Meadows."

"Your sister – it's nothing remotely resembling what you thought it was! It's - Just before Guanyin died, he sent her an encrypted message. She put it out to some kind of Pangaea community-thing to be deciphered, and the results came in this morning. It implicates the IMF, the British government, and of course Meadows and his gang of thugs. In other words, she's managed to uncover the whole sordid plot, and she's got proof. She's about to hold a press conference on Birdcage Walk. Irma Curzon's here. Switch the news on! It's live! Every journalist in London's here! It's packed to the bloody gills. We've *won*, in other words. *You've* won! They won't dare do anything to you now! I've got to go – Hannah's about to start speaking. Get over here." She hung up.

"Bloody... hell," Mordred said.

"That sounds suspiciously like a non-negative 'bloody hell'," Fleming said.

"We've, er, won."

"Right."

His phone rang again. *Annabel.* He was in too much of a daze to wonder what she might want. He picked up.

"It's just as you speculated," Annabel said calmly. "Ruby Parker's back in charge. McFarlane's nowhere to be seen. She wants to know where you are."

They had arrived. The taxi slowed. Fleming told the driver to drop them at the Royal Exchange.

"Tell her to meet us at Mansion House," Mordred said. He hung up and switched his phone off.

Fleming paid and they got out. He really needed the fresh air. His head felt light. He strode towards Mansion House. Too late to do anything else now. He was on autopilot.

"What did you mean, 'we've won'?" Fleming said, catching him up.

"It's over. For them. Guanyin's spoken from beyond the grave. Why didn't she tell me earlier?" He was addressing himself now. "Because someone in MI5 might overhear, of course. It was all she had. She didn't know what she was supposed to do with it, but then when I told her what I'd found at The Frederick and Elizabeth, she finally realised its significance. It was something in the nature of a last will and testament, only more so."

"Are you sure you're okay?" Fleming said. "We don't have to go through with this. There's still time to turn back."

The steps to the front entrance of Mansion House were gated and chained. They couldn't get to the doors, but they looked locked.

"Round here," Fleming said. He gestured down Walbrook where a side-door stood open. A group of what looked like domestic servants rushed out at speed, as if escaping a bomb. After a few metres, they slowed and started hurriedly talking. Some of them looked back furtively. One put a phone to her ear. They didn't stop.

Mordred and Fleming entered where they'd exited. They found themselves inside a narrow ascending stairwell lit by a strip-light at the top. Fleming closed the door behind him. The top of the stairs brought them into a sumptuous, well-lit gallery. Mordred had been here twice before, but could remember next to nothing about it. There was no one about.

Yet there was a noise, a kind of long ghoulish yowling, as of several intertwined voices. For a moment, Mordred couldn't make out what it was. Then he realised he'd heard it before. It was a small group of men, crying.

He'd only heard anything similar once before. During MI7's Iran season of films and texts, a year ago, in a documentary called *Once Upon a Time in Iran*. A tiny part showed a bunch of Iranian conscripts in a poorly-lit marquee on the eve of a huge Iran-Iraq War offensive in which, statistically, most of them couldn't conceivably come out alive. It was odd, and yet entirely natural, to see about a hundred young men in combat fatigues, sobbing their hearts out and hugging their comrades. Because they were terrified.

Fleming looked at him. "Is it - ? What is it?"

"More to the point, where's it coming from?" Mordred said.

There was a smell of burning. Someone had tried to set fire to the curtains. And pulled up a rug and tried to burn it. Whoever it was, they'd failed.

A door somewhere upstairs suddenly banged open. The crying intensified.

"I was expecting to be shot at, not this," Fleming said in a voice that indicated he didn't know which was worse. "Is it... men crying?"

"I think so," Mordred said.

Meadows suddenly appeared on the balcony, his face streaked with tears. He looked down at Mordred and Fleming as if their being here was entirely natural.

"Look what you've done, John!" he yelled. *"Look what you've done!"*

No sign of a gun. Somewhere in the background, mixed with the wailing, he could hear his sister's voice. Presumably, they'd switched the TV on, full volume. She must be live. He couldn't catch exactly what she was saying, but her tone was relentless and authoritative.

Suddenly, Raymond Carvell rushed into Meadows's arms and sobbed. Then Hilal Al-Ghaith joined the huddle. They pulled back from the balcony and disappeared from view.

"What do you want to do?" Fleming said.

"Wait for the police to arrive, I suppose," Mordred said. "It's surreal."

Mordred didn't know whether they should stay put or go back outside again. If they left, things might change and re-entry might become impossible. The police might need someone on the inside - assuming they were even on their way. Of course. They were implicated in all this, so it might take them a while to readjust to new circumstances.

Mordred sat on a chair. Strange to see the bad guys weeping, but in some ways, perfectly natural. They were pathologically self-centred by nature, so probably more than usually inclined to self-pity when things turned decisively against them. Surprising it didn't happen more often.

"Mind if I have a look around?" Fleming asked. "It seems a shame to sit idly. Frans Hals's *The Merry Lute Player* is in here somewhere."

"That's fine."

"You might want to put yourself somewhere a little less exposed, John. If they do decide to take a pot shot at you, you're a sitting duck."

"I'll be fine. Thanks for the thought."

The door on the next floor banged shut again. Fleming's footsteps receded. The crying became muffled, then seemed to die out altogether. All that remained was Hannah's voice, quite distinct in some ways, but without individually distinguishable words. Then that stopped too.

What took its place was an eerie silence. He was alone. It seemed to be getting warmer, as if someone had turned the radiators to max.

Suddenly, Meadows appeared alone coming down the stairs. He didn't look in any hurry, nor – as far as Mordred could tell – was he armed. All traces of his earlier grief had disappeared. He looked directly at Mordred, but without hostility. He wore an evening suit, as if about to embark for a formal dinner and ball.

He pulled up a chair opposite Mordred, and another, at an angle. He brought a coffee table over and set in between them. He showed no sign of the bruise he'd received on the Thames Embankment only a few hours ago.

"I could, of course, kill you now," were his first words. "As your friend just pointed out, you're a sitting duck. But that would be beneath me, and it wouldn't achieve any-thing."

As usual at the end of a mission, Mordred was presented with a choice. Either engage in stereotypical *bon mots* of the type Meadows had just proffered, or not. Say things like, *I think you've proved nothing's that far beneath you, Faris,* or per-haps, *Don't overestimate your options, Faris.* Or not.

As usual, he chose not.

"What are you going to do when you come out of prison?" he asked. The most genuine question he could think of - albeit a tad morbid.

"We're not going to prison, John," Meadows said quietly. Another *bon mot.*

"We'll see."

"You've frustrated the last chance to make the coming world more democratic, you realise that? The one thing the elites don't want is for the crisis to come before they're ready. They want to be the ones to precipitate it, ensuring as much control as possible. Thanks to you, the future world is likely to be ruled exclusively by Goldman Sachs."

"Me? I didn't do anything. Martin Curzon sent my sister an encrypted email, and she hired some acquaintances to decipher it. That would have happened even if I'd never existed."

"Look, John, you'd be a good leader, someone the world could believe in. I'm not joking. Just say the word and I'll arrange for you to get more gold than you've ever dreamed of. Because that's all it'll take. No one need know."

"You mean the gold buried beneath this building?"

"I mean, my own personal stock. How did you find out about that, by the way? No, don't tell me. We haven't time."

"I'm going to pass."

It suddenly occurred to him: where was Fleming?

Lady Julia Greysonwell appeared from a door on the opposite side of the room. She bore a tray laden with cakes, otherwise she too looked like she was going to a banquet. Hair perfectly coifed, understated party dress, high heels. She walked up to them and placed the tray on the table. She sat down next to Meadows, and across from Mordred. She took Meadows's hand and squeezed it. He looked teary again.

She turned to Mordred. "I imagine you're wondering where your friend is. Don't worry, he's quite safe, but he's outside the building now. It'll take him a few minutes to come round. He'll have a headache; otherwise he's unharmed. He can't get back in. All the doors are bolted. There wasn't time to make tea, by the way. And all the servants have fled, for obvious reasons. Please have a cake. They're not drugged. As Faris just pointed out, we'd have nothing to gain from anything like that. And obviously, it would be sordid."

Somehow, he knew she was telling the truth, and it seemed rude to refuse. He took a Fondant Fancy; Meadows picked a slice of Battenberg, and Lady Julia took a slice of

Victoria Sponge. There were no plates, so they held their free hands under their chins to catch the crumbs.

Funny how in episodes of crisis and confrontation, the mundane inevitably intruded. The exam arrived that you'd dreaded for weeks, and still you thought about a specific football match; the interview came to secure your future, and what you mainly noticed was a loose thread in the carpet. Occasionally, as here, the intervention came from outside; everyone involved desperate to shut out the magnitude of what was really occurring.

"Really nice," Mordred said, sounding mildly absurd, even to himself.

"Mmm," Meadows agreed.

"Thank you," Lady Julia replied. "I bought them myself."

It was getting hotter. Even she was slightly flushed. Beads of sweat stood on Meadows's forehead. Nevertheless, they all finished their cakes in silence, without looking at each other. Then, without knowing exactly why, they each took a second.

"When you said you had nothing to gain from drugging me," Mordred said, "I took that to mean you're resigned to your fates."

"We are," Meadows said.

"So why have you locked the doors?"

He uttered this question at the exact moment it appeared fully formed in his head. And instantaneously, as part of the same process, he knew the answer.

Because they expected to die in here.

That explained the terrible crying. Like those Iranian conscripts, they'd decided on a course of action from which they had no chance of emerging alive.

Lady Julia smiled. "I see you've realised what's going to happen. Don't worry, you've every chance of making it out alive. When the fire starts to take, go upstairs, and follow the notices. We signposted it on Friday, for the party. There's a ladder onto the roof. I've already called the fire brigade. I did so not because I particularly care about the building - it's too late for that – but because I think you deserve to live.

"I'm sorry you never got to meet Henry," she went on. "He was really disappointed when you couldn't attend the other day. He was looking forward to meeting you so much. Still, what's done is done.

"Before you go, Mr Mordred, I feel it's my duty to tell you that everything Henry said at his press conference the other day was, and is, true. Everything else – the 'conspiracy' poor Martin Curzon uncovered, and which your sister has just finished elucidating to five hundred assembled worthies – is a fabrication. It's damning for those implicated, obviously, especially since we made sure there's a lot of evidence to back it up – fabricated evidence. Heads will roll. But it's far less shocking than the truth, and that's partly what matters."

A section of the floor on the other side of the room suddenly caved in. Mordred jumped slightly, but Lady Julia showed no signs of noticing.

"The fact is," she continued. "Everything that's happened over the last few weeks – since you were stabbed - has had a very, very specific purpose. Just not remotely the one Martin Curzon supposed. Thanks in no small part to you, we've achieved exactly what we set out to achieve."

Another part of the floor collapsed with an almighty crash, leaving a hole from which flames leapt. In the same instant, Meadows's four friends appeared at the top of the stairs. Like him, they wore evening suits. Somehow they looked unperturbed by the devastation.

"Goodbye, Mr Mordred," Lady Julia said. "You probably need to go now. There isn't much time left."

"Sorry, this is insane," Mordred said. "You can't - "

Meadows laughed genially. "Don't try to save us. You'll only die futilely."

"Whereas we're not going to die," Lady Julia said.

He hesitated a moment, but he could see they were determined, and, given their utter inflexibility, they were right. He went upstairs without hurrying, and passed the four men going the other way. They didn't look at him. Like Meadows, they showed no signs of their recent grief.

There was an explosion somewhere in the basement. Smoke poured through the fissures in the floor. Flames ran up the curtains and across the ceiling, and crawled like living creatures over the furniture. Objects curled and discoloured and blistered and split.

Another detonation deep underground. The foundations shook.

Mordred felt deathly tired. Clearly, the cake *had* been drugged, after all, just not in the conventional way. Enough to make it impossible for him to turn and attempt some sort of mad rescue. Through the smoke, he saw them form a circle and hold hands. They stood as if waiting, then the floor beneath them shattered as if someone had hurled a grenade at its underside. They dropped through it as one unit, leaving only the view to a seething pit of red and yellow.

He followed the trail to the roof, as instructed. By the time he reached fresh air, he was staggering. He went to the parapet. A thousand miles below, he saw Ruby Parker and Annabel and a fire engine and an ambulance and a dense crowd of people. He could feel himself losing consciousness.

A clear blue sky, a white sun. The view was spectacular. Surely Mansion House couldn't be this tall?

Could it? Why had he never noticed before?

My God, you could see the whole world from here!

Chapter 29: Canteen Talk

"So you just sat there," Alec said incredulously, in the canteen, seven days later, "eating cake? A bit like we are now? And the whole bloody place was on fire?"

"I maintained my steely cool," Mordred replied.

10.15am. He and Alec sat opposite each other at the table closest to the serving hatch. Each had a cup of tea. Alec had a bag of *Monster Munch* and an Eccles cake. Mordred had an individual apple pie. Before them, spread out across fifty square metres of dining furniture, colleagues and acquaintances sat with laptops, stared into space, or chatted with friends. Behind them, the catering staff shouted orders and clattered pans about. Outside, the sun shone. The topmost tips of the plane trees shivered in the breeze.

"What did you say in your report?" Alec went on. "I hope to God you didn't cede the possible existence of alien life on Earth."

Mordred smiled. "I put down that she was making it up. Which of course, is the truth. It was nothing more than a final mischievous attempt to muddy the waters, possibly facilitated by grief at her son's death."

"Still, she managed to get the others on board. Meadows and his troupe."

"They were under her thumb. And they had nothing to gain from not going along with it."

"Plenty to lose, though. I mean, falling through the floor into a pit full of molten gold. More than a mid-level bummer, in my opinion."

"Probably a quick way to go. And they were together. And they were all slightly deranged."

"Understatement of the 21st century. They probably had millions in secret bank accounts that the government

274

couldn't even find out about, let alone confiscate. They probably wouldn't have been in prison long, either. And they were young. They must have been *really* under her thumb."

"So what's *your* explanation?" Mordred said.

Alec shrugged gloomily. "Same as yours, I suppose."

They stirred their teas. Alec offered Mordred a *Monster Munch*. "Seriously, though," he continued, "we should be bloody scared. None of it makes the slightest sense unless you assume that both the IMF and the British Treasury are *absolutely convinced* there's going to be a financial meltdown no later than 2026. And it's not like they wouldn't know."

"Pointless, worrying about what you can't change."

"Really? And that's your best response, is it?"

"What's yours?"

"I've just told you: fear. I call it the 'It may be stupid, but sometimes you can't help it' response."

"Don't worry."

"Thanks. But that doesn't help because it's an exact repetition of what you've already said." He sighed and looked at his phone. "I see your sister's front-runner for *Time* magazine's person of the year."

"Fallen on her feet yet again. The aliens clearly love her."

"The *Guardian* actually had a 'Hannah Lexingwood supplement' yesterday. An entire *supplement*. Ten pages. She's even more famous than Soraya."

"The perfect happy ending."

Alec frowned and clicked his tongue. "You're in a very odd mood, John. What's wrong?"

Mordred met his eyes. "I don't know what you mean."

"I mean, I'm finding it hard to engage you in conversation. Every time I say something meaningful, or try to, you respond with an inane one-liner. *I maintained my steely cool* or, *Pointless worrying about what you can't change* or, *The perfect happy ending*. You're too intelligent to imagine you're be-

ing witty, so I guess something else must be going on behind your 'steely cool' exterior. Such as the fact that you're
in an odd mood."

"If I told you the truth, we'd only argue."

"What's wrong with arguing? We're not a couple. We
don't have to find ways of tiptoeing our way back to intim-
acy with uneasy grins on our faces."

Mordred laughed.

"So?" Alec said.

"Seven or eight weeks ago I was stabbed. I lost something that night, I don't know what. A sense of my own in-
vulnerability, maybe. Like all the really personal stuff, it
doesn't have a name, or even a precise description. Then I
was herded into something that looked like a government
conspiracy to hide a clutch of murders. But before she died,
Lady Julia Greysonwell thanked me. *Thanks in no small part
to you, we've achieved exactly what we set out to achieve.* Those
were her actual words. Now, she's dead. But she didn't die
unwillingly. And she said her son was telling the truth in
that press conference of his. I said I thought she was lying,
a moment ago, but the truth is, I don't know what to think.
It sounds mad, but perhaps there really are aliens."

It was Alec turn to laugh. "What I hoped you'd say all
along."

"It goes counter to the laws of physics as we know them,
but maybe we just don't know them well enough."

"It would certainly make the world a more exciting place
to live in."

"Until they show themselves, that is, and make us their
slaves."

"Don't be so pessimistic. They'll probably uphold the
Prime Directive. They won't all be Klingons and Romulans.
Some of them will be Vulcans or Bajorans."

Mordred scowled. "Right. You see, this is what I was afraid of. Not that we'd argue, but that you'd simply laugh at me."

"I'm not laughing *at* you, John. I'm laughing *with* you. Come on, admit it, part of you thinks the same thing. And even if you don't, you normally have a good sense of humour. Where is it today, by the way?"

He smiled. "In counselling."

"You're serious?"

"Ruby Parker advised it."

"As a result of your report."

"My written report was exemplary. It dismissed Lady Julia's claims as delusional and plumped entirely and unreservedly for Hannah's version of events."

"However…?"

"My oral debrief was a different matter. I voiced my doubts. Among other things, I owned up to the fact that I'm having vivid dreams about Henry Greysonwell on a regular basis."

Alec chuckled. "I shouldn't imagine Phyllis is too pleased about that."

"Very funny."

"Sorry, I forgot your sense of humour's in therapy. What happens in these dreams?"

Mordred knitted his brows. "Nothing much. I meet Greysonwell. We speed through the universe together. On the way to our destination, we pick up Ian and Thelma."

"They're in it too, eh?"

"Not always. Most times."

"Where are you all going?" Alec asked.

"Somewhere reasonably pleasant. No one ever says. And we never arrive."

"Speaking as a colleague, I'd say what you're experiencing is normal."

Mordred gave him a thumbs up. "Thanks, Freud."

"*Nichts zu danken.*" Alec put his phone in his pocket. "We get to the end of a case – any case – and it's never like a Sherlock Holmes story: all clues seamlessly accounted for in a full explanation of what happened; when, why, who was responsible. We deal with fuzzy hypotheses. They 'succeed' by getting us to a place we can stop fretting and move on to something else. Take McFarlane for example. Where did he come from? I don't know. Who was he? I don't know. Where did he go? I don't know. I don't expect to know. Ruby Parker probably knows, but I don't anticipate her sharing anytime this side of the third millennium. Nothing's ever 'solved' in the detective novel sense. We're dealing with the whole world. It's too complicated for that."

"The reason I can't 'move on' is it's difficult to know whether I've uncovered a global financial collapse or an alien conspiracy. Two equally awful futures. It's not because my theory was too vague."

"How's Fleming? I'd imagine he's in the same boat as you. Can't you talk to him? I mean, instead of getting counselling?"

"He can't look me in the eye. He's cut up because he was overpowered and left me alone with Meadows and Lady Julia and a plate of cakes. I told him that's stupid, obviously."

"What about Murgatroyd?" Alec asked. "Ever see him again?"

"Nope."

"Which probably means he's happy."

"At least he knows why we had to fill in those forms."

"The reason being that one way or another, there's going to be a worldwide crisis?"

"Yup."

"I bet he's sorry he asked."

"Be careful what you wish for," Mordred said.

"Serves him right, the creep."

"Check. Do you know, I'm starting to feel a bit better now?"

"Good, because I've a surprise for you."

Annabel and Phyllis arrived in the canteen.

"I don't mean those two," Alec added.

They gave Alec and John a little wave, bought coffees at the hatch and came over. Phyllis put a copy of the *Times* on the table. "Would you bloody Adam and Eve it?" she said.

"Believe what?" Alec replied.

"BRF," she replied. "The American-Japanese company that the government's hired to recover Square Mile Gold's molten reserves. Guess what? It's published its initial findings into the viability of the recovery process." She picked up the paper and read. *"Due to a small but interconnected network of sinkholes beneath Mansion House, and the incredibly high temperatures generated by the blaze, much of the gold could now be as deep as one mile underground. Nevertheless, BRF claims full recovery is well within the margins of economic viability. The Home Secretary is expected to give the go-ahead for excavation within the next forty-eight hours."*

She tossed the paper onto the table. They sat in silence for a few moments.

"Still, it's not our problem," Phyllis said.

"Forget Greysonwell," Alec said. "Let's just take it at face value. I was just about to tell John about our surprise."

"Oh, that," Annabel said.

"Don't build your hopes up, John," Phyllis added. "It's really not that exciting."

Alec rolled his eyes irritably. "Fine. We'll just forget it."

They sat in silence again.

"What was it going to be?" Mordred asked.

More silence. Alec finished his tea.

Phyllis and Annabel exchanged looks. "Sorry, Alec," they said in unison.

"You tell him then," he replied.

"We decided we all needed to get together socially a bit more," Phyllis said. "You, me, Alec, Annabel, Tariq. Edna and Ian if they're interested, although they're young: they probably go clubbing or something. And Suki and Victor. Remember our game of Monopoly in The Electress Palatine, that night. Yes, I know it's got bad associations, but we all had a good time while it lasted. We were thinking of making it a regular thing."

"We realised we'd have to get the okay from Ruby Parker," Annabel said. "You can't just have seven or eight spies getting together all the time. We might be 'taken out', as the Americans say."

"It was Annabel's idea to ask for Ruby Parker's approval," Alec explained.

"And she said no," Annabel said.

Mordred laughed. "The end. Well, you tried."

"But she thinks it *is* a good idea… if you subtract the vulnerability factor," Annabel said.

"So we've all got to wear face-masks," Phyllis said.

"Ignore Phyllis," Annabel said. "That was a joke. No, we've got the exclusive use of seminar room T15 every second Friday. She'll provide a selection of board games. We can put music on. We can order drinks from the canteen – they'll keep a supply especially for us. Kevin will take us home in the company car at eleven, *gratis*."

"In short, it sounds disturbingly like a nonagenarian's dream," Alec said. "But we thought you'd like it. And tragically, we're also oddly attracted to the idea."

"It'll seriously reduce your chances of meeting a member of the opposite sex," Mordred said.

"I'm allowed to take an MI7 woman," Alec said. "I just haven't found one yet. I mean, whoever she is, we've yet to meet. Anyway, not all enjoyment has to involve an audacious frisson of amour. Sometimes, it's enough to be a top hat on a piece of cardboard."

"Ruby Parker won't be there, of course," Annabel said. "But guess who will?"

"The Queen?" Mordred said.

They all looked witheringly at him.

"We're trying to be constructive here," Phyllis told him.

"Sorry," he said. "It's just, sometimes I have dreams in which they're interchangeable."

"My God, I have that," Alec said.

"I thought it was just me," Phyllis put in darkly. "I thought I was weird."

"Ditto," Annabel said. She considered for a moment and added, "You see, we may be different on the surface, but underneath, we're all quite similar."

"That's right," Alec said. "Similarly weird, let's not mince words. Anyway, to answer Annabel's teaser, Nicholas Fleming is coming with his wife. Special dispensation from the RP, because they used to work here. Nothing to do with her trying to lure them back. Probably."

"I actually can't wait till Friday!" Annabel said happily.

"Should be good, clean fun," Alec said.

"Nothing beats a good old-fashioned board game," Phyllis put in.

Mordred looked at each face in turn.

My God, they were serious.

He suddenly thought about Ian and Thelma in Syria, those last photos of them grinning together; about the way he and Henry Greysonwell had narrowly missed becoming friends; about how often he and Phyllis and Annabel, Alec, Edna, had been to the ends of the earth together, how frequently they'd saved each other's skins, how readily, once reunited, they resumed their contented routines and ways of interacting. How much they took it all for granted.

The end of the world wasn't important. Not much, anyway. Let it come. Only the quality of the present really mattered: nice food, drink, a roof over your head, intimate conversation, ease in each other's company, laughter.

Meanwhile, he needed to make an early grab for the railway stations, avoid Park Lane and Mayfair, and snap up the orange properties.

Acknowledgements and afterword

"There's going to be a global financial crash," Hannah says in chapter 19. She adds, "2026 at the absolute latest. More knowledgeable people than me have written carefully-argued books about it."

What books, the reader might ask?

Well, one source for this aspect of *The Square Mile Murder* was Mitch Feierstein's carefully-argued 2012 bestseller, *Planet Ponzi*. Feierstein does not put a date on the allegedly coming global economic meltdown, but he stresses its scope and immanency. It will be global. "That moment of awakening is getting closer – and so is the kicking" (p34).

Another source was James Turk and John Rubino's 2013 *The Money Bubble*. "The end game – the destruction of the major fiat currencies – is inevitable. But how the world gets from here to there is currently unknowable. So rather than predict a single path, we outline a number of possibilities with names like 'crack-up boom', 'currency war', 'catastrophic failure', and even 'cyber war and debt jubilee'." (p2). They expect their money bubble to burst "soon" (p4).

The idea that the IMF might take a leading role in managing a worldwide economic downfall, and might, indeed, even be preparing for it, was suggested by James Rickards's 2016 New York Times Bestseller, *The Road to Ruin: The Global Elites' Secret Plan for the Next Financial Crisis*. Rickards employs the metaphor of 'ice-nine', taken from Kurt Vonnegut's 1963 Cold War novel, *Cat's Cradle*. "Ice-nine had two properties that distinguished it from regular water. The first was a melting point of 114.4 degrees Fahrenheit, which meant ice-nine was frozen at room temperature. The second property was that when a molecule of ice-nine came in contact with a water molecule, the water immediately turned to ice-nine... Ice-nine is a fine way to describe the power elite's response to the next financial crisis. Instead of reliquefying the world, elites will freeze it. The system will be locked down... Ice-nine fits with an understanding of financial markets as complex dynamic systems. An ice-nine molecule does not freeze an entire ocean simultaneously. It freezes only adjacent molecules. Those new ice-nine molecules freeze others in ever-widening circles... Financial panics spread the same way... A global financial crisis, worse than any before, is imminent for reasons explained in this book. A liquidity injection of the kind seen in 1998 and 2008 will not suffice because central bank balance sheets are stretched. There will be little time to respond. Ice-nine account freezes will be used to buy time while global elites convene an international monetary conference. They will attempt to use special drawing rights (SDRs) issued by the IMF to refloat the system. SDRs might work. But a more likely outcome is that citizens will see through the sham of resolving a paper money crisis with more paper money. Investors will grow impatient with ice-nine. They will want their money back. The money riots will begin... There will be blood in the streets, not metaphorically, but literally" (p22, 23, 53).

Feierstein, Turk and Rubino, and Rickards are, as far as I can discover, respected experts within their fields. All of them – Feierstein especially, repeatedly and explicitly – stress that they are reporting on the basis of publicly-available statistics universally recognised to be fundamental.

A big caveat, however: I am not myself an expert within that field, and I accept that, despite my best efforts, I may have misjudged the plausibility of their analyses. Hopefully, the reader will judge the evidence for him or herself.

As for the year 2026, that is Hannah's rough estimate of the latest date of the supposed crisis, based on cyclic theories of economic history such as the Elliott Wave, the Kondratiev Wave, and the Fourth Turning, all of which can be interpreted to suggest widespread adversity is imminent.

Again, there is not space to go into more detail here. And Google is only a click away.

The section on 'Dutch bank ABN Amro' in Chapter 27 is factual.

Also discussed in Chapter 19 is Bitcoin and the blockchain on which it is built. Together these are probably among the greatest achievements of the present century. They, and the related cryptocurrencies, again discussed in chapter 19, are supposed, by some, to have been intended as a panacea to any coming crisis. The anonymous creator of Bitcoin, Satoshi Nakamoto, wrote: "The central bank must be trusted not to debase the currency, but the history of fiat currencies is full of breaches of that trust. Banks must be trusted to hold our money and transfer it electronically, but they must lend it out in waves of credit bubbles with barely a fraction in reserve. We have to trust them with our privacy, trust them not to let identity thieves drain our accounts... With e-currency based on cryptographic proof, without the need to trust a third party middleman, money can be secure" (quoted in Dominic Frisbee, *Bitcoin: The Future of Money?* p141). There can only ever be 21 million Bitcoins, which makes it the antithesis of our current economic system of (purportedly) highly noxious fiat money. Its appearance in the aftermath of the 2008 crash may also have been no coincidence. And its transactional anonymity creates a space for political anarchism, even today, as it gets snapped up by venture capitalists.

The blockchain's possible origin in the work of the cypherpunks in the 1990s, and its rise to prominence via the Silk Road and the sanctions against Wikileaks in 2011, ensures something like an edgy libertarian glow still surrounds it. The latest manifestation of this is undoubtedly Bitnation, also mentioned in chapter 19. There are no readily-available books on Bitnation, but its website is fully developed and I urge interested readers to visit it. It aims to bring about nothing less than a complete revolution in human affairs. If some of its ideas seem overly-idealistic ('create your own nation'? 'Do-it-yourself space exploration'?), that may lie in our normal inability to process radical futures. If the past fifty years have taught us anything, though, it is that sometimes, when things seem like pipedreams, they aren't, and that, by the time their plausibility becomes generally obvious, we are often left with a dispiriting feeling of having missed the boat.

As for the sections on alien life in *The Square Mile Murder*, I based these partly on Timothy Good's 2013 *Earth: An Alien Enterprise*. I do not think there is any convincing empirical evidence that extra-terrestrials have visited our planet, but, on rational grounds, I would not necessarily rule it out. We know an awful lot about the laws of physics today, but there is undoubtedly much more waiting to be discovered. The Fermi Paradox ("If there is intelligent life out there, why hasn't it shown itself?"), while a good question, is by no means unanswerable. However, even if someone were to prove to me conclusively that aliens have been to Earth, I would not know what to do with the fact. As in all such cases, agnosticism seems reasonable.

In any case, in *The Square Mile Murders*, the alien motif can also be taken as Henry Greysonwell's sense that there is an awful lot happening deep beneath the surface of civilisation in 2017. So much so that another decade may be all it takes to utterly transform the world.

Or not. We shall see.

JW November 2017

~

Books by James Ward

General Fiction
The House of Charles Swinter
The Weird Problem of Good
The Bright Fish
Hannah and Soraya's Fully Magic Generation-Y *Snowflake* Road Trip across America

The Original Tales of MI7
Our Woman in Jamaica
The Kramski Case
The Girl from Kandahar
The Vengeance of San Gennaro

The John Mordred Tales of MI7 books
The Eastern Ukraine Question
The Social Magus
Encounter with ISIS
World War O
The New Europeans
Libya Story
Little War in London
The Square Mile Murder
The Ultimate Londoner
Death in a Half Foreign Country
The BBC Hunters
The Seductive Scent of Empire
Humankind 2.0
Ruby Parker's Last Orders

Poetry
The Latest Noel
Metals of the Future

Short Stories
An Evening at the Beach

Philosophy
21st Century Philosophy
A New Theory of Justice and Other Essays

CPSIA information can be obtained
at www.ICGtesting.com
Printed in the USA
LVHW111634260721
693715LV00009B/184/J